DAMAGED INNOCENCE

Nancy O. Bush

PublishAmerica
Baltimore

ISBN: 978-1-4489-8938-6
PUBLISHED BY PUBLISHAMERICA, LLLP
www.publishamerica.com
Baltimore

Printed in the United States of America

This book is dedicated with love to my husband Bill, my mother Tootie, my father J.B., my brothers Rick, Bill, John and Tom and to the memory of my brother David.

PROLOGUE

Wilke Spenzi was buried alive, but then he was already dead. He was born on April 3, 1943 to Mattie and Joseph Spenzi. It was a fairly normal labor and delivery. Her water broke at the local Piggly Wiggly supermarket when she and Joseph were buying some groceries and last minute baby things. They also picked up some condoms for the future. Marceline, Missouri was a very small town and the Piggly Wiggly store was even smaller. So, when Mattie's water broke, everyone in the store gathered around and as she and Joseph left, they all followed her to St. Francis Catholic Hospital. There was a motorcade of at least seven cars.

Wilke was born at 7:12 p.m. that night. It was after much huffing and puffing and swearing on Mattie's part that little Wilke finally came out. From the very start of his life, he was looking fierce and acting angry. He cried so much that Mattie could hardly nurse him in between his bouts of wailing. She asked the nuns if they were sure she had the right baby and they assured her there was no mistake. She had to stay in the hospital for four days and Wilke wailed most of the time. When Mattie was finally released, the nuns wrapped the screaming baby in a blanket and unceremoniously plunked him in her lap as she sat in a wheelchair. Then they rolled mother and baby to the front door of the hospital where Joseph had their car waiting at the curb with the motor running. It almost seemed like a cellblock escape straight out of the movies. The nuns were glad to see them go and made the sign of the cross as they drove away.

Wilke seemed to be normal for a new baby. He peed, he pooped, he had bouts of colic, he cut teeth, but he did it all with such anger and determination. He definitely had an attitude. Mattie and Joseph swore they had given birth to the devil's child. The baby never seemed to smile. He scowled and grimaced. His most common expression was a glare. It was like he was thinking, "I'm going to get you for this!"

Mattie and Joseph met at the annual taffy pull at the Wien picnic. It was held every August and was one of the biggest social events of the year. Joseph knew that Mattie was one of the Doman girls. He'd seen her around town a few times, but she didn't go to his school, so he didn't know much about her. There was an instant attraction between them. They were both 15 and knew that it would be a while before they could get serious about a future together, but they knew they wanted one. They got married when they were 20. It had been a long time coming, but they both felt it had been worth the wait. Joseph owned a gas station, the only one in town and Mattie worked with him, pumping gas and doing the books. They tried to have a child, but it took three years and two cinnamon pills from Dr. Smith.

Joseph and Mattie were not sure if little Wilke was different because of the cinnamon pills, but whatever the reason, they soon decided that he really was different. Even something simple like breastfeeding him was a challenge. Mattie tried to nurse Wilke when she was in the hospital, but it was impossible. He sucked so hard it hurt, and as if that wasn't enough pain, he bit her nipples with his hard gums. So she decided to bottle feed him. He would take a whole bottle of formula, but then throw up like a broken fire hydrant. Eventually the nuns were able to get him to keep the formula down. Mattie wasn't quite sure how they did it.

He was not only different in a lot of ways; he wasn't really a cute baby. When Mattie would take Wilke out in his baby carriage, it seemed to her that no one would stop to coo over him or say what a darling baby he was. Passersby would just glance at him and then at Mattie and walk on by. It wasn't that Wilke was deformed or a mutant in any way, but he just had a look about him that put people off…sometimes even his parents.

They knew that being new parents would be challenging, but they had no idea how really scary it was going to be. They had named Wilke after Joseph's father William Kenneth. His middle name was Adam just because Mattie and Joseph thought Wilke Adam sounded like such a strong name. But soon,

Wilke had a different idea. In his early years, he decided that he didn't like his first name or his middle name or his last name, so he told everyone that he wanted to be called by the nickname "Was." He made sure everyone knew it was pronounced like "wuzz" and not "wass."

PART I

THE FAMILY TREE

CHAPTER ONE
Will and Fannie

William Kenneth Spenzi came to America on a boat from Ireland. He landed with boatloads of other immigrants at Ellis Island in the Upper New York Bay near the New Jersey shore. After several days of processing and acclimation, he and other able bodied men and women boarded a barge that took them to a city in New Jersey named Hoboken. The train station in that city was one of the main hubs where Midwest-bound trains ferried hundreds of thousands of much-needed workers to less populated areas of the growing American landscape. William Spenzi had no specific destination in mind when he boarded the Santa Fe train, so he rode and rode until he liked the looks of the area of the country that passed by his window. He saw miles and miles of rich green farmland and forest and it reminded him of his Irish homeland, so at the next stop, he picked up the one battered suitcase that held everything he owned and stepped off the train on the platform. This was the area of this new country that he would call home.

There were plenty of farms all across the Midwest and those farms needed workers. In Marceline, Missouri, it was no different; jobs were plentiful. William was working on a farm near town the day after he got off the train thanks to a local, one-eyed farmer by the name of Porter. Porter seemed to know every farmer in the area and they seemed to know him. At first, William was an itinerant laborer, meaning he moved around a lot. Some jobs lasted for days and sometimes weeks. He went from farm to farm, dropping Porter's name as a reference, taking whatever jobs were available. The pay was low, but he always had a barn, shed or bunkhouse to sleep in at night and three square meals a day. The farmers' wives seemed to pride themselves on feeding their help well. He hoed rows and rows of vegetables or worked in the orchards trimming trees or picking the fruit at harvest time. It was a wonderful life in America he thought.

It wasn't long before the word "wonderful" took on new meaning for William when he met Fannie. She was a beauty, with long, dark hair that hung in curls around her freckled face and the daughter of Edgar Clark, a crusty, but warm fellow who owned a farm in the area. It just so happened that Porter Wilson, the farmer that had befriended William when he first arrived, was a best friend of the Clarks and suggested that they give him a job. Porter knew that Edgar's health was failing and he thought that William might have the maturity and personality to fit in.

William was getting tired of moving around from farm to farm and when he met Edgar Clark and then feasted his eyes on Miss Fannie Clark, he was determined that he'd make this job last and last. He soon developed a perfect angle to reach this goal…as luck would have it, the only tractor on the farm had a cantankerous personality and Edgar himself had no mechanical skills and no patience with the "rusty bucket of bolts." Now, along came William, a "Mr. Fix-It," if there ever was one! He soon overhauled, tweaked, tuned and tamed the pesky tractor like a lion tamer with a chair and a whip and he therefore became indispensible to Edgar as the only person on the whole farm that could handle the belligerent machine. His days in the vicinity of Fannie were now assured as he settled into a fulltime job around the Clark's farm, regardless of the season or the work to be done. He could hardly wait for mealtimes when he would sit at the big table in the farmhouse and watch Fannie bustle back and forth from the kitchen as she fed him and the other hungry workers. His world was wonderful as Fannie became part of his life.

He nicknamed her "Peach" because of her smooth, creamy complexion. She would always blush when he called her that, but she secretly liked it better than her given name. Fannie and Will, as she liked to call him, would sit on her father's front porch swing at night after dinner and talk of his life in Ireland and her life in Missouri. Will loved to look into her blue, inquisitive eyes.

She questioned why if he was from Ireland he didn't have a very Irish name or speak with an Irish brogue. He told her that his family had stole pigs and so they removed the "O" from their last name as punishment. He vowed someday to get the "O" back. Fannie would laugh and tell him that he may not have the Irish brogue, but he certainly had the blarney.

Their friendship grew as they spent more and more time together. Even in the winter, Will found plenty that needed to be done around the farm, so his job and his access to Fannie was secure. Various pieces of farm machinery needed to be maintained, the dairy cows in the barnyard needed to be fed and milked and the chicken coop got a weekly cleaning. Will seemed to always be busy with one project or another, but you can be sure that Fannie wasn't far away. Then one day, as Will was tinkering with the tractor in the barn and Fannie was looking on and handing him tools as he needed them, Edgar came up to them and asked Will Spenzi what his intentions were with his daughter. Will was caught off-guard, but he managed to sputter, "Well Sir…if Fannie will have me, I'd be proud to have a wife that looked and acted just like her." It wasn't the most romantic proposal, but Fannie accepted and her father approved. Two months later, Fannie and Will Spenzi were married in the only church in Salisbury, Missouri—population 65—and all 65 were at the wedding, even Porter Wilson, the one-eyed mayor.

Mayor Wilson had lost his left eye in a snowball fight when he was 12 years old. He and his best friend Jack Keenan were walking home from school through the drifts of snow and Jack decided to throw a few snowballs Porter's way. Of course, Porter took a few shots of his own. Jack kept the fight going and hastily picked up a chunk of hardened snow and rolled it around in his mittens. He threw it and hit Porter straight on in the left eye. Porter fell backwards, clutching his eye and screaming. At first, Jack thought he was just playing around, but when Porter kept crying and didn't get up, Jack bent over him and pulled Porter's hand off his eye. All he could see was a bloody socket. He couldn't even see an eyeball.

Jack knew his friend needed help so he ran across the field to home. His father drove him back to where Porter was and they took him to Dr. Noble, about 25 miles away in Brookfield. As it turned out it wasn't the snowball that blinded Porter, but a good-sized rock that was frozen in the chunk that Jack had picked up. The rock had hit Porter's eye like a small caliber bullet.

Porter lost the eye and Jack Keenan never quite got over what had happened. Porter tried to tell Jack that it wasn't his fault, they were just a couple of kids throwing snowballs and it was an unfortunate accident. Porter said he rather liked having just one eye—made him more interesting, less ordinary.

William and Fannie were honored to have Porter at their wedding. He was a jovial man and it made events seem more special to have him around. Everyone knew he was mayor in name only, because there really weren't too many mayoral responsibilities to be done in Salisbury, except to attend weddings and funerals and preside over any little feuds that might come up. A few people whose fights he'd gotten in the middle of secretly called him "Old Rocky Eye," but mostly the people of Salisbury appreciated what Porter had been through with the loss of an eye and then the loss of his best friend, Jack Keenan. Jack died when he was 14. They had said it was a hunting accident—his rifle misfired while he was squirrel hunting alone. Everyone pretended to accept that as truth, but they knew the real truth was that Jack never got over what he had done to his friend and had taken his own life near the same place where Porter had lost his eye.

Porter and Fannie's father Edgar had become friends while playing high school basketball. They were fierce competitors on the court, but good friends when the game was over. Edgar was the main person to console Porter after Jack's death. When they graduated from high school, neither of them had the money or the desire to go to college. They ended up working fulltime in the cornfields together. After a couple of years they had saved up enough money to buy some land of their own to farm. It turned out to be a good investment and they grew crops of wheat, potatoes, strawberries, corn, squash, beans and made them both a nice little bit of "chum change," as Porter called it. Edgar later sold his portion of the farm to Porter and bought a small home for himself and his daughter Fannie.

Porter Wilson was not married and had no children of his own. He thought of the people of Salisbury as his family and Fannie as the child he would never have. So, on her special day he wanted to give her something to show how much he cared for her. As a wedding present he gave William and Fannie a parcel of land to farm and a little house that was on the property. It would be a good start for them and it would be one less property for him to oversee. Since his partnership with Edgar, Porter had gone on to buy a number of other properties that had turned out to be good investments.

Fannie and William had planned to live with Edgar until they could afford a place of their own. They were surprised and grateful to Porter for his generous gift. This would be a great way for them to start their new life. William could farm the land and Fannie would take care of the rest. And they wanted children—lots of children. They had both been an only child and they knew how lonely that could be.

Will and Fannie had no money for a honeymoon, so they didn't race out of the church with people throwing rice or get into a car all decorated with cans tied behind it or "Just Married" written on the windows. They stayed to enjoy every moment of their special day. As they waved goodbye to the last of the wedding guests—they turned to look at one another and both knew that they were heading someplace they had never been before, but they were going there together, and together they would find their way. William put his index finger to his lips with a silent kiss and she did the same, and they touched fingers, as they had done many times in the past.

William said, "Mrs. Spenzi, I think it's time I take you home and put you to bed." Fannie replied in a soft, sensuous voice, "Well, Mr. O'Spenzi, I do feel a bit tired. Please, my good lad, take me home and put me to bed. I can think of no other place I'd rather be."

They went back to her father's house where Edgar had decorated her bedroom with some flowers from their garden. He had also bought a bottle of port wine and it was on the bedside stand with a couple of stemmed glasses. He had turned the old radio in the room on to a soft music station. What a surprise for the newlyweds! They were very touched. The scene intensified their excitement. They toasted each other with the wine, listened to the music, and drank in the moment. Fannie had bought a special nightgown for her wedding night, but it went unused. They just kissed and held one another for what seemed like hours, until they both drifted off into a blissful sleep—wedding clothes and all.

At about 8:00 the next morning they were awakened by a little tapping noise at the bedroom door. Fannie got up and opened the door and there stood her father with a big grin and he had a serving tray in his hand. It was filled with steaming coffee, orange juice, fruit and Edgar's great homemade whole-wheat pancakes with hot maple syrup.

Fannie wiped the sleep from her eyes and said, "Dad you are too much. This is wonderful. We are both starving. Thank you for last night and the wine and music and flowers. It made our night so special."

Will added, "Yes, Edgar, thanks so much for everything, but especially for Fannie. Would you join us for breakfast?"

Edgar passed the tray to Fannie and said to them, "No, this is your day. I need to get back out in the barn and get started on my chores. Just enjoy yourselves, and Will, you take good care of my girl." And then he was gone. They enjoyed the breakfast Edgar had made for them and they enjoyed each other…as they made love for the first time.

The newlyweds stayed with Edgar for a week. They were concerned that since he and Fannie had been together as just the two of them for so long, Edgar might have some problems with being alone for the first time, especially with his cough and his poor health. He assured them that he had prepared himself for this moment and jokingly told them that he was glad to be rid of Fannie. After all, without her around there'd be one less thing to worry about and now, he said, he could have his girlfriends over. They both knew it was farmer's blarney, but they loved him for making them feel comfortable about leaving.

The house on the property that Porter had given them was small and quaint, but without a bathroom. It had running water in the kitchen sink, two cupboards above and two below and a small stove with two burners. The living room was larger than they needed and what they had extra of in living room, they lacked in bedrooms. There was only one of those, but there was an attic where someone could possibly sleep and a basement filled with old fruit jars and a big metal tub. Porter had lived there himself for a short while and hadn't spent much money or time fixing anything up.

Though it was sparse, Fannie and Will thought it was the most beautiful home they had ever seen. They decided they could get by with no bathroom for a while. After all, there was a nice privy not far from the house and in cold weather they could always use a chamber pot. Will and Fannie had both learned to make do in life. Someday they would put in a bathroom, hopefully before any children came along.

After they had inspected every nook and cranny of the house and each fantasized about what they would change or what they would put where and what they would do with this or that, Fannie turned to Will and said, "I think we have forgotten something Mr. O'Spenzi."

He gave her a quizzical look.

Fannie looked at him with her beautiful blue eyes and said, "I don't recall being carried over the threshold of our new home."

Will took her hand and walked her back out onto the front porch. The screen door was covered with flies.

My Peach," he said with a big grin, "I think we are going to have to make this a quick carry unless you want a houseful of flies." With both of them giggling, he easily lifted her into his arms, yanked open the door creating a cloud of flies, and rushed inside.

She loved feeling his strong, muscular arms around her. Will was not just handsome—he was beyond that. His raven black hair and steel grey eyes were a striking combination. What she really loved about him was that he was as perfect on the inside as he was on the outside.

"Will that do, my Peach?" he asked. "Oh, and by the way, do you really want to be called Mrs. O'Spenzi?"

"That will do Will," she replied, "and yes I want us to put the "O" back in front of your name. If we have to, we will raise some pigs and send them back to Ireland to atone for your parents theft, which, by the way, I doubt there is really any truth to. I am sure they were very nice people and they would never steal pigs. How could they raise a wonderful son like you and be guilty of any crime like that?"

Will looked at her and knew that someday what he had neglected to tell about his short life in Ireland and the nightmare about his parents would have to be told. He hadn't really lied to her, he had just withheld some information, and Will knew that what you withhold can sometimes be worse than lying.

CHAPTER TWO
Edgar Clark

In 1927, the population of Wien, Missouri was about 47. Being such a small town, there were not a lot of businesses in town, and therefore, not a lot of job opportunities. Some of the early town's folk were responsible for what businesses were there. For example, The Stonewall Tavern was owned by Joe Bixman and his brother Ben. The Fesslers, Ida and Bud, ran the only grocery store in town. St. Mary's Catholic School and St. Mary of the Angels church were under the leadership of Father Luther. The Doman family had built on an addition on their home and made it into a dancehall, where people in the community could come and dance on Friday and Saturday nights. There weren't any hard drinks at the dancehall, just buttered popcorn, soda pop and root beer floats.

Many of the people in Wien were related through marriage. A Null had married a Bixman. A Fessler had married a Gladbach. Edgar Clark's father Eddie had married a Washam. They lived together. They worked together. They played together. It was a close-knit community.

Edgar, like most of the boys in Wien, was raised to be a farmer from an early age. When he was five, he could remember riding with his father on their tractor, baling hay. At six he was milking cows, feeding chickens and helping to shear sheep. He went to St. Mary's School, but only when he wasn't needed on the farm. His mother Edna was not always happy with this and insisted that he get an education. Edgar couldn't see the use for school, since he knew he was going to be a farmer no matter what education he got. Edna won out and Edgar did make it on to high school in the nearby town of Salisbury.

It was in high school that Edgar first noticed Hannah Wehner. They had actually gone to the Catholic grade school in Wien together, but he hadn't paid much attention to her in those days. She never raised her hand in class; she kept to herself on the playground and hardly ever talked to anyone. Physically, she was plain-looking with dark hair and freckles and was as quiet as a mouse. She wasn't the kind of girl you paid much attention to. The nuns seemed to like her because she did well in her schoolwork and never caused any trouble. Hannah was a middle child in her family. She had a brother Abe who was two years older than her and twin sisters Leona and Viola, who were two years younger.

At Salisbury High, Hannah had blossomed in several ways. The 16 year old tomboy's girlish figure rounded out and she became much more outspoken. She still did well at her schoolwork, but showed a real interest in what few sports were available at such a small school. She was good at basketball and softball. There were only 20 students in the high school and five of them played basketball. Hannah was one of them, along with Edgar, Porter Wilson and the Bore brothers, Ollie and Albert.

Edgar, Hannah and Porter became teammates on the basketball court and best of friends. They would walk home from school together and never ran out of something to talk about. Sometimes they would go to the little movie theatre in Salisbury or drop by Doman's dance hall to enjoy root beer floats. As the friendship deepened, Porter could see that Edgar was falling for Hannah and he was happy for his friends.

It was obvious that Edgar's future included Hannah.

On October 15, 1937, Hannah and Edgar were married and Porter was best man. Her twin sisters were bridesmaids and Abe, her brother walked her down the aisle. Edgar didn't think he could be much happier, until two months later Hannah announced that she was pregnant. The first person they told was Porter Wilson and then Edgar's parents, Edna and Eddie. Edna was thrilled and couldn't wait to start knitting hats and booties and painting the old cradle that had been Edgar's.

Hannah wished that her parents could have been there for the good news, but they had died when she was 15. There was a terrible accident on the big hill at the Stonewall Tavern. Johnny Gladbach had left the tavern with a little too much beer in his belly and drove out onto the road just as Hannah's parents were coming up the hill. All three of them were killed.

Hannah's brother Abe was 17 at the time and after the accident he pretty much raised the family with the help of some of the townspeople. Hannah looked up to Abe and so did her twin sisters. He had been the strong one to see them through the worst of times. He had given up high school and sports and all of the things he enjoyed just to take care of them.

Abe needed to make money for the family, so he did odd jobs and construction work. When Father Luther and the parishioners decided they wanted to add a steeple to the church, Abe was hired to do the job. It was a hot day in August and Hannah was nearly nine months pregnant. She decided to take a cold pitcher of lemonade down to the church for Abe. She called to him to come down and take a break. He looked down at Hannah and headed for the ladder and lost his balance. His shirt caught on one of the shingles, then tore and Abe came tumbling down. His body hit the ground with a loud thud.

Father Luther heard the commotion. He came running from the sanctuary and found Abe on the ground, dead as the dirt beneath him. Hannah had fainted and fallen on the broken glass of the lemonade pitcher. When Father Luther realized Abe was beyond help, he went to Hannah, put her in the old church truck and drove her to Dr. Noble's in Brookfield. By the time Edgar got there, Hannah had given birth to a baby girl, but the trauma had been too much for her and she was, as Doc Nobel put it "in God's hands now." And so on that day, Edgar had gained a daughter, but lost a wife and a brother-in-law.

Edgar and Hannah had planned to name the baby Fannie if it was a girl and Jacob if it was a boy—so Fannie it was. The loss of his wife was so great that for awhile he could hardly look at the baby or be around her for very long. Edna and Eddie took care of her for the first couple of months until Edgar was able to deal with some of the loss. He eventually took her home and the twins Leona and Viola moved in with him. Together they raised little Fannie until she was a teenager and then the twins decided it was time to get on with their own lives. They had become teachers at St. Mary's School and both decided to become nuns. They were placed together in a convent in Kansas City.

Edgar and his daughter Fannie were alone and they would be until William Spenzi came along.

CHAPTER THREE
Little Fannie Clark

The Stonewall Tavern was located, oddly enough, right across the road from the small playground at St. Mary's School. The children could swing on the squeaky swing set and see men coming and going to the tavern all day long. At some point in each day, almost every man in Wien paid the tavern a visit. Some dropped by for lunch or a quick snack, some for a cold beer and some just came to sit and drink away the hardness of the day.

Six year old Fannie was in first grade at St. Mary's. Almost everyday she could see her father's truck parked at the tavern. She never knew how long he stayed because there were only two recesses in the day, but his truck was there during both of them. When school was over, she would find him at home, usually sitting in his wooden rocker on the porch or in the back room, smoking a cigarette and gazing off into space. He wore the same combination of clothes: striped farmer's bib overalls, an old, dark-colored T-shirt and a beat-up, sweaty old baseball cap.

Fannie's Aunt Leona and Aunt Viola had been raised in the Catholic Church. They were devout in their beliefs and never missed a Sunday service. When they came to live with Edgar, it was a difficult adjustment for all of them. Edgar wasn't prepared to take care of a baby and neither were they.

Grandma Edna came as often as she could to help out and show Leona and Viola what needed to be done. The maternal instinct soon kicked in and they became the main caretakers of little Fannie. That arrangement was fine with Edgar. He would go off to work the farm with Porter Wilson and leave child-tending to the twins.

The only time Edgar was left alone with Fannie was on Sundays when the sisters went to church. He was left with strict instructions and he ignored all of them. He let Fannie just play on a blanket or crawl around. He never fed her or changed her. This so concerned the sisters that they tried to get Edgar to let them take Fannie to church with them. He was adamant that neither he nor Fannie would ever set foot inside of that evil church again. It had taken the life of his wife and brother-in-law, and it wasn't getting anyone else in his family. He could not understand how Leona and Viola could go to the place where their brother and sister were killed.

Leona and Viola got jobs teaching at St. Mary's School, but they had to take turns with the teaching. One of them always had to be with Fannie, so Leona would teach Monday through Wednesday and Viola would teach the other two days and a catechism class on Saturday. This arrangement worked for awhile, but the sisters were increasingly concerned that Edgar took so little interest in little Fannie. They felt that he needed to start playing a bigger part in his daughter's life.

Often life deals a card that causes certain issues to be met head on, and when Fannie was five years old her Aunt Leona became very ill. Doc Noble didn't know what was causing her sickness, so he arranged for her to see a specialist in Kansas City. The specialist told Leona that she had a large cyst in her uterus. He said he did not think the cyst was cancerous, but he recommended that the cyst and the uterus should be removed. She would be in bed for at least six weeks. Viola went to Kansas City and stayed with Leona through the procedure and the recovery. So the card was dealt and Edgar was left alone with little Fannie. Luckily, Grandma Edna could step in to watch her during the days until Edgar came in from his farm chores, but in the evening and at night, Fannie and Edgar were alone.

One night after he had fed Fannie a bowl of cereal for dinner, she looked up from the table and asked him, "Why don't you ever smile, Mister Edgar?"

He looked up and answered, "I don't like to smile, and there is nothing to smile about. And why do you call me Mister Edgar? I am your father."

Little Fannie looked at him for a long time and finally said quizzically, "I didn't know I had a father. Does that mean you were married to my mother?"

Edgar was annoyed and responded, "Of course I was married to your mother and you are our child."

Fannie edged down out of the chair and took her cereal bowl to the sink. She stopped and looked back at Edgar saying, "Oh, then should I call you 'Father'?"

"Well that's better than 'Mister Edgar', wouldn't you say?

"OK Father, if I call you that, would it make you smile?"

"Yes," he said. "I suppose so." He broke into a grin and it seemed that a connection had finally been made between them.

That night after she had taken a bath, Edgar let her listen to a few radio shows with him until she fell asleep. He picked her up and carried her to bed and as he lay her down and tucked her blanket around her, he marveled at the sweet soapy smell of a little girl fresh from her bath. He was tucking her in bed for the first time, and now he felt the warmth of love he had been denying himself.

When Leona and Viola finally returned from Kansas City, they saw a different Edgar and a different little Fannie. They were amazed at the change. Edgar and Fannie were constantly chatting and she loved to laugh at his jokes and Edgar actually laughed himself. Edgar would take Fannie to the fields with him on certain days and let her help pick corn, chat with Uncle Porter, or just play around. He still insisted that she couldn't go to church, but she could go to the Catholic school, when she was old enough.

There was no kindergarten at St. Mary's, so Fannie started first grade when she was six years old. There were seven students in her class: four girls and three boys. As with most church-affiliated schools, they had a strict dress code and the girls wore navy blue jumpers with a white blouse and the boys wore dark blue trousers with a white shirt. Fannie's Grandma Edna was quite the seamstress and she made up several school uniforms for Fannie to wear.

Sister Albertina was the head nun and she taught math and history. Fannie didn't like either one of those subjects and did poorly in both. Her Aunt Leona taught English and spelling and she excelled in those subjects. Aunt Viola taught the same subjects on the days that Leona didn't teach. She also taught catechism. With a couple of teachers in her family, Fannie did get some special attention but it was not at school. In the evenings, her aunts would help her with her schoolwork. Maybe she had an unfair advantage, but in life she was finding out, you needed every advantage you could get.

Fannie was about four months into the school year when she started seeing her father's truck parked at Stonewall's Tavern. She never brought it up directly to him, but she began to wonder why he was there so often and why he was home so early everyday from the fields. Her curiosity got the best of her and one day after school, while there was still plenty of sunlight, she didn't go straight home from school. That morning she had heard the twins tell Edgar that they wouldn't be home until later in the evening. Fannie didn't want to go home and face her father all alone with the way she was feeling. Instead, she walked a mile or so to her Uncle Porter's house, believing that perhaps he could help her understand what was going on with her father. She found Porter in his kitchen peeling potatoes and sipping on a cold glass of lemonade.

"Why Miss Fannie, what a nice surprise," he said with a jovial grin as he picked her up and gave her a big hug. "Did you forget where you live or did you just come to see me?"

As he set her back down on her feet, he was concerned that she had a serious look on her face that he hadn't seen before.

After a few seconds to get her thoughts composed she said, "Uncle Porter, I'm worried about my father. I see his car at Stonewall's everyday and when I come home from school; he's always at home early. I thought he was working in the fields with you, so I don't know what's going on."

"Now Miss Fannie, your father works hard in the fields and sometimes, I guess, he just needs a break," Porter said. "He's been coming to work, but some days he's just not himself. He gets too sad to work I guess. You know he still misses your momma very much. You know he loves you, but I think maybe sometimes you remind him of the woman he loved and married and lost. That's not a bad thing, but for him it can be a sad thing."

"Uncle Porter I try to understand my father's sadness," she softly said. "But I don't think him being at the tavern everyday is a good thing. And I don't like it when he just sits and smokes every night."

"Well, I guess maybe you and me and your father need to have a talk," he replied.

It was nearly dark when Porter's car drove into Edgar's driveway. Edgar was waiting at the door with a belt in his hand. Fannie had never seen that kind of look on his face or a belt in his hand. Porter entered first.

"What you planning to do with that belt Edgar?" he asked. "You going to punish this child for coming to visit her Uncle Porter?"

Edgar looked at both of them and just stood there holding onto the belt.

"Edgar, let's sit down," Porter said. "Put the belt away and let's talk a little over a nice big glass of iced tea. You've got some iced tea, don't you Edgar?"

Fannie could see there was an adult confrontation coming so she quietly headed off to her bedroom. She got out of her school clothes, hung them neatly in the closet and pulled her nightgown over her head. She could hear the mens' raised voices and it scared her, so she crawled into her bed and pulled the covers over her head. The noise from the kitchen was muffled and not so scary. She didn't want to make her father mad, but she feared that now both he and Uncle Porter would be mad at her and with each other. She closed her eyes and soon was fast asleep.

The next day at recess, Fannie saw her father's truck once again at Stonewall's, but he wasn't at home when she got out of school. An hour or so later he came in the door with a big bag of groceries and surprised her and the twins by making a delicious dinner of fresh corn from the fields and sliced tomatoes, bread and fried liver and onions. Whether they liked it or not, they cleaned their plates and asked for more, just to show Edgar how pleased they were with his effort.

Fannie never again saw Edgar's truck regularly at Stonewall's during the day. He would stop in from time to time to catch up on guy talk with a friend or have a quick beer, but it was never a long stay and it wasn't every day as it used to be. The smoking behavior went by the wayside as well. Fannie found a crumpled pack of Edgar's cigarettes in the trash. It seemed that he had turned a corner either because of what Porter had said to him or perhaps because of his love for little Fannie. Whatever the reason, she was grateful that Edgar was able to change and find a place in his heart for the wife he had lost and the daughter she had given him.

Change was everywhere, but sometimes it took some extra pressure. He had even agreed to attend the ceremony for Leona and Viola at St. Mary's Church. They were going to recite their final vows as the sisters of Jesus Christ. It took some tearful pleas from Fannie for him to agree, but after she reminded him of how important it was to the twins and how much they had done for the family, he gave in. It was difficult for him. He thought of his sweet wife Hannah lying on the broken glass on the church steps and her brother Abe lying beside her.

Edgar tried to put those thoughts out of his head for this one special day.

The twins were pleased to see him there. They had loved taking care of Fannie, but now that the girl was 14 and in her first year of high school in Salisbury, it was time for them to move on with their own lives. They had been accepted as teaching nuns at St. Jude's Catholic School in Kansas City.

When they left on this new mission, the house seemed empty without them, but Edgar and Fannie soon settled into their own routine. She went to high school, and he went to the fields with Porter. At night Fannie cooked their dinner and Edgar would help her with her homework. They still listened to radio programs together, or played a game of checkers. Sometimes Fannie would ask Edgar about her mother and he would tell her as much as he felt comfortable with at the time.

In May of that year, Edgar came home one night all excited. He had brought Uncle Porter with him. Fannie was making a big pot of spaghetti sauce for dinner, so there was plenty for all three of them. She could tell that her father was almost bursting to tell her something, but they ate their dinner and then, when the table was cleared; she could see that he could wait no longer. "Fannie, your Uncle Porter and I have some good news. As you may know, we have been doing very well on the farm. Our harvests have been good for the past several years and we've made some good investments. Both Porter and I have been able to put some money away. I have decided to sell my share in the farm to Uncle Porter. With the money from selling that share, added to what I have saved, you and I can now buy our own home on our own land and we can farm our own property."

Fannie wasn't sure quite what to think, but she had never seen her father so excited. So, they celebrated with a sweet dessert and Porter assured her that it was good idea for both of them. They had lived in a house that Edgar's parents, Edna and Eddie, had let Edgar rent from them when he married Hannah. It had provided a good home for Hannah and Edgar and eventually for little Fannie and the twins, but Edgar wanted his own home and his own property to work the land for he and his daughter.

In July, they bought their new home just outside of town. It had two, nice-sized bedrooms, a big kitchen, indoor plumbing and a fancy parlor. Fannie started cleaning and putting things in their place and Edgar couldn't wait to get on his old tractor and start plowing his own fields. It was a good time for both of them. Fannie went on to finish high school in Salisbury and was planning to go onto college at the University of Missouri. She wanted to be a teacher like her aunts Leona and Viola. Nobody in the family had ever gone to college and Edgar and Uncle Porter were excited for her, but had some trepidation about letting her go that far away from home for the first time.

Two months before Fannie was to start college, Edgar got sick. He was diagnosed with a bad case of a lung disorder called pleurisy. Everyone thought the nagging cough was just a leftover of his smoking habit of the past, but the cough got worse and worse. Doc Noble said there was little treatment for it. Unfortunately, it meant that Edgar would have to stop doing a lot of the heavy farming alone. He was going to need help. He talked with Porter about the situation and Porter said he had been hiring boys from the trains coming in from the East Coast. Most of them were immigrants and they were good workers. He admired their motivation to make a better life for themselves in America. He paid them decent wages but he expected a lot. Porter told Edgar he'd send one of the boys up to talk to him and see if Edgar would agree to hire him.

William Kenneth Spenzi showed up at Edgar's doorstep the next evening. He had jet black hair and the bluest eyes Edgar had ever seen. He looked strong and healthy and had a smile that was hard to turn away from. Edgar invited him to stay for dinner. Fannie had made a couple of pork chops and a few ears of corn for her and Edgar. Once she saw they had a hungry guest, she cut everything in halves and shucked some fresh peas from their garden and sliced up a loaf of homemade bread that she had made the day before. They all enjoyed the meal and two days later William Spenzi was working for Edgar.

William and Edgar got along well right from the start. Porter Wilson had told William about Edgar's pleurisy disease and William soon learned when the sound of Edgar's cough meant he should stop what he was doing and rest until the cough subsided. He gladly picked up the slack of farm work that he knew Edgar couldn't do and in a very short time, he proved himself especially skilled at making Edgar's rusty old tractor cooperate. It was a good arrangement. Fannie did not go off to college that year. She was worried about her father's health and she wanted to keep an eye on him as well as on the Spenzi boy.

CHAPTER FOUR
Will and Fannie

Will enjoyed having his own property to farm. It was small, but he made the most of it. He grew wheat, corn, tomatoes, potatoes, zucchini and any other crops that would be of value to harvest for the produce buyers. He also managed to maintain a small garden near the house where Fannie could pick fresh vegetables that she used for cooking and canning. Fannie, with the help of Edna, fixed up the house and made it comfortable and livable.

Edna enjoyed helping Fannie make curtains, bed linens and area rugs. They even made the stone-walled basement a nice place to take a bath. In one corner of the basement there was a dark, earthy-smelling root cellar with a low ceiling and a hard-packed dirt floor. It had rows and rows of shelves around the walls—floor to ceiling. It was in here that the temperature remained cool year-round, even when it was hot and humid outside in the summer. Fannie canned every kind of vegetable and fruit in season and the shelves quickly became stocked with shiny glass Mason jars of tomatoes, peaches, pears, cherries and jams. The Spenzi household was becoming very self-sufficient.

Porter Wilson was a frequent visitor and would drop by about once a week. He always said he just needed to check in on them, but Fannie knew it was to enjoy another of her delicious cooked meals. He promised that he would help them build a bathroom once the babies started to come. Will continued to help Edgar with his farming when he could and he could see and hear that his father-in-law's pleurisy was getting worse. It was getting obvious that any strenuous farm work was becoming impossible for Edgar.

Two years into Fannie and Will's marriage, the crops were doing well and Porter, Edgar and his father Eddie started working on a bathroom for the house. They were getting anxious for a grandchild. They thought if there was a bathroom, the child would be soon to follow. Well, as it turned out their premonition came true. Just nine months after the bathroom was finished, the grandchild came. He was a beautiful boy that Fannie wanted to name Joseph Buford. Will didn't have a problem with the name, but was never quite sure where it came from. There wasn't anyone in either of their families named Joseph and the name Buford…well; it would forever remain a mystery.

Joseph Buford or JB as they called him was a beautiful child. He had jet black hair like his dad and blue eyes like both Fannie and Will. He was adored by his parents and everyone he met. Will wanted to take him everywhere. He even took him to the tavern just to show him off. The whole town seemed to dote on JB. They all knew when he took his first baby steps, cut his first teeth, had a fever or when he said his first word, which was "dah." Will was sure he was trying to say "Dad." Fannie didn't care because she didn't think they could be much happier.

When JB turned two years old, Uncle Porter gave him a golden retriever puppy for his birthday. Porter had heard they were good with kids, gentle and protective. JB was thrilled with the puppy. Fannie and Will named her Molly. JB and the pup were inseparable. Molly slept in JB's room every night. If he woke or seemed to need something, Molly would go to Will and Fannie's room and wake them up. She was the perfect baby monitor.

As everyone predicted, Edgar's health got to the point where he couldn't keep up with the farm work and when crops weren't planted and fields were not worked, the land was choked with weeds. He sold the farm to the Schiltz boys, Larry and Jack. They were young and ambitious farmers and he knew they would make good use of the land. With a good part of the proceeds of the sale, Edgar built an addition on Will and Fannie's house where he could live near them but in his own area where everyone could have a degree of privacy.

Fannie was thrilled to have her father back under the same roof with her.

JB loved having his doting granddad around and Edgar was still able to wander around the farm with Will and help out where he could. It seemed like an excellent arrangement for the whole family.

May 24th was JB's fifth birthday. Fannie had decorated the house, baked a cake and invited most of Wien to the party. Her aunts, Viola and Leona, were coming to the party from Kansas City. Edna and Eddie were there to help out. Porter had threatened to buy JB a pony, but Fannie had said no and so he just came with bags of other gifts. It was early afternoon and Will was still working in the field. He came through the house around 2:00 o'clock and hugged his son and said "Looks like somebody is having a birthday—I wonder who it is? Don't worry son, I'll be done in time for the party, I just need Grandpa's help for a minute."

Will had a knack with the mechanics of the tractor, but in order to move it about 75 feet from the driveway to the barn, he needed Edgar to steer it and manipulate the transmission and clutch while he fiddled with the carburetor linkage to keep the engine running. Edgar climbed up on the tractor and plopped in the seat while Will stayed on the ground next to the engine compartment.

"Hold the clutch in will ya'? Will asked. "I'll push the starter from here."

The engine coughed a few times and started right up.

"Okay, put 'er in gear and let the clutch out slow," he said.

Edgar kicked on the clutch pedal and tried to get the gear shift lever to engage, but it would just grind and clank and, with that, the tractor lurched and stalled.

"Oh damn," said Will as he walked around to the back of the tractor to see if he could help Edgar get the gear engaged. "Try 'er again," he said as he leaned against the rear tractor tire.

Edgar hit the starter and as the motor sputtered to life, the tractor lunged backward and the balky transmission dropped into reverse gear as Edgar's foot slipped off the clutch pedal. Will was caught by surprise and fell on his back as the tire rolled on to his body. Edgar didn't immediately know the seriousness of what had happened until he looked back and saw Will on the ground with the huge tire on his chest. He tried to get the tractor in gear to get it to move off of Will, but he forgot to engage the clutch with his foot and the shift lever wouldn't budge. He shut off the engine and jumped down. Will was unconscious and Edgar could see no breath coming from him.

What neither of them knew at the time was that JB had followed his Grandpa Edgar out the door and was standing on the porch and saw the entire scene. He just stood there—he didn't move and he didn't scream—he just stood there.

Edgar stumbled toward the house, coughing and yelling for help. Eddie, Porter and the Schiltz boys came running. Jack Schiltz leaped into the tractor's seat and jammed down the clutch pedal with his left foot. That freed the tractor to roll forward as the others yanked on the tires and pushed on the back of the tractor's frame. In seconds, the huge tire rolled off of Will's body. Though there wasn't any obvious blood on Will, it looked like his chest was crushed in where the tire had rested and he wasn't breathing.

"Will…Will!" Porter shouted as he bent over the broken body. "Hang on Will! We're going to get you some help! Just hang on!"

They carried him to Porter's car and laid him across the backseat. Eddie climbed in and rested Will's head on his lap. Porter and the Schiltz boys jumped into the front seat. Edgar collapsed on the porch, coughing and spitting up gobs of phlegm. The activity and stress was too much for him. Porter drove at breakneck speed to the hospital in Brookfield. The doctor and nurses in the emergency room did all they could, but Will was pronounced dead at 3:42 that afternoon. The tractor had crushed the life out of him.

Leona and Viola drove Fannie to the hospital while Edna looked after JB. When Fannie got there she saw Porter sitting on a chair inside the emergency room. He looked up at her with an ashen face and said, "Fannie he's gone—our Will is gone." In an instant, life changed. JB turned five and Will was dead.

The whole town turned out for the funeral. Porter delivered a proper eulogy and everyone got a chance to speak about their love for Will. Fannie had been crying for three days straight. JB was there and he tried to be brave, even though it hurt and he didn't really understand. He said how much he loved his dad, but couldn't quite grasp yet what had happened to him. Edgar did not attend the service. After the accident, he barely came out of his room. He blamed himself, and as much as Fannie tried to convince him differently, he could see the sadness in her eyes and he couldn't bear it.

Two months after Will was buried, Edgar had dinner with JB and Fannie. It was still early evening and he said he felt like going fishing at the Schiltz pond. He gathered up his pole and a bag of what Fannie thought was more fishing gear. She didn't argue with him because she thought he needed to be alone. She knew that fishing relaxed him.

"Please Dad, don't stay out too late," she cautioned. "You know how sometimes the evening air gets you to coughing. Besides, I need for you to tuck JB into bed and read to him. He loves that. "

JB saw his granddad heading out the door with a fishing pole and begged to go along. Edgar bent down and kissed JB on the top of his head and told him, "No, not this time JB—maybe another time."

Edgar never returned that night and as it got later, Fannie called Porter and Eddie and Edna around 10 o'clock. They went down to the Schiltz pond and found Edgar floating face down in the water. There were two empty liquor bottles on the small wooden dock. In one bottle they found a piece of paper. It read,

I can't stand your pain anymore and I can't stand mine.

Please tell JB how sorry I am. I love you Fannie.

CHAPTER FIVE
Joseph Buford Spenzi

Within two months, JB had lost a father and a grandfather. For a child of only five, he had experienced a great deal of sadness in his life. His father went off to fix a tractor and never came back to him and his grandfather went fishing, and never came back to him. JB lived in fear of who he would lose next. He became anxious and terrified if his mother left the house for any reason. When Fannie had to go out alone, Edna and Eddie would stay with JB and he would pace the house or stand glued to the window until his mother returned.

Porter Wilson delivered the eulogy at Edgar's service, as he had done a few months earlier for Will. This time he broke down and couldn't go on. The loss of his best friend was just too much to bear. Leona and Viola were at the service and went forward to calm him and take him back to his seat. JB just sat quietly holding his mother's hand. He didn't cry. He had cried so much at night in his bed, that he had no tears left. After the service, some of the town's people stopped by the house to pay their respects to the family. Many brought food and they all expressed true sympathy. When Fannie would go outside to thank them and say goodbye, JB would be right behind her holding onto the back of her dress. When friends tried to reach out and touch JB with a kind hand, he would hang on even tighter to his mother.

In just a few short months, Fannie found herself alone with a son to raise and land to farm. She wasn't sure how good she would be at either one. Her immediate family's resources for support were dwindling. Edna and Eddie were getting up in their seventies. Eddie was through with farming, so he sold their property and they moved into the addition that Edgar had built. It was important for them to spend as much time with JB as they could and they knew Fannie needed all the help she could get.

In the fall, JB went off to first grade at St. Mary's School. He still suffered from the loss of his father and grandfather and there were many times that the nuns reported to Fannie that he had acted out his sorrow and disrupted the class or had just disappeared. Whenever he went missing from class, he would go home early and tell his mom the nun got sick and school let out early. Fannie forgave him for his fibs for a while because she knew all that he had been through and what great losses he had suffered.

JB was too young to understand that Fannie had suffered the same losses. She had lost her wonderful, loving husband Will, and a father that she had shared most of her life with. She felt so alone, even with Edna and Eddie nearby and Porter stopping by nearly every day. No one could really know the grief that she felt on a daily basis. She couldn't show it to her son and she had no mother to help her bear this burden of loss and sorrow.

On a chilly day in February, Porter stopped by the house. As he came into the kitchen he said, "Anybody got a hot cup of coffee for an old one-eyed man?"

"Oh Porter, you silly goose," said Fannie. "Sit down at the table. I just made a fresh pot."

He eased into the chair and cleared his throat as Fannie put a steaming cup in front of him. She poured a cup for herself and joined him at the table. She knew he had something important to say. She could see it in his face and she could feel it in the air.

He slowly began to speak. "Miss Fannie, you are a young woman. You have a farm to deal with and a child to raise. Now you hear me out. Your father and I both had dreams of you going to college and getting that teaching degree you always wanted."

At that, Fannie tried to interrupt but Porter would have none of it. He raised his hand to silence her and continued, "You deserve to have a life too Fannie. You'd be the first one in this town to get a college degree. You'd be an inspiration to all of our young ones and to your son. So, here's the thought. The Schiltz brothers are interested in your farm property. They would work it for you and give you 20 percent of any profit. You keep the house as is and I'm going to pay it off for you. I don't need the money and have no one else to give it to. "

Fannie jumped up and grabbed her Uncle Porter around the neck, almost tipping him over in the chair. "Oh, Porter you are just the kindest man and a wonderful uncle, but you know I can't leave JB," she said. "I know I have Edgar's parents here, and I have you. But, I can't saddle all of you with fulltime responsibility for a heartbroken five-year-old. My college degree will just have to wait."

"Well now Miss Fannie, if we plan this out right you'll only have to leave JB for a few weekdays at a time depending on your class schedule," he suggested. "The University of Missouri in Columbia is only a three hour drive from here—you can go there during the week and come home on the weekends. Besides, I have another idea. You know that the Schiltz brothers have a sister. Her name is Alfreda. She's a good, kind woman that loves kids. I've already talked to her about this whole idea and she thinks it would work out fine."

Fannie knew Alfreda. She cleaned the church and Father Luther's living quarters and sometimes helped the nuns teach Sunday school. She was a nice lady, in her thirties, had never married and the word was that she was unable to have children of her own. She kept house for her brothers Jack and Larry. She seemed quite satisfied with those chores and tending to her churchly duties.

"Well Uncle Porter, you certainly have given me something to think about," Fannie said.

"Fannie, don't just think about it—call up the school tomorrow and find out what you need to do to apply for admission. C'mon, life is short woman. Let's get this dream going for you!" he said with that famous Porter Wilson grin as a hug turned into an impromptu dance twirl around the kitchen floor. Fannie couldn't believe the anticipation and hope she was feeling in her life again.

A few days later, with a trembling voice, she presented the idea to Edna, Eddie and JB. At first there was silence, but then Edna was the first to speak, "Well dear, I think it's a wonderful idea, you need to do something for yourself and you need to keep busy and you know we'll be here for JB. You'll make a wonderful teacher!"

Eddie wasn't as enthusiastic and didn't have much to say. He just looked at Edna and nodded his head, which seemed to mean he agreed with her. JB, on the other hand, understood what was happening and had quite a bit to say.

"Mom, why do you need to go to school?" he asked "You are already smarter than anybody I know, and we have the farm and Molly and Edna and Eddie and Uncle Porter. Why would you leave me with scary Alfreda? "

"JB, why do you call her scary Alfreda?" Fannie asked. "She's a very nice lady."

"She walks kids home from school and they disappear," he announced. "And…," he continued, making fists with his hands on his cheeks, "And…if they do come back, their fingers and toes are missing!"

"Oh really JB?" said Fannie with a grin. "Are you sure that Alfreda cuts off the childrens' fingers and toes? Why on earth would she do that?"

"She needs the fingers and toes to feed to her brothers for dinner," JB replied knowingly.

"Now Mr. JB," she admonished. "Surely you know that none of that is true—there are no children missing from your school and as for fingers and toes…I don't know of one child that is missing any."

"Well…well," he stammered. "If that lady, Alfreda, comes here, I'm going to hide under my bed and never come out…except to feed Molly."

"Let's give her a chance," Fannie said. "Alfreda wants to come by tomorrow and officially meet all of us—and JB, if, after you meet her, you want to hide under your bed—then that will be your decision. And, I'll make you a deal Mr. JB. If I see her carrying a bag of toes or fingers, I will get rid of her right away—agreed?"

JB wasn't sure if he'd won or lost the battle, but he felt a change was coming and her name was Alfreda.

CHAPTER SIX
Alfreda Schiltz

Frank and Katherine Schiltz owned a big turkey farm just east of Salisbury. At any one time they had a couple of thousand turkeys and it was a joke in the area that you could hear Schiltz's turkey farm before you could see it. They would get poults—that's what you call baby turkeys—in the early spring and tend to them until just before the holiday season. In late October or so, big trucks would come and fill up with turkeys and off they'd go to the processing plants in Kansas City and St. Louis. It made Frank and Katherine and their three children a very good living. When the turkeys had gone and they waited for the new ones to come in the spring, they also had 60 acres of land that they farmed with various crops.

Their house was huge in comparison to most of the homes in the area. Everyone thought of them as royalty. Katherine was not royalty at all. She was a hard worker—always wore an old apron and work boots. She was either out feeding the turkeys or working in the fields with Frank. She appreciated what she had, but took none of it for granted. When they had a good year with the turkey and crops, they always gave a substantial donation to St. Mary of the Angels Church. Many times when someone was sick in town or needed help, Katherine was the first one to arrive with some hot turkey soup or with whatever financial aid the person might need.

She had raised her children to be the same way. Her first born was

Alfreda. Frank had really wanted a boy and would have named the boy Alfred, but since he got a girl, and to make him feel a little happier, Katherine named her baby girl Alfreda. The gender change wasn't a problem as Frank adored Alfreda, and she soon had her daddy right where she wanted him, wrapped around her finger. But, as luck and destiny would finally have it, boys were in the genes. It took four years, but along came baby Jack and just a year after, brother Larry was born. Since Alfreda was the oldest, she became a very responsible child at an early age. When Katherine was out feeding the turkeys or doing other chores, Alfreda took care of Larry and Jack. When they were toddlers it wasn't too great a task, just change diapers, feed them and put them down for a nap, but as they got a little older it was a whole other story.

Alfreda was happy to start first grade. It got her away from the responsibility of watching and tending to her brothers every day. Of course, Katherine had to stay closer to home, but sometimes she and Frank would take the boys out to the turkey pens and let them scatter some of the feed. When chores were done for the day and dinner was over, there would be music in the house. Frank and Katherine were talented musicians. They both played various instruments and wanted their children to appreciate music as well. There was one room set aside in the house for these activities. Katherine played the piano and guitar and Frank loved to accompany her on the drums. She also played the accordion and taught Jack to play the piano. Larry learned the clarinet and Alfreda was challenged by the flute. It became a family ritual every night that they would practice their chosen instruments and cook up some melodies together. If they sounded good, there would be ice cream afterwards. If they sounded bad…there would be ice cream afterwards. It was family time and they all had fun.

When Alfreda was nine years old, she and her mother went to the Wien cemetery to put some flowers on Katherine's parents' graves. Alfreda had always loved the adventure of going to the cemetery, with its rows and rows of big gray headstones and blocks, some of which were so old they were covered by a greenish moss. She would wander down the rows and look at the names and the writing on the headstones. She especially liked the larger stones and the square blocks of granite. By climbing up on top of a headstone or on a memorial block, she could see all the way across to the other side of the cemetery. She did the same thing on this day, but she wasn't aware that the stone she had chosen was wobbly on its concrete base. Without warning, the stone, and Alfreda, toppled over. She landed on her side with the stone pinning her legs so she couldn't move them. Her screams of pain and terror brought her mother running to her side.

Katherine tried to push the stone off Alfreda's legs, but it was too heavy. Both she and Alfreda screamed for help. After what seemed like an eternity, they saw a truck crunch to a stop on the gravel lane that wound its way through the cemetery and two men jumped out and came running toward them. Porter Wilson and his friend Ben Bixman had been driving around in the area and heard the screams. While Ben and Porter lifted one end of the stone, Katherine pulled Alfreda out from under it. She was crying and patches of skin on her legs were scraped and bleeding. They gently carried Alfreda to the truck and had her stretch out in the back with her head in her mother's lap. They drove her to Doc Noble's office in Brookfield. He checked her over and was amazed that she didn't have any broken bones, but her left ankle was twisted, badly bruised and sprained. He put a splint on the ankle and over the next few months it healed, but her left foot pointed off on a strange angle and Alfreda walked with a limp from then on.

She was a pretty girl, with light brown hair and blue eyes, but she was terribly shy and other than the time she spent with her family, she kept mostly to herself. She wrote poetry and could usually be found quietly reading alone in her room. She had accepted her limp, but was always self-conscious about it. Her brothers went on dates and to dances, but she never had an interest. Her life was complete as it was. Katherine and Frank were concerned that she seemed to have no motivation in meeting a man or having children, although she loved little children. She worked hard on the turkey farm and was always available to babysit for neighbors and friends. Her high school years came and went without fanfare and she graduated when she was eighteen. In her mid-twenties she took a job cleaning the church and working for Father Luther. She also enjoyed walking some of the children home from school just to make sure they got home safely. The younger children didn't seem to notice or mind that she limped.

When Porter Wilson approached her about the job for Mrs. Spenzi and her son JB, she wasn't quite sure. She had never taken care of a child on a full time basis. She was aware of what the Spenzi's had been through and she certainly wanted to help. She told Porter that she would meet with Fannie and JB and see how it went. Porter felt that was fair enough. Alfreda thought she owed it to him—he had been there in her time of need many years ago in the cemetery.

It was about 6:00 o'clock when Alfreda knocked on the door at the Spenzi house. Fannie answered the door with JB right behind her. As she came in, it became obvious to JB that she was carrying a big plastic bag. He let out a howl, "I told you Mom—she has fingers and toes in there! Don't let her in!" he yelled as he turned and headed for his bedroom.

Fannie laughed at his antics and put her hand on a shocked Alfreda's shoulder. "Please excuse my son," she said with a grin. "He just needs to know that you don't have fingers and toes in that bag."

"No, Mrs. Spenzi," she said. "I brought your family a roasted turkey that I made for you this afternoon. I'm sorry that I don't have any fingers and toes. It seems that's what Mr. JB Spenzi was expecting. Believe me, they aren't nearly as good as a roasted turkey."

"Alfreda, meet the rest of the family," Fannie said. "We so appreciate the turkey and will have it tomorrow night for dinner. Tonight we are having a grilled cheese sandwich with tomato soup and cherry cobbler for dessert. It is Mr. JB Spenzi's favorite meal."

Alfreda said hello to Edna and Eddie, whom she had seen many times at church and Porter was there and JB's dog Molly. JB had made his way back to where everyone was and he hid himself just around the corner in the hallway.

Alfreda could see that JB was hiding nearby, so she said, "JB you have a very nice dog. I like the name Molly."

Molly heard her name being mentioned and came running to Alfreda and jumped up to be petted while she madly licked Alfreda's hands.

JB became upset and rushed into the room waving his arms at Molly. "Get away from her Molly! Get away!" he said to the dog.

"Why JB," said Alfreda, "I think she likes me, and I hope you will too."

With that, they all sat down to dinner and chatted, while JB just nibbled on his food and ignored everyone. He pretended that none of them were there.

After dinner, Edna offered to do the dishes and clean up while the men went to the front room to chat. That gave Fannie and Alfreda a chance to settle down in a couple of chairs on the porch where they finally had an opportunity to talk.

"Alfreda, I am sure you are aware that JB has been through some very difficult times," Fannie began. "He has lost a father and a grandfather and now I am going away to school. He is a wonderful child, but he can be very trying and difficult. Do you think you are really up to this?"

"Mrs. Spenzi…, I guess I should be calling you Fannie…, I am very good with children. I love them. JB seems like he will be a challenge, but I believe the Lord has brought me here for a reason and I will do my best with him. Why don't we give it a couple of months and see how it goes."

Fannie thought for a moment and then agreed with Alfreda's suggestion. She would be leaving for college at the University of Missouri in Columbia within the next 10 days so Alfreda would move in with them and get acclimated. Initially, Fannie would come home every weekend. When Alfreda needed to clean the church or help Father Luther, Edna and Eddie would be there for JB.

Plans were made and Alfreda got ready to leave by thanking them for the meal. She tried to give JB a hug, but Molly was the only one willing to get that close to Alfreda at this point. JB went running to his room reminding Alfreda that she would never get his fingers or toes.

Fannie was excited to start college, but concerned about JB at the same time. She kept telling herself—let's just see how it works. On a cool fall day in September she left for the state university in Columbia. She would live in a girl's dormitory on campus during the week and drive home on weekends. Edna and Eddie, Alfreda and Porter were there to give her a send off—but JB was under his bed with Molly. Fannie had talked with him the night before for a long time and he seemed OK, but he couldn't say goodbye to his mom. He just knew she was never coming back. He believed that everybody he loved seemed to go away and never come back.

Alfreda had only brought a few of her personal belongings to the Spenzi house. She would be using Fannie's room while she was gone during the week, and she didn't want to make JB feel like she was taking over his mother's territory. It seemed, however, that no matter what she did, JB was not going to be happy with this new arrangement.

The first night after Fannie left, Alfreda made JB's favorite meal of a grilled cheese sandwich, tomato soup and cherry cobbler. Edna and Eddie and Porter all sat at the table with Alfreda, but JB refused to come out for dinner. When Alfreda went to check on him, he was still hiding under his bed with Molly.

"JB do you think Molly would like some food? she asked. "It's been a long day and she's probably hungry."

There was no response. "Well," she said in a loud voice. "I'm just going to leave some food for Molly and some food for you in the kitchen and if either of you get hungry in the night, It'll be there for you. Goodnight JB. Goodnight Molly."

The next morning the food was gone. Alfreda took that as a good sign. So she made a breakfast of pancakes and sausage and went to his room. He was still asleep on the top of the bed. "Joseph, it's time to get up," she said. "I made breakfast for you and when you are ready, I'll walk you to school.

With sleepy eyes and tousled hair, JB mumbled, "My name is not Joseph."

"Well," said Alfreda, "did you know that Joseph was the husband of Mary in the Bible and he became the father of Jesus? He was a fine man, and I think you are going to be a fine man. So I'd like to call you Joseph."

By now JB was wide awake and he countered with, "Well I don't like the name Alfreda, so what should I call you?"

Alfreda said, "Why don't you call me what my brothers do. They call me Tootie."

JB said, "Why do they call you Tootie?" and she replied, "It's because I play the flute and that flute goes 'toot-toot' because I'm not very good at it yet."

That hit JB's funny bone and he laughed and laughed at the "toot-toot," but calling her Tootie was just fine with him. "Okay Tootie, I'm Joseph." A deal was made and Alfreda was pleased that they finally agreed on something.

"So Joseph," she said, "you need to eat some breakfast, take Molly for a short walk and then together we will walk to school. We don't want to be late. You know that Sister Raphael is not happy when children are late for school."

"I don't need you to walk me to school," he said.

"I promise not to cut off your toes or fingers," she said with a laugh.

Joseph actually managed a smile and said, "I'll let you walk with me, but only so far. I don't want anyone to see me with you or know you are living with me."

"That's fine Joseph," she said. "Let's just pretend that I'm invisible. Does that work for you?"

Joseph actually chuckled and quipped, "Yeah that's fine, but just stay away from my fingers and toes."

CHAPTER SEVEN
Porter Wilson

The people of the town of Salisbury kept re-electing Porter as mayor, year after year. Of course, nobody ever ran against him. He enjoyed being mayor, but there really wasn't too much to be done in the job. He tried to get somebody else to run, so he could retire, but nobody ever did. He had made good investments and lived in a nice home and even had a housekeeper. Porter never flaunted his wealth. He tried to do right with it, and the only people he wanted to make sure benefited from it were Fannie and JB. At this time in his life they were his only family.

He was pleased to be able to pay off Fannie's house on the farm and help her with her college expenses. Every thing he did made her seem more like the daughter that he never had. He went out of his way to plan for Fannie and JBs future. For example, she wasn't aware that Porter had set money aside for JB to go to college. He'd done that when Edgar was still alive and always kept it a secret. Edgar had been his best friend after Jack Keenan passed away. He and Edgar had grown up together and worked the fields together and shared so many sorrows and joys. He missed his good friend. Porter hadn't minded living alone all of these years, but that didn't mean that he didn't get lonely.

Almost every evening that first week after Fannie left, he would stop by to check on JB, Alfreda, Edna and Eddie. He generally seemed to come around supper time, so Alfreda made sure she had plenty of food for all of them. Porter always brought something to contribute to the supper, either a fruit pie that he had bought at the store or some ice cream or maybe a watermelon from his garden. Alfreda was glad to have him there because she knew how much JB loved and felt comfortable with Porter.

"So JB, tell me about school and how you and Alfreda are getting along," Porter asked.

"Uncle Porter," he said after a short pause. "There are three things that you should know. My name is Joseph now, because that's a name for a fine young man. And number two is that Tootie and I are learning to like each other. It works because she's invisible. And the good news is that I still have all of my fingers and toes—so far…"

"So, Tootie and Joseph it is now," Porter said while glancing over at Alfreda. "I like those names."

JB said, "But I just don't like Tootie walking me to school everyday."

"Why is that?" Porter asked.

"She has a bad foot and she shouldn't be walking that far," JB replied.

"Well, I have a bad eye, does that mean I shouldn't be seeing that much?" Porter asked.

"Uncle Porter…you ask the strangest questions," JB said.

"Well then, let me ask you a simple question," said Porter. "Would you and Alfreda, oops, I mean Tootie, like to go to the carnival in Marceline this weekend?"

"You mean like a carnival with rides and games and animals?" JB asked.

"Well, I don't know about animals, but I know they will have rides and games," Porter said.

"I'd like to go Uncle Porter, but my mom is coming home this weekend," JB said.

"Well, I talked to your mom today and she won't be coming home this weekend. She has a big paper to write and she needs the extra time in the library. She said she would call you and see you next weekend," Porter said.

JB looked panicked and tears started to well up in his eyes. He put his head down in his folded arms and all he could think about was that he remembered that his Mom was never coming back, just like his father and grandfather.

Alfreda caught Porter's concerned eye and she said, "Porter the carnival sounds like fun, but Joseph misses his mother. If she can't come to us, can we go to her? I know it's a bit of a drive and I know she has a paper to write, but maybe Joseph and you could go to lunch with her, and Joseph could see where she's going to school. I think it's important for him to see his mother after this first week that she's been away."

JB looked at Alfreda and she wasn't invisible anymore. At that moment she could have taken all of his fingers and toes and he wouldn't have missed them. He was so happy with her suggestion.

"Well I do declare Tootie Schiltz, that is one of the best ideas I have heard in a long time," said Porter. "I've got this big old car that never gets to go anywhere and I think a little trip to Columbia would be good for it and for all of us. Edna and Eddie, would you like to come along for the ride?"

Edna wanted to do some gardening and Eddie had a lot of little odd jobs to do around the house, so they found good reasons to decline. After all, they would see Fannie the following week and it would also be nice for the two of them to just have some time alone.

Porter said, "Okay, then it's settled. Everyone get a good night sleep and I'll be back in the morning at eight o'clock sharp. Even if we take our time, we should be there by noon and we can surprise your mom JB and take her to lunch.

JB said to Alfreda, "You are coming with us, aren't you Tootie? "

"No Joseph, you and Uncle Porter go and see your mother. She doesn't need to see me," she said.

But I really want you to come," he pleaded. "This was your idea and it was a good one. After all, I need you there to explain to my mom why my name is Joseph now."

"Well alright Joseph, but then you have to explain why my name is Tootie," she said.

They said good night as Porter left and went off to bed excited about what they'd experience the following day.

Alfreda had a strong feeling that some progress in their relationship had been made. Time would tell.

CHAPTER EIGHT
Fannie Spenzi—Mizzou

The University of Missouri, affectionately known as "Mizzou" was the largest college in Missouri. In 1942 they had over 7,000 enrolled students. Fannie Spenzi was one of them. She was in her late twenties and felt like a misfit, but a determined misfit. She knew that once she got her teaching degree she could make a better life for her and JB and set a good example for the young children of Wien.

Her first week was stressful, with getting registered and selecting classes, buying books and settling into dorm life. She missed JB so much and there were a few times that she just wanted to run out of the classroom and go home to her son and forget about this education stuff. She tried to be strong and kept telling herself that in the long run, this would all be worth it.

She called JB every night, if only to talk for a minute or so. He seemed to be doing okay. Alfreda always gave her a positive report, but Fannie still doubted how well things were really going. She was looking forward to coming home on that first weekend, but one of her professors had assigned a research paper that was due by Monday. Fannie knew that she couldn't drive all the way back to Wien, spend time with JB and write the paper. She called Porter and asked him if he could explain the situation to JB.

Porter picked up JB and Alfreda at 8 o'clock as promised. When he drove up they were standing on the porch, ready to go. JB jumped into the backseat of the car and wrapped up in a blanket that Alfreda had brought along.

It was quiet for awhile and nobody spoke and then they heard JB breathing softly. He had fallen asleep and he slept most of the trip.

Porter broke the early morning silence, "Alfreda this was a great idea and it will be so good for JB to see Fannie. Thank you for suggesting it."

"Porter, in just this one week, I have begun to understand this child and will understand him more as time goes on," she said.

"You seem to be so good with children," he replied. "Why didn't you ever get married and have some of your own? "

"I guess I have always felt damaged. After all, who would want to marry a woman that walks with a limp and can't dance?" she said.

"Well, I've only had one eye most of my life. Do you think I'm damaged?"

"Oh no Porter, I'm sure you can still dance with one eye," she said with a giggle.

"Well, I think you can still dance with a little limp," Porter shot back. "Why don't we try it sometime?"

After a couple of potty stops along the way, they pulled up at the university about noon. JB was groggy from sleep. Porter and Alfreda had chatted most of the way. She had laughed at his idea of going dancing, but he assured her that he was serious. They talked about all kinds of things. She told him how the Schiltz family raised turkeys. He told her about his eye and how at first he had worn a patch and then dark glasses and finally later in life he had a glass eye put in. He, of course, knew all about her ankle injury—he was there.

"Porter, you know how grateful my family and I have been to you through the years," she said. "I don't know what would have happened if you and your friend hadn't come along when you did and helped push that stone off of me and driven me to Doc Nobles' office. "

"Alfreda, I just wish I could have gotten there sooner," he said. "You were so young and helpless and I got you to the doc's office as fast as I could. I'm glad it wasn't worse. What's a little limp? I think it makes you more interesting and less ordinary…kinda' like me."

"Well Porter Wilson," she said. "I guess we are like two peas in a pod…as they say"

"Yes Alfreda and these two peas are going to go dancing one of these days," he said with a grin.

They parked the car in the visitor parking lot and headed up the esplanade leading to the main entrance of the university. The campus was beautiful and covered with mature trees, painted with the colors of fall. There was ivy on many of the buildings and a large fountain with two big sculptured fish squirting water from their mouths. JB had never seen a place so large and beautiful. There were people everywhere. Some were sitting by the fountain or at picnic tables eating lunch. Many of them were just walking around with books and chatting with others.

JB found it difficult to picture his mother here. She was his mother and belonged at home with him. He was afraid she would be too happy here in this beautiful place and that would make another reason for her to never come home.

They weren't sure where to start looking for Fannie, but Porter noticed a directional sign that pointed to an "Information Center." That seemed like a good place to start. The center was located in the front of a large impressive building. They entered through a pair of massive glass doors and were greeted by a woman behind a high desk. "May I help you?" she said.

"We are looking to visit Miss Fannie Spenzi. She is a student here," Porter said.

"Is Fannie expecting you," the lady asked?

"Well not exactly, we wanted to surprise her," he replied. "I am her Uncle and this is her son and our friend Alfreda."

"I appreciate it that you all want to surprise her, but everyone needs to be notified if they have a visitor," she said. "I will have to call Fannie's room to see if she is available."

She rang the phone to Fannie's room and her roommate answered. She said that Fannie wasn't in the room, because she had gone to the library to study.

With that information, the trio headed out to find the library.

It was in its own building and had huge wooden doors with a large, ominous sign warning "NO TRESPASSING—STUDENTS AND FACULTY ONLY!" Porter decided not to chance getting in trouble on their first visit to the campus at Mizzou, so he suggested they sit down on a bench and contemplate their next move.

As luck would have it, within minutes, a tall, skinny, friendly-looking fellow with thick glasses came out of the library doors. Porter jumped up, approached the young man and said, "Can you help us please? We came here to surprise Fannie Spenzi. We know she's in the library, but since we aren't students, we can't get in to see her. Could you just give her a message for us, so that she knows we are here?"

"Gee Mister, the library is huge. What does she look like?"

"Well," said Porter, "she has long brown hair and big blue eyes."

"C'mon Man, there's hundreds of female students with brown hair and blue eyes!" the fellow said incredulously.

"I know," JB piped up. "I gave my mom a big pin with my picture on it and the pin has writing on it that says 'I LOVE MY MOM!'—she told me that she always wears it. See if you can find a student wearing a big pin that looks like me." And with that, he flashed the guy a huge Cheshire cat smile.

"OK, just because of that smile, I'll give it a try," the guy said with a chuckle.

He went back into the library and within minutes Fannie came running out to greet them.

"Porter, JB and Alfreda what a wonderful surprise," she said.

JB ran into her arms and hugged her and Fannie said, "Porter this was a great idea.

Thank you so much!"

"Don't thank me Miss Fannie," he said. "JB will tell you about how the whole thing was Tootie's idea. She knew you needed to see him and he needed to see you."

"Tootie?" Fannie said, "And who is Tootie?"

"Mom, Alfreda's nickname is Tootie and my new name is Joseph…you'll just have to get used to it," JB said. "Tootie told me that Joseph was Mary's husband and the father of Jesus. And she knows that he was a fine young man like me."

Fannie put her arms around all three of them and said, "Well I don't care what your new names are, I am just glad to see all of you. Let's go get some lunch and get caught up."

Nearby was the on-campus Commons restaurant where they picked out soup and salad and a couple of sandwiches on the buffet line. It was a beautiful fall day and they sat outside and chatted. JB dominated the conversation. He had so much to tell his mother. He talked about school and Molly and Edna and Eddie and let her know how excited he was about going to the carnival in Marceline with Porter the next day. Fannie was so pleased and relieved to see him smiling again and talking with excitement in his voice. It looked like this just might work out. She could see that there was already a good connection between JB and Alfreda.

After lunch, Fannie took them on a tour of the campus and then went back to show them her dorm room and meet her roommate. It was a short, but good visit for them all. At about 3:00 o'clock, Porter suggested that it was time for them to get back on the road so they could be home before dark and in time for dinner. JB wasn't quite ready to leave yet, but after plenty of hugs and kisses from his mother, he took Alfreda's hand and headed for the car. To keep from being sad, he took only one last look at his mother and said with a grin, "Look Mom—I still have all of my fingers."

Fannie hollered back, "What about your toes?"

"Yep, I still got those too," he shouted. "I think Tootie likes grilled cheese sandwiches better than fingers and toes."

They all laughed and Porter, Alfreda and JB piled in the car and headed back down the road for home.

PART II

WILKE SPENZI

CHAPTER NINE
The Bad Boy

Wilke Spenzi, or Was, as he liked to be called, did not have an easy childhood because he was not an easy child. He was the kind of son that only a mother or father could love, and that was even at question sometimes.

When Wilke was born, Joseph Spenzi still owned the only gas station in Marceline. It was a town with a population of about 2,000, and it was located 10 miles from Wien through old gravel roads. It was a real town though, with Loman's drugstore, the Piggly Wiggly grocery, a small Macy's department store, a funeral parlor, and a Catholic school, church and hospital. Needless to say, the townspeople of Marceline were mostly Catholics. The only non-Catholic member of the community was Dr. Red, the dentist. It wasn't a booming metropolis, but when people in Wien said they were going to town,—it meant Marceline.

There was one blinking red stoplight in town and Joseph's gas station enjoyed a perfect location at that corner. People didn't have much other choice, unless they wanted to drive to Brookfield, 20 miles away. Joseph liked the fact that the stoplight was there—he always imagined that it made people stop and then think that they needed gas or a cold drink, or a block of ice or a Hershey's bar. It was a good location and a good business.

Since Mattie and Joseph both needed to work at the gas station, they would bring Wilke with them each day. When he was a baby they would put him in a little bouncy thing and let him chew on a cookie or whatever might keep him quiet. When he started to walk, it became more difficult for them. While Joseph was out pumping gas or working on the grease rack, Mattie would attend to customers inside the station. Sometimes, when they wanted a block of ice, she'd leave the station for a minute and go outside to the ice cooler located next door. Oftentimes, while she was gone, the mischievous Wilke would open up the candy case and swipe a Snickers bar, Three Musketeers or whatever else he could get his sticky hands on. As he got older, and taller, the little rascal found out how to open the cash register and he'd reach in and snitch some nickels to get a cold bottle of soda from the pop case. Needless to say, these shenanigans would certainly entertain the old guys who met almost everyday at the Texaco station.

There was a good-sized room intended for customers who were waiting on their cars that was located just off the side door to the office. It had a window in one wall that looked into the work area, lift and grease rack. It was here that a regular group of five or six old fellows would gather almost every day to swap stories, spin yarns and trade pearls of wisdom. The pop case was in this room and when Wilke would dart into the room with a couple of nickels that he had filched from the register, it was time for him to entertain this readymade audience. He became very adept at pulling an empty pop bottle crate up to the machine and after climbing up; he'd poke two nickels in the coin slot and slide back the shiny chrome pop case cover. The guys loved to watch the youngster deftly maneuver a bottle of Coke or Dr. Pepper down the maze-like rails inside the case until the bottle was positioned to pull up and out. He'd ceremoniously pop off the cap to the cheers of his appreciative audience. If he felt like it, sometimes Wilke would continue his entertainment by providing an impromptu tap dance on top of the case. The chrome cover was a perfect sounding board for his little feet as he kicked his heels ratta tat tat...ta ratta tat tat...ratta tat tat! and the old boys would always clap at the conclusion of every dance.

By the time Wilke was six and ready to start school, almost all of his teeth had cavities and were ready to fall out. Dr. Red, the local dentist, said there wasn't much he could do for him. He'd just have to be toothless until his permanent teeth came in. Mattie and Joseph could hardly wait to send him off to school. They figured that the nuns might be able to instill some discipline into him. They really wanted to have more children, but they had been so challenged by Wilke, they didn't know if they'd be able to raise him with other children, or if they should.

The first two weeks at St. Bonaventure Catholic School were not good ones for Wilke or the nuns. He didn't get along very well with any of them and they even had to resort to a round of extra prayers at vespers everyday asking God to give them patience with him. There were 10 children in the first grade class. Six were girls and four were boys. Sister Mary Ellen was their teacher. She was young and this was the first class she had taught on her own. She knew it would be a challenge, but she had no idea what lie ahead of her with Wilke Spenzi.

Mattie and Joseph tried to be supportive parents. They would all have dinner together at night after the gas station had closed. Mattie would ask about Wilke's day and how he was getting along. He just hung his head and had no answer. Mattie and Joseph would offer to help with his homework, but he said he had none. They were at a loss.

Within the next couple of weeks at St. Bonaventure, Wilke quickly and unfortunately cast his own fate. He racked up a list of misadventures that convinced the nuns that he was incorrigible. He managed to jab one of his schoolmates, Karen Ewigman, in the back with a pencil. He was told to stand in the corner of the classroom and he responded by peeing his pants in front of everyone. One day the nuns discovered that all the reading textbooks were missing from the shelf in the back of the classroom. After much prodding and threats, Wilke admitted his misdeed. He hated reading so much that he had taken the books and hid them in the freezer compartment of an old refrigerator in the nun's quarters. Enough was enough…

The nuns and Sister Mary Ellen felt they were no longer able to deal with Wilke's behavior and they demanded a meeting with Mattie and Joseph.

"Mr. and Mrs. Spenzi," Sister Mary Ellen began, "We have done our best with Wilke, but he is not a fit for this school. Perhaps he would be better off in a public school or you might want to look into some counseling for him. All I know is that we can no longer handle him at St. Bonaventure. He is a danger and distraction to the other students."

Mattie and Joseph were near tears, but they understood. They were just not sure what they were going to do with him. As they got up to leave, Sister Mary Ellen took them aside and said very seriously, "Maybe you should look into sending him to spend some time with the monks."

Mattie and Joseph didn't think that their son living with monks was the answer, but a

week after Wilke was dismissed from St. Bonaventure; Joseph made an announcement at the dinner table. "Wilke, as you know, you can't go back to school at St. Bonaventure, but you still need an education. Your mother and I have discussed this and next week your grandma Fannie is coming to stay with us for awhile. She will be your teacher and you will have school right here at home."

Wilke had heard all of the stories about his grandmother Fannie. How she had struggled to raise Joseph by herself and had finally gone to college and became a teacher and how she put Joseph through college with the help of some old guy named Porter Wilson. Wilke had gotten so tired of hearing how wonderful she was and how she survived the death of her father and Joseph's father and went on to become not only a high school English teacher, but the principal at Salisbury High School. Word was that she was an inspiration to all the young people of Wien. "Blah blah blah," Wilke thought. She was no inspiration to him.

He did remember her from when she had come to visit several times. She seemed like a nice enough lady, but he remembered that all she talked about was how important education was and how proud she was of Joseph. Wilke was puzzled that she was so proud of a son that went to college and became a grease monkey and gas pumper.

CHAPTER TEN
Matilda Doman

There was a saying that Mattie had remembered from early childhood. "You can make the plans, but you can't plan the results." She certainly had not planned the results of her life. She had fallen in love with Joseph Spenzi at an early age and waited so long to marry him and then a long time for them to have a child. Now, even though she knew life wasn't going to be perfect, it had gotten harder than she expected. She loved Joseph and as she tried to be a good mother, she had to admit that Wilke was a hard child to love.

She had grown up in a family as one of six girls. Her parents, Jerry and Bonnie Doman, were loving parents and their home was full of joy and laughter. The family ran the Doman dance hall and snack bar and the whole family helped out to run the business. Mattie did whatever her parents wanted her to do and she even sang and danced with some of the bands that would play on Saturday nights. She was a good dancer, but not the best of singers.

Although her given name was Matilda—her sisters started calling her Mattie at an early age and it had stuck. She was the youngest of the Doman girls. Her sisters were Carol, Ginger, Verna, Peggy and Joann. Mattie loved all of her sisters, but Carol was her favorite. She was the oldest and very protective of her baby sister. Ginger was a year behind Carol and she was not the nicest of sisters. She seemed to be jealous of the attention that Mattie got.

Ginger would play tricks on Mattie like hiding her pajamas or telling her there were snakes under her bed. Mattie was too young to understand why Ginger was so mean to her. Verna and Peggy were twins and they were 4 years older than Mattie. They were pretty much inseparable and didn't pay much attention to Mattie.

Joann was the closest in age to Mattie and she had been born blind.

Bonnie and Jerry Doman had never expected to have six children, but they were devout Catholics and the Pope said no birth control for Catholics. They loved their girls, but it was a financial challenge to raise all of them. The dance hall did well on the weekends and a few nights during the week, but funds were always tight.

Mattie's dad Jerry took on odd jobs to help out and her mother had a part-time job helping to clean St. Mary's School. She would also work for Ida and Bud Fessler at their country store when they needed it. When times had gotten really tough, Katherine Schiltz stepped in to help out and so had Porter Wilson. It was just that kind of community. People offered help where it was needed.

When Mattie met Joseph Spenzi at the Wien Picnic taffy pull, she couldn't take her eyes off him. They were on opposite sides and although she wanted her team to win—at that particular minute when their eyes met, she could have cared less who won. Joseph seemed to pick up on that and smiled at her as his team won.

Mattie was shy, but her sister Ginger was not. After Joseph's team won, Ginger congratulated him and offered to buy him a soda. They walked together to the soda stand and Joseph asked for three sodas. He gave one to Ginger as he said, "Sorry you lost, but thanks for being a good sport."

Ginger said, "But, Joseph, I was supposed to buy you a soda."

He smiled and replied, "Thanks Ginger. Enjoy your soda. I'm going to take this one over to the girl that helped me win."

Mattie was sitting by herself on a bench near the quilt stands. When she saw Joseph approaching, she wanted to jump and run, but he was in front of her before she knew it and he handed her a soda. She accepted it and thanked him, but she kept her gaze down, looking at the ground.

Joseph sat down beside her and said, "Hello my name is Joseph Taffy, the greatest taffy-puller in the world."

She couldn't resist looking up and laughing. What a silly thing for him to say. "Well, I'm Mattie Taffy, the worst taffy-puller in the world," she said shyly.

"This is great, we already have something in common," he replied. "The worst and the best at taffy-pulling. Alright Mattie, the worst taffy-puller, if you aren't planning on buying some quilts or playing bingo or doing the cakewalk, would you like to go for a walk with me? "

She was hesitant and told Joseph she was at the picnic with all of her family and she should probably not go off anywhere.

He said, "Okay then, enjoy your soda. It's hot out here, so I'm going to walk over to the pond that's just down the road and take off my shoes and soak my aching feet in the cool water. And do you know what I'm going to do then? I'm just going to sit there and watch the fish jump."

Mattie watched him walk away. Oh why not? she thought as she grabbed her soda and went after him.

They did exactly what Joseph said, they sat on the creaky wooden dock with their bare feet in the cool water at the Schiltz pond and watched the fish jump. He told her that this was where his Grandpa Edgar had died and how his father had been killed under a tractor tire and how his mother was going to college to be a teacher and about how Alfreda was called Tootie and Porter had saved her when she hurt her leg and Molly the dog slept on his bed and Edna and Eddie were his grandparents.

Joseph asked why he had never seen her before in school at St. Mary's. She told him that her sister Joann was born blind and that she needed to attend a special school in Brunswick, Missouri. Even though Mattie wasn't blind, she went to the same school as Joann in order to understand her special needs and be able to help her when she needed it.

This was the first of many nights that they would spend together under the stars, talking and sharing stories.

Mattie looked back on those wonderful times and wondered why she had been given such a difficult child, when she and Joseph were so full of love for one another, and had so much love to give. She sometimes wondered if her sister Ginger had not put some kind of curse on them. Ginger really never forgave Mattie for taking Joseph Spenzi away from her, although he didn't really have any interest in her. It was a childhood grudge that lasted throughout the years.

CHAPTER ELEVEN
Grandma Fannie

Wilke was not happy that Grandma Fannie was coming to live with them. He already had enough problems dealing with his parents. Why did they think he was going to treat her any differently than he had the nuns or his classmates? It would just be one more person he had to take his anger out on. Why couldn't they all just leave him alone and let him read his comics and hang around the gas station and entertain the old men that came by and gave him money from time to time, if he would dance on top of the metal soda pop case.

What Wilke didn't know was that Grandma Fannie wasn't any happier than he was to be coming to live with them. She had to take a sabbatical leave from Salisbury High School as their principal and leave her comfortable home and friends. But Fannie could tell from Joseph and Mattie that they were at their wit's end and really needed help. She loved her son and he had always come first in her life. She was doing this for him.

Fannie was used to challenges. She had graduated first in her class at the University of Missouri in a little over three years. Her grades were never below a "B." She had landed a teaching position almost immediately with Salisbury High School and within two years became their first woman principal. In the midst of all of this she was raising a son, with the help of Alfreda, Porter, Edna and Eddie.

In the past five years as principal at Salisbury, she had also started working on her Master's degree on a part time basis. Her hope was to someday be a professor at Mizzou, where she had learned so much and found a new life for herself. Fannie never remarried after Will's death. There were a number of men at the university that found her attractive and had asked her out, but she let them know in a nice way that her priority was her son and her education. She knew early on that after Will Spenzi, there really wouldn't be anyone else. The love he left her with and the son they shared was all she really needed to be happy.

She knew that she was going to have to be strong with Wilke. The years had taught her a great deal about being strong. She had buried a husband, a father and just a year ago, Edgar's parents, Edna and Eddie, and two months ago a beautiful, loyal dog named Molly.

She knew all about loss and sorrow and the strength you needed to get through it. Her solace through all of this, other than her son Joseph, was Porter and Alfreda. They were her best friends and she was the maid of honor at their wedding. They made an interesting couple with Porter's glass eye and Alfreda's limp, but their marriage was a delightful occasion and now they had opened a dance studio where Porter taught dance steps while Alfreda provided the piano accompaniment. Years ago, Alfreda had told Fannie that she knew the Lord had brought her to the Spenzi home for a reason. That had certainly proved to be true.

Fannie agreed to help with Wilke, but she insisted on several conditions. She was not there as a grandma to babysit him. She was not there to clean house or make the meals. She was there to tutor Wilke as best she could and try to prepare him to go back to the Catholic school or a public school, if necessary. Mattie would make the meals as usual and do whatever cleaning needed to be done. Wilke was to be ready to start his home schooling every weekday morning at 8 o'clock and they would go until at least 3 in the afternoon, perhaps longer if necessary. He could take a break for lunch when Mattie came home to make it and he would be allowed two 10 minute breaks during the day to go to the bathroom or just stretch a bit. After dinner, Wilke had two hours to work on homework and one hour to himself before bed. This was the schedule for the week and Fannie would go home on weekends and be back on Monday morning.

Mattie and Joseph had agreed to all of this. They were so grateful to Fannie. She really was their last hope. They just were not sure how they were going to get Wilke to comply with the restrictions. Their faith was in Fannie and they knew they'd all just have to take it one day at a time.

CHAPTER TWELVE
First Day of Home School

It was a chilly Monday morning in mid-October and Fannie had driven to Marceline early for an appointment at St. Bonaventure with Sister Mary Ellen. The purpose of the meeting was to tell the Sister about Wilke's new educational plans and to see if any first grade textbooks were available to buy. When the Sister heard that Fannie was actually taking on the challenge of educating Wilke herself, she bowed her head and made the sign of the cross.

"Mrs. Spenzi, good heaven on earth...you don't need to buy the books. You may have them with the blessings of all of us at St. Bonaventure," she said. "This is such an undertaking for you. May the Lord be with you and give you strength."

"Yes Sister, something tells me I'm going to need the Lord on my side," Fannie said with a wry smile as she embraced an armload of books and headed back to her car.

She arrived at Mattie and Joseph's about 8 o'clock and could see that they had just finished breakfast. She joined them at the table as they poured her a cup of coffee.

Joseph reached over and put an arm across Fannie's shoulders and said, "Mom I'm so glad you are here. Mattie and I realize what you are giving up to do this, but you are our last hope."

"Joseph, you are my son," she said. "I love you and Mattie and I promise I will do my best with Wilke, but please don't expect miracles. By the way, where is my grandson this morning?"

"Mom," Mattie began in a halting voice, "maybe today is not the best day to get started on this. Wilke said he wasn't feeling well this morning. He decided not to get out of bed."

"Oh no!" Fannie exclaimed in a very loud voice. "That's no way to start the first day of school. It sounds to me like Wilke just has what we call the 'first day jitters.' I'd like him to get out of bed and get dressed for school and get out here,,, and I mean out here…now!"

Mattie jumped up from her chair and headed for the bedroom to get Wilke. Joseph excused himself from the table and announced that he was going to be late for work as he banged out of the house through the screen door. "See ya' later Mom," he tossed over his shoulder. Fannie couldn't help a small grin as she witnessed all this activity.

In just a few minutes a dressed, but disheveled, Wilke crept into the kitchen at his mother's prodding.

"Well there you are Wilke," Fannie exclaimed. "It's so nice to see you again!"

He looked at her and said, "My name is not Wilke, it's Was."

"Yes, I know…and my name is Santa Claus," Fannie responded. "Wilke you were named after my late and wonderful husband, William Kenneth. He was very special to me and you are very special to me. I don't care if you want to call yourself Was or Where or When or Whatever. I will be calling you Wilke. We will be working at the dining room table—it will be known as the 'learning table' during the day."

Mattie sensed that Fannie needed to continue to be in charge of the situation so she gave Wilke a kiss on the head and reached out and gave Fannie's hand a squeeze as she headed out the screen door. Fannie and Wilke were alone.

There was silence as they stared at one another. Wilke broke the silence in a whiny voice, "I don't think you're a very nice grandma."

With that, Fannie stood up and directed him toward the table in the dining room saying, "Well Master Wilke Spenzi, today and for many days to come, I am not going to be just your grandma. I am going to be your teacher. I want you to sit down and let's start doing some reading."

"I already know how to read," Wilke said.

"Oh really," said Fannie. "You already know how to read. That's very nice. I know you like comic books. Go get me your favorite one and you can just read it to me."

Wilke went to his room and came back with a tattered comic book titled "Captain Bob and the Capture of Tyrannosaurus Rex."

"Oh, I can see this will be a very exciting story," she said as she sat down at the table. "So, Wilke, go ahead and read what Captain Bob is saying right here on the first page."

Wilke opened the comic book and smoothed the first page out on the table. Fannie looked at the comic attentively, waiting for him to start reading. He looked at page and then back at her. He ran a finger across the panels on the page and then looked again at Fannie. "I guess he's saying that he's scared of the dinosaur," Wilke offered.

"Oh come now," Fannie said. "Captain Bob's words are assuring all of his men that he's in charge and they have nothing to worry about. Look right here it reads, 'Okay all of you trusty shipmates. I am Captain Bob, the bravest of all. As long as you sail with me, you will be safe and the dinosaur will be captured.' See, Captain Bob is the hero. Wouldn't you like to know what your favorite characters are actually saying, and not just think you know by looking at the pictures? I bet you'll find out that it makes the story a lot more exciting."

"Well, maybe you're right, but I don't think I need to know all that," he said.

"Well, let's forget about Captain Bob for now," she countered as she picked up the reading textbook. Do you know who Dick and Jane are?"

"Nope," he responded."

"Well, I'm going to introduce you to some other characters that you will get to know," she said as she opened the book and placed it in front of him. "You'll meet Dick and Jane and Jack and Jill and a lot of new people."

"I hope they're all nicer than you," he said.

Fannie smiled to herself and realized that the challenge had begun.

Mattie came home at noon as planned and fixed lunch. They all sat around the kitchen table with tuna sandwiches and hard-boiled eggs. Mattie knew this combination was one of Wilke's favorites and after the shaky start to the first day at school; she wanted to try to make a special lunch to make up for it. Wilke was hungry, as usual, and ate all of his lunch and washed it down with a big glass of milk and a Hostess Twinkie for dessert.

Mattie and Fannie engaged in chit-chat, but the school day challenges weren't discussed. Mattie could feel the tension in the air. She made a sandwich and put it in a little brown bag with a couple of boiled eggs to take back to Joseph at the station. She quietly headed out the door and let Wilke and Fannie get back to their lesson.

They recited the alphabet and read the first chapter of the Dick and Jane book. After about an hour Fannie said it was time to move on to some arithmetic. It wasn't her strong subject, but she thought she could certainly teach first grade math. It turned out that Wilke actually liked numbers and it seemed to go better than the reading. They also worked on a little spelling, which Wilke hated. Not wanting to end the day on a bad note, Fannie asked Wilke to open his comic book again. She patiently prompted him to read a few of the words from several of Captain Bob's captions. It was about 4 o'clock and she thought they both had enough for one day.

When he was excused, she noticed that Wilke got up from the learning table with his comic book and went to his room, but interestingly enough, he took the Dick and Jane book with him.

That night, when they all gathered at dinner, they ate at the kitchen table so as not to disturb the learning table.

Joseph started the conversation, "Hey Son, what did you learn in your first day of school?"

Fannie put her head in her hands as she almost choked on her most recent bite of dinner when Wilke looked up from his bowl of soup and said in a very matter of fact tone of voice, "I read that a kid named Dick and a girl named Jane have this stupid dog that doesn't even know how to fetch a bone."

Joseph said, "Wilke, if you do well in your schoolwork, maybe we can look into getting a dog. I had a wonderful dog named Molly when I was growing up, and she was my best friend until I met your mother."

"Yeah, I know and your father died and your grandfather died and Molly died," Wilke responded. "Why would I want a dog that's going to die?"

They finished their soup in silence. Wilke went off to his room. He really didn't have any homework that first night. Fannie had gone easy on him. He fell asleep with the Captain Bob comic book on his chest and the Dick and Jane book in his right hand.

Fannie, Mattie and Joseph watched a little TV and went off to bed. Fannie told them it had been a good first day, but reminded them, and herself, that they had a long way to go.

CHAPTER THIRTEEN
The Field Trip

One morning about a month into the home schooling, Fannie woke to find Wilke standing beside her bed. He had a small duffle bag in his hand.

"Wilke, are you alright?" she asked as she sat up.

"Yes Grandma, but I wanted to let you know I wouldn't be at school today," he said.

"Oh and why won't you be at school?" she asked.

"Grandma I don't like any of this. I want to be a dancer. The old guys at Dad's gas station tell me that I'm a good dancer and they pay me to dance on the soda pop case," he said.

"Well, those old fellows should know a good dancer when they see one," she said knowingly. "They've been around for a while. So, what do you have in that bag?"

"I have a couple of shirts and some underwear and an extra pair of jeans and a box of Rice Krispies and a couple of Twinkies," he explained.

"Oh I see," she replied. "If that's the case, don't you think you should take something to drink—some water or maybe one of those Coca-Colas you like so much?"

Wilke said, "Thanks Grandma, that's probably a good idea. I could be gone for a long time."

Fannie said, "Wilke, if you are going to be a dancer, you need really good dance shoes. You'll probably need some with taps on them. Do you have some like that?"

Wilke said, "Well no, where do I get shoes with taps on them?"

"If you can wait a few more days, you and I will find shoes with taps on them. I want you to have the best dance shoes before you leave town," she said.

Wilke had a perplexed look on his young face. It was quiet for the longest time as he thought and finally blurted out, "Well, maybe I could wait a couple more days, but no longer."

"We've got a deal. Now go put your bag away before your parents see it and let me get another hour of sleep," she said with a smile.

Later that morning, after Mattie and Joseph left for work, Fannie said she would make good on her promise and she and Wilke would go looking for tap shoes. She called it a field trip. Wilke had never been in Fannie's car. It was Mercury, and even though it had some rust around the fenders, it was painted dark blue and orange on the outside. The inside had nice seats and there were all kind of little gadgets that Fannie seemed to always be fidgeting with. Wilke noticed at once that there was a statue of Jesus on the dash. It was just standing there and as they started to move, he was afraid that the statue would fall down, but it didn't and he was amazed. It stood there, no matter how fast they went. He thought that perhaps he had seen his first miracle.

"I need to make a few stops before we go to find your tap shoes," she explained as she pulled into the parking lot at the Santa Fe train station in Marceline. "I need to get a couple of tickets for Porter and Alfreda while I'm on this side of town. They have planned a trip to the Ozarks next month and I promised to get the tickets for them. If you'll wait here, I'll be right back.""

While she went into the depot, Wilke stayed outside by the car and stared up and down the tracks. He hoped a train would come along. He liked the sound of trains and the wail of the whistle. Some movement up the tracks caught his eye. There was what looked like a man squatting down by the tracks and he had a bundle on a stick slung over his shoulder.

When Fannie came out of the ticket office, Wilke pointed out the man on the tracks. She didn't act surprised. She just said, "Oh, that's Hobo Joe."

"Grandma, how do you know his name?" Wilke asked

"Wilke, men like him are all called 'Hobo Joe'," she said. "Most of them have never known a home. They go from place to place by hopping in open boxcars on the trains, never knowing where they are going next. Most can't read or write. They just jump from one trackside town to another. They either do odd jobs to get a little bit of money for food or many of them are known to be thieves and steal food and money. It's a sad, dangerous life for them, but that's the kind of life they choose."

"Okay, let's go," she said as she headed to her car. "I have one more stop to make to see an old friend named Seth Nemire. I haven't seen him in a long time. He was a friend of your grandfather's and he works in the coal mines a little way out of town. I'd like for you to meet him."

As they bumped down a dirt road to the coal mine, the statue of Jesus still stood rooted securely on the dash.

Wilke didn't really know what a coal mine was, so he had no idea what to expect when they finally got there. When the car stopped, they were in front of what looked like a huge cave with a bunch of men milling around. They all had black faces. He was surprised that his grandma had so many black friends.

Grandma Fannie walked up to one of the men and asked to see Seth. They told her he was down in the mine, but they'd let him know someone was here to see him. Wilke watched the men as they walked around and he heard them talking to one another, but mostly he heard coughing...loud coughing.

A big man with a black face came walking toward them and Fannie ran forward to meet him with a hug. With Wilke by her side, she introduced him to Seth as her grandson.

"Well, Mr. Wilke, mighty nice to meet you," he said. "I've heard Fannie talk about you and how much you look like your grandfather and I must say, you do! Your grandfather was a good man and tried to get me out of these mines years ago, but I wouldn't listen. So, I'm still here. I hope you never end up mining coal Wilke. Your grandfather wouldn't like that."

They chatted for a while and then said goodbye. Fannie made a point of reminding Seth that if he or any of his family needed anything, they knew where to come.

As they walked back to the car, Wilke told Fannie, "I've never seen black people before Grandma."

Fannie laughed as she told him that the black on the faces and hands of the men is just coal dust from inside the mine. She also made a point to explain that the men cough because the coal dust gets into their lungs and over many years in the mines, it causes them to get a disease where they can't breathe and they die.

Wilke seemed to take in all this information and asked, "Grandma Fannie, how did you and Grandpa Will know this Seth fellow?"

"Your Grandpa came across Seth one day when our old truck broke down," she recalled. "Seth was just walking home from work. He was all covered in black coal dust and sweat but he took time out to help your Grandpa with the truck. He knew what to do to get the truck running again and your Grandpa wanted to thank him by inviting him and his wife to dinner at our house the next weekend."

She explained that the coal miners knew the job was hard and dangerous and the coal dust was unhealthy, but they all needed to work to earn money to support their families. "Your Grandpa felt sorry for Seth," she said. "He knew that Seth needed an education in order to get a job out of the coal mine and he wanted to help Seth get that education. He tried to encourage him to get back to school and at least learn reading and writing, but Seth had to work hard to provide for his family. He stayed at coal mining even though his cough was getting worse."

"Okay, enough of that," she finally said as they started back down the dirt road. "Wilke, are you ready to go find those tap shoes, we have about an hour before dinner?"

"Do you know what Grandma," he said. "I'm really tired. Can we just go home?"

"Sure Wilke…but tell me, will you be at school tomorrow? I don't want you to run off without those tap shoes."

Wilke said, "I'll be at school tomorrow, but I'm keeping my bag under my bed just in case."

"Okay," Fannie said with a grin, "but remember that you can't leave town without those tap shoes."

Wilke just looked at her grin and smiled and then he turned his attention back to the miracle happening on the dashboard. There was Jesus still standing up tall.

They arrived back at home and at dinner Fannie was amazed by how much information Wilke had gathered from their field trip. During dinner he talked non-stop about how he and Fannie had gone for a drive to do some errands for her and he saw Hobo Joe and a black coal miner. Mattie and Joseph looked up from their meals with a questioning look.

"It was just a little field trip," she explained with a wink. "I wanted to show Wilke what can happen to people that can't read or write. I think you got the picture, didn't you Wilke?"

"Well all I know is that I don't want to be a hobo or work in a place where everybody coughs all day," he admitted as Joseph returned Fannie's wink.

After Mattie cleaned up they all settled down to watch the Lawrence Welk TV show. Wilke loved to watch the dancing, but soon fell fast asleep wondering if dancers needed to read and write...

CHAPTER FOURTEEN
Let's Dance

It was now early spring and Wilke had been doing well in his studies. He seemed to have a new respect for Grandma Fannie, since they had some shared secrets. She knew he had tried to run away and he knew he was going to need her help in getting tap shoes. He was still doing poorly with spelling, but his math knowledge was way beyond a first grader. His reading had greatly improved and he could now read most of what his comic book hero Captain Bob had to say.

Fannie was pleased with his progress. He still threw tantrums from time to time and would show up late to the learning table, and one time Fannie found the table in disarray, with school supplies dumped on the floor and books with torn pages. But she found that the damage was just because Wilke had gotten frustrated with a math problem or a bad grade he earned on a spelling test.

Joseph and Mattie were very pleased with the changes in Wilke. They talked to Fannie about getting him a puppy to reward him. Fannie said absolutely not. Wilke had a long way to go and a puppy would be a distraction. She still needed his full attention.

Fannie told them that what Wilke really needed was some interaction with children his own age. He had no friends and saw no one except Mattie, Joseph and Fannie. The only time he interacted with others was on the weekends, when he would go over to the gas station and talk to the customers that happened to be hanging around. They all liked Wilke and gave him their spare change when he danced for them. He put all the money toward his tap shoes. So far he had saved about $7. He thought he would soon be able to buy the best tap shoes around, and he might even have some left over to catch a train to the Ozarks, where he heard people danced way into the night.

When Wilke would get an A on a test, Fannie would reward him with a trip to Loman's drugstore and they would have a chocolate soda or sometimes a banana split. Unfortunately they didn't get to make this trip too often, because Wilke got very few A's. He was an average student, but he had come a long way from those first days at St. Bonaventure School.

One morning in early May, when Wilke had a difficult time with his spelling and English lessons, Fannie asked him if he'd like to go for another field trip. He was more than happy to get away from school work.

"Where are we going?" he asked.

"I need to visit some friends," Fanny explained, "and, I'd like for you to meet them as well. You met them before, but I think you were too young to remember."

Wilke was excited to get into Fannie's car again. He could hardly wait to see the miraculous statue of Jesus, and he watched it closely as they drove the 10 miles of gravel roads to Wien.

First, Fannie made a stop at her own house, where she checked up on a few things and got her mail.

Wilke thought the house was big, way too big for one old woman. There were all kind of rooms filled with stuff and pictures of Grandfather Will and Wilke's father Joseph on almost every wall. There were at least four or five pictures of his father and mother at their wedding. There was also a picture of Joseph's dog Molly. Wilke came across a picture of Edgar, Fannie's father and he had a big smile, but hardly any teeth. Wilke thought he looked most like Edgar. They both had no teeth.

What really interested him was the orange-striped, tabby cat he spotted on the back porch. He opened the screen door and went out to pet the cat. The cat at first backed away and made a hissing sound. Wilke sat down and picked up some of the hard food in the bowl nearby and held out his hand. The cat came closer and ate a piece of the food and stood still just long enough for Wilke to touch the top of his head.

Grandma Fannie looked out the screen door and said, "I see you've found Chester."

Wilke said, "Is he your cat Grandma? I didn't know you had a cat."

Fannie said, "Well I guess in a way he is my cat. Nobody has ever come to claim him. He showed up one day at the back door—a stray I guess. I started feeding him, and when I'm gone, the Schiltz boys keep food in his bowl. He helps around here by catching rats and mice and he sleeps in the barn. He's not allowed in the house."

"Grandma, he seems lonely," Wilke said. "I bet he likes to be petted and there is no one here to pet him. Can we take him home with us?"

"Oh my, no," Fannie said. "Your parents would not agree to that, I'm sure. Let's go Wilke, say goodbye to Chester."

As Chester seemed to realize that Wilke was going to leave, he paced on the porch and rubbed his head around Wilke's ankles and made a few meow sounds.

"Grandma please," Wilke begged. "Chester likes me. I'll explain to my parents. I know they'll understand. I'll take care of Chester, I promise."

Fannie answered by clapping her hands and the cat bolted for the barn. She brought Wilke in the house and closed and latched the back door.

Wilke was sullen in the car and had his fierce face on.

Fannie broke the silence by saying, "Wilke, now we are going to see my best friends, Porter and Alfreda."

"Oh great, you mean the 'crips,'" he said.

"Now, now, that is very unkind and disrespectful," she said. They were at your baptism and they have done more for you and this family than you could ever know. They helped raise your father and put me through college. Yes, Alfreda walks with a limp and Porter has a glass eye, but we do not, ever, call them 'crips.' Do you understand?"

They pulled up in front of a small wooden building behind the church and went to the door. Fannie knocked and Porter welcomed them in. He was in his early sixties now, but still had a warm, jovial smile. He called for Alfreda and a lady in her mid forties appeared. Wilke thought she looked frail, but noticed that she had the most beautiful sparking blue eyes.

They all hugged and Fannie introduced Wilke. "I know you haven't seen him for a few years," she said. He's nearly seven now. Say hello, Wilke."

He shifted anxiously from foot to foot, but managed a weak "hello" and shook their hands. In the big room with a wood floor, he saw a piano in one corner with a flute sitting on the bench and a record player on a shelf that was filled with all kind of shoes.

Porter said, "Wilke, Fannie says you like to dance. Well, this is our dance studio. It's here that we teach people to dance."

Alfreda said, "We were just finishing up a ballet lesson with Betty."

It was then that Wilke spotted a short, blonde girl in ballet shoes standing in the corner. She wore black tights and a white top. She looked over at him and waved with a smile. He hadn't had a girl his age smile at him in a long time. Maybe this trip wasn't so bad after all he thought to himself.

Porter said, "Wilke if it's alright, we'd like to show you some dance steps. What kind of dancing do you like?"

"I like to tap dance, but I don't have any taps on my shoes," Wilke replied.

"Well then you are in luck," Porter said. "We have all kinds of shoes here and I'm sure there are some tap shoes in a size that fits you."

Wilke thought for sure that the Jesus guy on Fannie's dash had reached out and touched him. A girl had smiled at him and he was actually going to get to put on a pair of real tap shoes.

Porter checked up and down the shelf and found a pair of tap shoes that seemed right and when Wilke tried them on, they were a little tight but he wasn't about to complain.

"Okay, young man," said Porter. "Show us some of your dance moves."

Wilke was shy at first and just nipped the toes and the heels of the shoes lightly on the floor. He was surprised at how loud and crisp the shoes made the sounds. He'd never had a pair of tap shoes so this was all new to him.

Porter said, "Do you need some music boy? Alfreda plays a mean piano."

"No thanks, when I dance on the pop case at the gas station for the old guys, there isn't any music. I guess I make music in my head," he explained.

He started to tap a little harder and as the music in his mind filled his head, he just let go and tapped his heart out. Ratta tat tat, he went. Ratta tat tat tat tat!

When he finally stopped, everyone, including Betty the ballet girl, clapped.

Porter said, "That's not bad for somebody that just dances on a soda pop case."

Wilke looked embarrassed, but his heart was soaring.

Fannie asked Wilke if he would like to come to the dance studio every week and take some dance lessons. "If it's alright with you Wilke," she said. "I can drop you off and then go check on things at my house and stop over at the high school in Salisbury."

Wilke thought it was a wonderful idea. They said their good byes and Fannie told them she would be back next Wednesday about 1 o'clock.

On the way home, Fannie was amazed that he was so animated. He couldn't stop talking about how much he loved to dance.

As she pulled the Mercury into the driveway at Mattie and Josephs, she wondered to herself if dancing might be the key to open the door that Wilke still hid his unhappiness and anger behind.

CHAPTER FIFTEEN
The Birthday

Wilke looked forward to every Wednesday when he could put on the borrowed tap shoes once again. Fannie told him that on the days that he had dance practice, he would have to finish more homework that night. Wilke agreed. She was pleased to have found something that might motivate her grandson to want to learn.

As to Porter and Alfreda, they weren't such "crips" after all, Wilke thought. Alfreda wasn't a dancer with her bad ankle, but she did play the piano and flute very well. He was impressed by Porter, who seemed to know every tap dance step. They would both put on their tap shoes and Alfreda would pound out a rinky-tinky tune on the piano. The 62-year-old Porter Wilson would tap away and Wilke would imitate the steps. He showed Wilke the clamproll, the ball change, the step toe and a basic stomp. Alfreda enjoyed accompanying them and loved seeing the two of them having so much fun. One of his favorite moves was the double clamproll that Porter said was the finale of every great tap routine. Ratta tat tat, ratta tat tat and a ratta tat tat tat tat!

Every Wednesday, on the way home from dance class, Wilke would ask Grandma Fannie if they could just stop for a minute at her house, so he could pet Chester.

"OK, but only for a few minutes, we have to get back home soon," she'd always say.

Wilke would run to the back porch and there would be Chester. It was almost like the cat was waiting for him. He'd stroke and talk lovingly to the cat and made sure Chester had plenty of food in his bowl and fresh water in an old pie tin. As they headed for the car, Chester would run to the end of the porch and just stand there looking as they drove away.

It was nearing the end of May and Joseph's birthday was coming up. Mattie knew it had never been a day of celebration for him, since his father died on that day. She respected that and always made May 24th a low key day. She would cook his favorite meal, which still was a grilled cheese sandwich, boiled egg and cherry cobbler. There would always be a card by his dinner plate. It wasn't a birthday card, just a nice card that said "I Love You." There was never a gift or a cake with candles.

This year was going to be Joseph's 35th birthday and Mattie thought it was time to let go of the past and celebrate his birthday in a special way. She didn't want to surprise him, because she worried what his reaction might be. So, she just asked him and said she'd like to have a few of their friends over and that Fannie's aunts Leona and Viola would like to come down to visit. They had not seen them in a long time. She told him that she wanted to celebrate not only his birthday, but how well Wilke was doing. They had a lot to be thankful for. Joseph agreed. A small party would be fine. It was time they all had a little fun.

Mattie told Wilke and Fannie about the party. It would be the Saturday evening coming up, just five days away. Fannie was pleased to hear that Joseph was finally able to celebrate his birthday.

Fannie asked Mattie who was invited to the party and she said, "Well, Porter and Alfreda are coming and your aunts are coming in on the train.

Wilke was originally excited about the party, but once he heard the nuns were coming, he wasn't too happy. He thought that it was bad enough to have them in school, but you sure didn't want them in your house.

"I'm going to invite some of our good customers from the station," Mattie said. "Why don't you see if your friend Seth and his wife can make it?"

"Sounds like a good group to me," Fannie said. "Wilke and I will even let you use the learning table for this special occasion."

They all smiled.

On their trip to dance class that Wednesday, Fannie asked Wilke if he might like to surprise his father for his birthday and show how well he was doing with his tap lessons. She thought it would be a fun idea if he and Porter could put on a little tap show for the birthday crowd.

Wilke looked at her and said, "No, I don't think we're ready for that. Besides, I don't think nuns like tap dancing."

"Well now, what would make you think nuns don't like tap dancing?" she asked. "I'm going to have Porter bring the tap shoes along, just in case you change your mind.

"I won't," he said.

"Don't forget, after the lesson, we need to stop and check on Chester," he said.

"How could I forget to stop for Chester," she said. "You remind me of that every Wednesday."

"I wouldn't pester you if you'd let me bring him home with us," he said.

"I told you before Wilke, that I'm allergic to cats and that's why I can't let Chester in the house," she said.

"Well, you're not going to live with us forever," he reminded her.

"No, but while I am living there, we can't have a cat in the house," she said.

Mattie was busy making preparations for the party. She was not going to bake a cake, but she had three or four cherry cobblers and planned to put candles on top. Everyone was bringing a dish, and she would have other food prepared. The dining room was decorated with crepe paper and there was a big sign she had made that said HAPPY BIRTHDAY JOSEPH. It was so exciting. This was the first real party in their home.

The Sisters Leona and Viola were to arrive late Friday afternoon by train. They planned to spend the weekend. Fannie and Wilke had finished their lessons by 4 o'clock.

Fannie said, "Wilke, go comb your hair and wash your face. We need to go pick my up my aunts at the train station. Do you remember them? They are very nice."

Wilke said, "I never met a nice nun."

Fannie said, "Let's go Wilke, or we'll be late."

As they drove along, Wilke was hoping that the Jesus statue in Fannie's car would take care of any curse these two nuns would put on him. He saw them get off the train and his heart started to race. Fannie got out of the car and went up to greet the Sisters. Wilke was in the front and they got into the back, but not before opening his car door and giving him a big hug. If ever he wanted to be invisible or dead, it was at that moment.

The nuns and Fannie chatted on the way home and Wilke just kept looking at the Jesus statue. Please don't fall off the dash. I really need you now he said to himself. He didn't know how he was going to get through a whole weekend with nuns in his house. He just hoped they knew who they were dealing with. His reputation with nuns was not good.

That night, there was a nice family dinner around the real dining room table. All the adults chatted and chatted and Wilke, feeling out of place, complained that he didn't feel well and excused himself to go to his bedroom. He piled every comic book he had in front of his door. Those nuns were not going to sneak in on him in the night.

The next day, Joseph got up and went to work at the gas station as usual. Mattie stayed home to continue the preparations for the party. Wilke had never seen his mom quite so alive and full of energy. He was glad to see her happy.

Joseph closed the station early and came home to take a shower. He popped open a bottle of beer and sat down at the kitchen table. Wilke didn't generally see his dad drink beer. He wasn't sure what beer was, but he knew it wasn't the same as root beer. He saw his mom make a drink for herself that they called a Tom Collins. Wilke wondered who Tom Collins was and why they'd named a drink after him. He'd have to ask Grandma Fannie.

The guests started to arrive about dinner time. Each one brought some kind of food dish to share. Rosie and Tony McGanna brought some scalloped potatoes. Penny and Bernard Peski had made a roasted chicken. They all kept coming with food. Somebody even brought some pickled pigs' feet. The table and counter in the kitchen were overflowing. It looked like quite a feast.

Mattie and Fannie greeted everyone and offered drinks. Joseph was making a lot of Tom Collins and something called whiskey and handing out cold bottles of beer. Wilke walked around and when someone wasn't paying attention, he would take a sip of a Tom Collins. It was sweet and sour and tasty. He preferred that to the beer and whiskey. He was having quite a good time until Grandma Fannie caught him taking a sip of another Tom Collins. His drinking time was over.

A big guy walked up to Wilke and introduced himself, "Hello there

Master Wilke, it's good to see you again. I'm Seth from the coal mine and this is my wife Loretta."

Wilke was taken aback. "You really are white," he stammered.

"Well yes, I am white. Are you disappointed?" Seth asked.

"No, I just thought you had a black face when I saw you," Wilke said.

"I have a black face during the day and a white face at night," he said with a grin. "What you saw was the dust and dirt from the coal mine on my face. Remember, you don't ever want to work in the mine."

Seth and Loretta walked away to talk with Joseph and Mattie. Wilke looked around at the other guests. He knew most of them from the gas station. Some were the old guys that paid him to dance on the soda pop case. There was one fellow he recognized, but Wilke wondered why he was there. It was Homer Goss. Homer was known as the town drunk. Even though Wilke didn't yet know what a drunk was, he knew that Homer was not quite all there most of the time. He wondered why his parents had invited him. Maybe, he thought, they just felt sorry for him.

Wilke was curious how the nuns were doing and what they thought of all of this drinking and partying. He wandered into the living room and found the nuns sitting in front of the TV and each one of them held a bottle of beer. They were laughing and seemed to be having a great time. He thought for the first time, that maybe nuns really were human after all.

As he left the living room, he ran into Porter and Alfreda. It was reassuring to see them.

"Hey there Mr. Tap Man, I brought your shoes along and I brought mine, just in case you want to do a little dance for this crowd tonight," he said. "I think it would make your dad really pleased, but I'll leave it up to you."

Wilke had sipped just enough Tom Collins, whiskey and beer—that he said he would do it.

By about 7 o'clock, most of the guests had finished their drinks and everybody had feasted on the food. It was about time to light the candles on the cobblers. They all seemed to be having a good time and Homer Goss had certainly downed his share of drinks. Fannie tried to make sure that he had some food to help soak up some of the alcohol. Food or not, he was still looking a little wobbly.

Porter stood up and announced that he and Wilke would like to do a special dance for Joseph's birthday. It was one they had been practicing, an old Fred Astaire number and Porter had even brought some canes that went with the routine. Alfreda had a record that she put it on the old record player. Everyone made a circle around the performers as the music started.

Porter and Wilke tapped to the music. Wilke was having so much fun and all the steps just came naturally to him. It was only about a two-minute dance, but at the end everybody clapped. Joseph and Mattie were so proud. Fannie had the biggest smile on her face.

Just then, Homer Goss staggered into the middle of the circle and blurted out, "Well now, that was pretty good for an old geezer with one eye and a queer little boy with no teeth. You two should join the circus. You'd be a great freak show. They pay good money for freaks you know."

At that, Joseph grabbed Homer and dragged him toward the door. "Homer get the hell out of here! He yelled. "You are no longer welcome in my house."

"Oh, Joe, you're a horse's katupi," Homer said as he pulled away from Joseph's grip. "Ya' know what that means, Joe? You're a horse's ass! "You don' know shit about shit. You're just a grease monkey. Now, your son here—he's got real talent and might just end up a better grease monkey than you. Imagine that, a queer, toothless, dancing grease monkey!"

At that, Joseph had heard enough. Though Homer was a big man, Joseph had no trouble knocking him off his feet. He shoved him to the floor and started to punch him in the face. It took three of the other men at the party to break up the mêlée.

At that moment, Joseph saw his father's death all over again and he swore he would never celebrate another birthday. It was a bad day and it always would be.

CHAPTER SIXTEEN
The Lost Boy

As Joseph was pummeling Homer, Wilke dropped his cane and bolted out the front door. Fannie saw him go and she headed out the door behind him. "Wilke, stop!" she shouted but to no avail. Wilke was a fast runner.

She watched him for a few seconds, but since it was getting dark she lost sight of him as he was out of the yard and across the road. She hollered his name and tried to run after him, but she knew she would never catch up with him.

Seth and several of the men got Joseph off of Homer and they dragged him to Seth's car since he had offered to take him home. Mattie slumped down at the kitchen table with her head in her hands. She was devastated by what had happened and knew that this would be one more birthday for Joseph that turned into a bad memory.

Fannie ran back into the house out of breath and told everyone that Wilke had taken off running down the street in the dark. The remaining guests went out looking for him. They searched everywhere. Mattie went to the gas station and checked all around there and the ice house. There was no sign of him. Some guests went down to the train tracks; others went door to door to neighbors to see if they had seen Wilke. There was no sign of him.

Joseph and Mattie were frantic. It was dark—nearly 8 o'clock. In desperation, someone called Sheriff Nelson and told him what had happened. He said he would join the search and drove up and down every street in the neighborhood. There was no sign of Wilke.

Porter and Alfreda also combed the streets of town in their car. There was no sign of the missing boy anywhere.

After a couple of frantic hours, most of the searchers ended up back at Mattie and Joseph's house. Still no sign of Wilke. Joseph thanked them and assured everyone that Wilke wasn't far away and would return when he was ready. He assured them that if he needed help in the morning, he'd let everyone know.

Fannie, Joseph and Mattie collapsed at the dining room table. It was still stacked with dirty dishes. The Sisters sat with them and they all held hands and prayed for Wilke's safe return.

In the midst of the prayer, Fannie looked up and said, "I think I might know where he is. Joseph, Mattie, get in my car. Sisters you stay here in case he comes back to the house. "

They piled in Fannie's Mercury and she spun tires in the gravel as she headed out of the driveway. "Where are we going Mom?" Joseph asked.

"Just keep praying and keep hoping I'm right." she said.

She roared down the gravel road to Wien, wheeled into her driveway and slid to a halt in front of her house. They all piled out of the car. Fannie let them in the front door with her key and she immediately went to the back door and looked out on the porch. There, as she suspected, was Wilke. He was curled up in a ball and had Chester in his arms. He had walked and ran all the way there in his tap shoes.

Mattie and Joseph just wanted to pick him up and hold him, but didn't want to scare him. They had never been happier to see their little boy.

Fannie said, "Let's get him home to his own bed. Joseph, you pick him up very gently and get in the back of the car. I think we'll bring Chester along to keep him company."

Joseph said, "Mom, are you sure? You know you are allergic to cats."

Fannie said, "Joseph, I love this little boy, just like I love you. So, from this day on, I am no longer allergic to cats. Right now Wilke needs a friend, and his name is Chester."

Joseph carefully picked up a sleeping little boy in his arms and settled in the back seat of the car. Mattie snuggled in beside them and she held Chester on her lap. Fannie locked up the house and slowly headed the car back down the road.

Joseph felt that he had just had the best birthday of his life. He had found his son alive and well. He reached forward and squeezed Fannie's shoulder and said, "Thank you Mom."

Fannie kept her eyes on the road but reached up and grasped his hand saying, "Let's go home and light the candles on that cherry cobbler."

CHAPTER SEVENTEEN
The Aftermath

It was very quiet at the Spenzi house the next morning. Joseph got up at seven but he called Ray McGanna and after telling him that Wilke was home, he asked him to open business at the station. He said he'd be over later. Ray understood. He told Joseph that he would get the word out to the others who were at the party so that everyone would know that the boy was safe. Joseph thanked him and went back to bed with Mattie. They cuddled in each other's arms and fell back to sleep.

Fannie got up once about 7:30 and checked on Wilke and he was still curled up in his bed with Chester beside him. She went back to bed. It had been a long night for all of them.

The Sisters were up early as usual. They had said their morning prayers and had given thanks for Wilke's safe return. In the kitchen they busied themselves with brewing the coffee and they planned on making pancakes and eggs for everyone when they got up. Leona and Viola's train was due to leave at noon that day and Fannie would take them to the train station. They wanted to be as helpful as they could before they left.

Fannie smelled the fresh-brewed coffee and decided it was time to get out of bed. She went to the kitchen and gave the Sisters a hug. They all sat down at the table and had some coffee and juice.

Fannie said, "Thank you both for your help and prayers last night. I'm sorry it didn't turn out to be the party we had hoped it would be."

Leona said, "The main thing is that Wilke is safe. We just feel bad that Joseph has had so many sad birthdays."

Soon, Mattie and Joseph made it to the kitchen in their robes. They still looked tired.

"Good morning you two," said Fannie. "Come'n sit down. We have hot coffee and juice and the Sisters have plans to whip us up some eggs and pancakes."

"Oh my heavens, what a treat," said Mattie. "That sounds wonderful! Thank you all for being here."

"I think the Lord wanted us to be here," offered Viola. "He always seems to know where we need to be."

Joseph went to check on Wilke. He opened the boy's door and found him still fast asleep with Chester. He closed the door. It's best to let him sleep as long as he needs to he thought.

As the adults were starting on breakfast, a sleepy-eyed Wilke showed up in the doorway with Chester at his ankles. "How'd Chester get here?" he said.

"Well, it looks like he just followed you home," said Fannie with a smile.

"Grandma," said Wilke. I don't understand. We can't have a cat because you are allergic to cats."

Fannie walked over and bent down to give Wilke a hug and Chester a scratch on his ears, "Don't worry, we'll work it out," she said. "I'll go to Loman's drugstore and get some medicine for my allergies. Besides, I'm only going to be here for a couple more weeks. School will soon be out and you'll be on summer break and I'll be going home to tend my garden and get back to my own schoolwork."

"So Chester can stay with us?" Wilke asked.

Mattie smiled and said, "Yes Wilke, Chester can stay with us. We'll go out later and get him some food and whatever he needs."

Fannie escorted Wilke to the breakfast table and they sat down. Chester seemed to realize that he was now part of the family, so he sat down patiently beside Wilke's chair.

While they were in the middle of breakfast, the doorbell rang. Joseph went to the door and to his astonishment; there was Seth and Homer Goss. He glared at Homer and not a word was said for at least a full minute. "What the hell do you want Goss? Joseph bellowed. "I don't believe you have the gall to step foot on this property."

Seth blunted the verbal attack by saying, "Now Joseph, wait a minute. Have an open mind. Mr. Goss here has come to apologize to you about last night." Joseph just glared at both of them.

In a sheepish tone of voice, Homer spoke up and said, "Joe, I'm sorry that I ruint your party. I guess the hooch just got me."

Joseph, obviously unimpressed by this apology, said, "Homer you not only owe me an apology for what you said at the party, but you owe a special apology to my son. What you said was cruel and hurtful and it was nothing a young boy should ever have had to hear. You made him run away last night after what you said and the whole town was looking for him. He could have been seriously hurt or worse."

"Okay Joe, well…let me say I'm sorry to the boy," Homer said.

Joseph opened the door and Seth and Homer followed him toward the kitchen. When Wilke saw Homer headed his way, he flew out of his chair and bolted out the screen door into the backyard with Chester in pursuit.

Joseph could see that Wilke wanted nothing to do with an apology from the likes of Homer Goss. He turned to the men and said, "Homer, you know you've got a drinking problem. You have had it for a long time. What you said and did last night was unforgiveable. I don't want to see you around the station anymore or anywhere near my family. Seth, take Homer out of here. I know you meant well, but the damage has been done."

Seth realized that Joseph was serious and after saying goodbye to everyone and giving Fannie a hug, he escorted Homer back to the front door and they were gone.

Joseph was perplexed, but he went out the back door to find Wilke. He was sitting under a tree petting Chester.

"Wilke, Homer is gone and he won't be back. I'm sorry for what he said, but Homer drinks too much and when he does, he has no control over what he says. I'm not asking you to forgive him, just understand that he's not a well man," Joseph said. "Let's go back in and finish our breakfast."

Wilke wasn't really hungry anymore, so he just picked at his food and then went to his room. The Sisters and Mattie busied themselves cleaning up the kitchen and Joseph gave hugs all around and headed for the gas station. Fannie announced that it was time to head for the train station so the Sisters wouldn't miss their train. Wilke appeared and asked to go along. They were all surprised, but happy to see him want to be involved.

Fannie, Wilke and the Sisters loaded up the Mercury and drove to the train station. They checked their tickets and were assured that the train was running on time. Fannie and Viola went into the station for a soft drink and Leona and Wilke settled down on a wide bench along the wall. Wilke looked intently into Leona's eyes and said, "You really are human aren't you?"

"Yes Wilke," she said. "We are and we love you. I'm sorry that you had to hear those terrible words from that poor man Homer Goss."

"Sister Leona," Wilke said. "What is a queer? Homer Goss called me a queer. Is that a bad thing?"

"No son," she replied as she took his hand in hers. "There are sometime things in the world that are out of the ordinary or different and those things are sometimes called queer, but you are not queer."

"But Homer Goss told me that I am queer so he must have meant that I am different," said Wilke.

"But you aren't," she said. "There are people who think Viola and I are out of the ordinary and different because we are nuns and we dress different in our habits and we act different. Do you think that makes us queer?"

Well no Sister Leona," Wilke said after he'd thought about what she had said. "You and Viola are different…but in a nice way."

"Well, that's exactly what we think about you. You are different in a nice way. There is nothing wrong with being different. It can make one very special. "Viola and I think you are special," she said.

Her words were almost drowned out by the sound of the train as it pulled into the station. Fannie and Sister Viola came out with sodas for everyone and they all hugged their goodbyes as the conductor took their luggage and disappeared up the steps on to the train car. Wilke had a new image of nuns now and he hugged both Sisters especially hard.

The whistle blew and the train began its slow motion move out of the station. Fannie and Wilke waved and waved as the Sisters rolled off down the track. Fannie took Wilke's hand and they headed for the car. "Thank you," she said giving his hand a squeeze. "I'm so proud of you. Thank you for being so kind to the Sisters."

When they got home, Porter and Alfreda were with Mattie in the kitchen. When they saw Wilke, they both hugged him and were so glad to see he was safe.

Mattie said, "Let's go to the store. We have to get food and supplies for Chester."

They all piled into Porter's big car and drove to the pet store in Brookfield. Fannie stayed home with Chester. She didn't want to leave him alone on his first day in his new home.

When they were gone, she said to Chester, "I know you're going to miss the farm and catching all of those mice, but I don't think you could have found a better home or a better friend. I can only imagine what all they are going to buy for you today. My old barn cat is about to become a very spoiled cat. I think maybe some good may have come out of all this turmoil."

CHAPTER EIGHTEEN
Summer Break

Though it was now the first week of June and the school year was over, Fannie and Wilke still worked on. He had a lot of catching up to do so they maintained their usual weekday schedule. The only change was that Chester was generally in Wilke's lap or under his chair when he was at the learning table. Fannie didn't complain, as long as Chester didn't distract Wilke from his work.

The cat had fit in to family life at the Spenzi household quickly. His litter box was in Wilke's room and he slept on the boy's bed every night. Wilke dutifully fed him and brushed him. They were inseparable.

Wilke was doing better at his lessons, but Fannie didn't think he could afford to take the whole summer off. She talked to Mattie and Joseph about him coming to live at her house during the week. St. Mary's School in Wien had a summer program and she thought it would be helpful for Wilke. It would be good for to him get used to being taught by nuns again. Mattie and Joseph agreed and so the arrangement was made that Wilke would live with Fannie during the week and Joseph and Mattie would pick him up on Fridays and he would spend the weekends at home with them. Wilke was fine about it, as long as Chester could come along.

Fannie said, "Well of course Chester can come along, I need my mouse catcher back."

Near the end of June, Fannie and Wilke packed their bags, said their goodbyes to Joseph and Mattie, and drove off in the old Mercury to Wien. They put a blanket in the back seat for Chester and he slept most of the way. Wilke was glad to see the Jesus statue still standing strong on the dashboard. Somehow he thought maybe all of this would work out, even though he didn't look forward to spending the summer in school.

They got settled at Fannie's house and on the first day of school at St. Mary's, she took him to the school and met with his teacher, Sister John Marie. Fannie was good friends with the past head nun at the school, Sister Raphael, but she retired several years before. Her replacement was Sister John Marie. She was a young nun, but seemed to be well-qualified for the job. She and Fannie hit it off quite well and when Fannie headed back home, she looked over at Wilke and nodded and winked as if to give her okay to the new teacher.

Wilke looked around at the other students and could see there were only four others besides him. He recognized only one of them. It was Betty the ballet girl from Porter and Alfreda's studio. Betty also recognized him and she walked over to say hello.

"Hello there," she said. "I think we met at Porter's dance studio. I'm Betty Barnes. Do you remember me?"

Of course I remember you Betty," Wilke replied. "My name is Wilke Spenzi. Are you still dancing at the studio?"

"I still dance there whenever I can," she said. "I want to be a ballerina someday. Do you want to be a tap dancer?"

"I don't know, I haven't tapped in a long time," he said.

"Well, if you feel like going back to Porter's studio sometime, I'd be happy to go with you. I thought you were very good," she said.

"Why are you in summer school?" he asked.

Betty smiled and traced a small circle on the floor with her toe before she answered, "I'm a slow learner I guess, but I have a lot of chores because my parents have been sick and I just haven't had a lot of time to study."

"Sick? Wilke asked innocently. "What are they sick with?"

"I hate to admit it," she replied, "but I think my parents drink whiskey too much and that's what is making them sick. They tell me that the stuff in the brown bottle is medicine, but I know it's whiskey."

"Oh my," said Wilke as he reached over and took Betty's tiny hand in his. "I'm sorry that they are drinking whiskey. I once saw a man drink too much whiskey and it turned him into a crazy man. My dad says the man is a drunk and he said bad things at my dad's birthday party."

"Well my parents aren't bad people," Betty said in a defensive tone as she pulled her hand away from Wilke's grasp. "I don't mind taking care of them…most of the time. But I know that one of the reasons I like to dance is that it gets me away from them and their problems."

At that moment, Wilke missed his parents and was grateful for how good they were to him and thankful that drinking whisky didn't influence their lives. He was also thankful for Grandma Fannie and Chester and felt sorry that Betty didn't have anyone like them in her life.

As the summer wore on, Wilke did well in school and developed learning skills way beyond the first grade level. Sister John Marie was very proud of his progress. She knew that Betty and Wilke had formed a connection, but tried to make sure it did not become a distraction for either of them.

One day after school in late July, Fannie came to pick Wilke up from school and he asked if Betty could come home with him so they could study together. Fannie had no problem with that but she worried if it was okay with Betty's parents. Betty assured her that her parents wouldn't mind. So, that afternoon, Betty and Wilke did their homework together. It was the first time that Betty had met Wilke's cat Chester and she loved how he rubbed against her ankles and purred when he was petted.

As afternoon turned to evening, Fannie was beginning to put some dinner together and she went to Betty and asked her if she would stay and eat dinner with them. "Oh no," Betty said as she jumped up from the table where she and Wilke had laid out their books. "I really need to get home. I didn't realize it was that late."

Fannie said, "Betty, if you feel you really should get home, I understand. Wilke…come on…let's hop in the car and take Betty home."

Betty looked disturbed as she stacked up her school work, but knew she had no choice, so they all piled in Fannie's car.

Fannie didn't know anything about the Barnes family. She had heard the name, but they weren't church goers and they weren't well known in town. It seemed that they just kept to themselves. After all of the years Fannie had lived in Wien, she didn't even know where they lived. Betty would have to direct the way.

They got to the end of Betty's driveway at about 6 o'clock and Betty wanted Fannie to just drop her off. She said she'd walk the rest of the way to the house.

"Young lady, it's late," Fannie said emphatically. "You have an armload of books and papers and it'll take two seconds to drive you up to your door." With that she swung into the Barnes's dirt driveway and headed toward faint lights in the distance. Betty didn't have a chance to object.

As Fannie's old Mercury approached the house, chickens scattered from the driveway. Fannie pulled up in front and Betty quickly got out of the car, thanking them for the ride. Before she could get very far, the porch light snapped on and an old man with a long dark beard came off the porch and approached the car. "Hi Daddy," Betty said.

Fannie spoke first, "Mr. Barnes, I'm Fannie Spenzi and this is my grandson Wilke. We're bringing your daughter Betty home. She and Wilke did some homework together tonight."

"Much obliged for bringing Betty home Mrs. Spenzi," he said as her turned toward Betty who was headed for the front door. "You...Betty...git in the house! You know you have chores to do after school."

Fannie tried to break the tension by saying, "Betty is a good student and I hope some of that rubs off on Wilke. I was happy to see them working so hard on their school work today. By the way, Mr. Barnes, I've lived in Wien a long time and never met you or your wife. Is your wife here? I'd like to meet her."

"My wife ain't too well tonight," he said. "She's in bed and the girl here needs to get in and tend to her. You all go on now. Thanks for bringing the girl home." With that, he turned and disappeared into the house. The door slammed shut and the porch light snapped off.

Fannie and Wilke sat speechless in the dark. Neither Wilke nor Fannie had a chance to say anything to Betty. It was obvious that she was afraid of her father and both of them thought it was probably for good reason. They were worried about Betty, but there was nothing they could do at that moment. Fannie turned the car down the driveway and they headed home.

Betty didn't show up for school the next day or the next. A week went by.

Wilke told Fannie about it and they drove over to the Barnes home on Saturday afternoon. They slowly made their way up the long dusty driveway and parked in front of the house. Fannie got out and went up on the porch and knocked on the door.

The same bearded guy answered the door and Fannie asked if they could see Betty. Before he could answer, a voice shouted from inside the house. "Jimmy…who you talking to?"

"Mama, we got vis'tors," he yelled to her over his shoulder. "It's the Spenzi folks and they're lookin' for Betty."

Before anything else was said, a wrinkle-faced, old lady with scraggly gray hair appeared at the door. She squinted at them in response to the sunlight and looked like she hadn't slept for days. "Listen to me now…," she warned. "There ain't no one by the name of Betty here. You go away. We don't cause no trouble and you don't cause us none."

Fannie was taken aback and blurted out, "We brought Betty home last week. This is where she said she lived. Where is she? How can you say she's not here?"

"I tole you to listen…Betty's gone to Wichita to stay with her grandma. She won't be back," the old lady said. "You better git outta' here now."

Feeling threatened, Fannie and Wilke backed off the porch and headed toward where Fannie's car was parked. At the side of the driveway under a scraggly shrub, Wilke noticed pink ribbons sticking out of the dirt as he was getting in his side of Fannie's car. He reached down and grabbed the ribbons and pulled—a pair of ballet shoes appeared—caked with dirt from where they had been buried. With shoes in hand, he jumped in the car and told Fannie that they better get out of there. She turned the car around and headed down the driveway. "Grandma," he said. "These are Betty's ballet shoes. I think maybe something bad has happened to her."

"You are right Wilke," she said. "I'm worried also. We'll talk it over with your dad and mom tonight, but I think we should go talk to Sheriff Nelson "

When they got home, Fannie called Joseph and Mattie and discussed the situation with them. They all agreed that Sheriff Nelson should be alerted to the situation. The next day they drove into Marceline and told their story to Sheriff Nelson. He said he would check it out.

A couple days later Sheriff Nelson showed up at Fannie's door. He told

Fannie and Wilke that he had checked out the situation and found out that Betty was living with her grandma in Wichita and was just fine. She would be continuing school there.

Wilke was glad to hear she was safe. He took Betty's ballet shoes and put them in his closet.

He hoped that maybe someday she would come back for them.

CHAPTER NINETEEN
Life After Betty

Sister John Marie was aware of what had happened with Betty. She tried to be sensitive to Wilke's feelings of despair and his sense of loss. Betty was the only friend he had in school. Now that Betty was gone, there were only four children left in summer school. There was Alfred Null, a quiet boy who barely spoke to anyone. There was Joyce Hughes who was a big mouth and Sister John Marie was constantly trying to calm her down, and there was Buddy Meinhart who was every nun's dream—a perfect student. Wilke didn't relate to any of them. He missed Betty.

As the summer went on, Wilke found it hard to focus on his schoolwork, but still managed to read at a 2nd grade level and his math skills were almost at a 4th grade level. His spelling had improved and Sister John Marie thought he would be well prepared for 2nd grade in the fall.

Wilke liked staying with Grandma Fannie during the week. He learned all about the farm and helped her pick strawberries and tend to the potatoes, green beans and other vegetables that she grew. Chester was never far behind. He followed Wilke everywhere. Chester roamed the barn during the day and slept in Wilke's bed a night. Sometimes Wilke would have to let him out in the middle of the night, because the cat needed to prowl and catch mice for Fannie.

Every Friday night, Mattie and Joseph would drive to Wien and have dinner with Fannie and Wilke and then take their son home for the weekend. Wilke looked forward to seeing his parents on the weekend. He would go to the gas station and help his dad and mom and hang out with his old buddies, but he didn't dance on the pop case anymore. They seemed to understand, and never asked why.

At home, he would have dinner with his parents and Chester was always nearby. He would watch some TV with them and then go to bed and read his comics. Mattie and Joseph always tried to make the weekend special for him. It was their quality time together.

On one particular weekend, close to the end of August, Mattie and Joseph had asked Fannie if she would drive Wilke home on Friday, have dinner with them and spend the weekend. Fannie thought this a bit odd, but agreed.

When Wilke and Fannie arrived, they found the house lit with candles and Mattie had quite a spread prepared. She had made scalloped potatoes, fresh corn on the cob, peas and pork chops. There was also a homemade chocolate cake sitting on the counter.

Fannie said, "Mattie you have outdone yourself here. Did we miss a birthday or anniversary?"

Mattie said, "No Fannie, you haven't missed a birthday, but soon there will be a new birthday to celebrate. Joseph and I are going to have a baby."

Fannie was left speechless for the moment and Wilke was as well. They just stood frozen in place.

Mattie said, "Come on you two, let's sit down and enjoy this dinner together. I'm eating for two, so excuse me if I take bigger portions," she said with a smile.

When Fannie came to her senses, she congratulated them and told them how happy she was.

"It's about time Wilke had a sister or brother," Mattie said.

Wilke still wasn't able to speak. He just stared at his mom.

When she asked if he'd be happy with a baby brother or sister, all he could say was, "Can I still keep Chester?"

"Well of course dear," his mother said as she gave him a hug, "Chester is part of our family, just like the new baby will be."

Wilke still looked puzzled by all of this and asked if could be excused to go to his room with Chester.

"Don't you want dinner or cake?" Mattie asked.

"No thanks," he said as he picked up his cat and headed for bed. "I'm tired and I've got to go talk to Chester about all of this."

Mattie was taken aback and looked to Fannie for an explanation. "Just let him get used to this whole thing at his own pace," she advised. "A new baby will be a major change in everyone's life."

They finished their dinner and chatted about baby things and names and how they would turn the little sitting room into a nursery. Fannie was happy for them, but concerned about Wilke.

That night while cleaning up the dishes, Joseph asked his mom a question that he had always wanted to ask.

"Mom, I know our name has always been Spenzi and I've told people my father came to America on a boat from Ireland. They just kind of laugh and ask me what kind of Irish name is Spenzi. They say it sounds more like German. Did Dad ever tell you the story of why we have a German name, but we're Irish?" he asked.

Fannie took a deep breath and cleared her throat before answering him. "I was wondering if someday you would ask that question and I always wondered how I would answer it. I guess that time is now."

CHAPTER TWENTY
William O'Halloran

Mattie could sense the tension and feel the pressure on Fannie caused by Joseph's question so she excused herself from the kitchen and headed to check on Wilke. She felt that it was best to give them some time alone.

"Joseph, your father Will didn't tell me much about his past life until we were into our second year of marriage. I hadn't asked any questions, I just loved him and was happy to be with him, but I knew that there was something he'd feel better about if he finally told me. I didn't push, I just waited," she said.

She told him that one evening after dinner they had returned from a walk and had sat down on the porch swing to watch the sun go down. Will told her that he needed to tell her something. She knew it was something that was important to him.

"He said that his given name was William O'Halloran," Fannie began. He was born in Cork County, Ireland to Mary and John O'Halloran and they ran a local pub in town named The Shamrock. John poured the beer and Mary served it. The business was going well, but Mary and John drank up most of the profits. They were both big drinkers, not only beer, but whiskey and whatever made them feel good.

"When Will was about five, his parents got into a terrible fight one evening. It was probably fueled by the liquor they had been drinking at the pub. He was upstairs in his bed and heard the commotion. The noise stopped when the door slammed as someone left the house and Will crept downstairs to see what had happened. There he came upon his mother unconscious on the floor and there was blood everywhere. He tried to wake her but she was out cold. He ran to the neighbors, and eventually the police came. His mother was taken to the hospital and never came home. She had died that night of blunt force trauma to the head—probably several blows from a beer bottle. The police questioned Will and he told them the truth…that he had heard his mother and father in a terrible fight and then the door slammed and it was quiet. A search was launched for his father and he was caught and jailed for murder. Parentless, and with no relatives nearby, William was sent away to his first orphanage.

"Throughout the next 15 years, he was sent to several orphanages. One of the owners of William's orphanage sold a group of the children to an orphanage in Germany. That was common in those days. Will was put on a ship with a large group of children and ended up in Bayreuth, Germany. He learned quickly that Germans didn't take kindly to Irish Catholics. He figured that to stay alive, he'd have to change his last name A few weeks after his arrival in Germany he looked out the window of his small room and saw a truck pull up out front. It had the words SPENZI BEER painted on the side. From that point on he became William Spenzi. He tried to fit in and cover up his Irish brogue.

"Eventually, William reached age 18 and he was released from the control of the orphanage. They no longer had room for him and since no one wanted to adopt him, he was on his own. From his various jobs in Bayreuth, he had squirreled away a substantial amount of money. He paid for his own passage on a ship to America and landed at Ellis Island in the New York harbor.

"In those days, agents representing various growing areas of the Midwest recruited workers from the legions of immigrants as they arrived in America. They were transported by train from New York and New Jersey to rural areas of states like Oklahoma, Iowa, Illinois, Kansas and Missouri. Farmers needing hired hands to work their land came to the train depots and offered men a job and a place to settle down. William got off the train and took a job in Missouri, which is where we met. He had a difficult life, but my love, my father's love and your love healed him. He was a very happy man at the end."

Joseph was quiet for awhile and then said, "Thanks Mom for telling me this about Dad. You know that I don't remember much about him, but I know he loved me. I can still see him lying under the big tractor wheel and everybody running toward him. I wish I could get that out of my head, but it will never go away."

Fannie got up from her chair and put her arms around Joseph. "I know son, I know...," she said. "Try to replace that memory with all of the times your dad carried you on his shoulders, took you to the pond fishing and sat you on his lap to read to you every night before you went to sleep. You were his greatest joy and accomplishment in life. He would be so proud of you."

They held on to each other for the longest time, and that evening they both went off to bed thinking of William O'Halloran/Spenzi.

PART III

THE CIRCLE

CHAPTER TWENTY-ONE
Change

The hot and humid Missouri summer had come and then slowly faded into fall's red, brown and gold leaves. It was time for Wilke to go back to school, and Fannie to resume her duties as principal of Salisbury High School and continue with her Master's degree. On a crisp fall day in the first week of September, Fannie went to St. Bonaventure Catholic School to meet with Sister Mary Ellen.

The nun greeted Fannie cordially and asked her how Wilke was. "Sister, I have come to return the books you were so kind to lend me," Fannie said. "Our star student Wilke studied every one of them and passed all of the necessary tests. He can now read at a second grade level and his math skills are excellent. He may still need a little help with his spelling. I would be pleased if you would agree to accept him back into St. Bonaventure."

"Mrs. Spenzi, I'm sure you've done a wonderful job teaching Wilke," the Sister began. "But it's not just his learning skills I'm concerned about. I'm also worried about his social skills and behavior with the other students. Last year he was a distraction to everyone in his class. We can't have that kind of behavior since students, as you well know, need to focus on their studies."

Fannie assured her that she understood the need for appropriate behavior. "Sister, Wilke has changed. He's learned some valuable lessons this past year. He understands how important it is for him to be able to read and write. I also think he's found some compassion for others. He now has a cat that he takes good care of and loves very much, and he's about to have a new brother or sister. I think you will find him a different boy and a very different student here at St. Bonaventure."

Sister Mary Ellen was quiet for a moment as she fingered the silver crucifix that hung on a chain around her neck and seemed to be seeking divine guidance for this decision. Fannie held her breath.

"Mrs. Spenzi, I am willing to give Wilke another chance, but only under the condition that, if after the first month, we experience any behavioral problems with him, he will have to leave the school once again. I'm not a counselor or a psychiatrist. I'm here to teach children that need and want to learn. If Wilke wants to learn and behave, then we have a place for him here."

Fannie let out the breath she had been holding with a whoosh…which startled the Sister who exclaimed "Oh my goodyness!" She reached out and took hold of Fannie's arm. It seemed so natural and appropriate that Fannie put her arms around Sister Mary Ellen and gave her a quick hug.

Sister Mary Ellen broke off the embrace with, "School starts in two days; I expect Wilke to be here on time."

"He will be Sister…and thank you," Fannie said as she turned and headed home wiping a tear of joy and relief from her cheek.

Joseph and Mattie were pleased to hear that Wilke was accepted back into St. Bonaventure School. They appreciated all that Fannie had done to home school him, but it was time for him to interact with other children. They were also excited about the new baby on the way. Mattie was already four months pregnant and a little bulge on her midsection was becoming visible. She still helped Joseph at the filling station everyday, but he made sure she didn't overdo and if she looked the least bit tired, he sent her home to rest.

The night before Wilke was to head for his first day back at school, Fannie drove to Marceline and they all had a nice dinner together. Fannie wanted to be sure to be there to give Wilke encouragement.

Joseph said, "Mom, Mattie and I and Wilke can't thank you enough for what you have done this past year. You've changed all of our lives for the better."

"Yes Grandma, I've learned a lot," Wilke offered. "I know I don't want to be Hobo Joe or Seth the coal miner or a drunk like Homer Goss and I even learned that nuns might be human. And thank you for Chester, he's my best friend."

After dinner, Mattie and Joseph cleared the table and they let Fannie and Wilke have some goodbye time together.

They went out on the back porch and sat holding hands in the porch swing. Wilke said, "Grandma, can I ask you for a little favor?"

"Well," she replied. "I guess so. Let's hear what it is."

"Can we just go for a short drive in your car, maybe around the block?" he asked.

"Well, I can do better than that," she said. "Let's just hop in the car and we'll go all the way to Lohman's for some ice cream."

Wilke jumped up and ran to the screen door telling Mattie and Joseph that he and Fannie were going for a drive and they'd bring back a surprise. He and Fannie got in the car and away they went.

"Okay Master Wilke Spenzi," said Fannie. "Why did you want to go for a ride in the car?

"Well Grandma," he replied. "I just needed to see the miracle again."

"Miracle?" she asked. "What miracle would that be?"

"I think your Jesus statue is a miracle," he told her. "No matter how fast you go or if you go over a bump or around a corner…he never falls over! It's got to be a miracle."

It was all she could do to keep a straight face. She didn't have the heart to tell the boy that the base of the statue had sticky adhesive on it and it had been stuck to the dashboard for years.

"Well Wilke, if you want that to be a miracle, then I guess it is," she said as she patted his leg on the seat next to her. "Miracles in our lives come in all sizes and shapes and colors and, God knows, we all need to believe in miracles. You are my miracle and tomorrow is going to be a very special day for you."

At Lohman's they got ice cream cones of their favorite flavor and sat on the bench in front of the store and talked and licked the cones before they melted. They brought home a small carton of ice cream for Joseph and Mattie. Soon it was time for Fannie to head for her house. She gave hugs to all, with a big one to Wilke, and off to Wien she went in her car with Wilke's Jesus miracle still perched on the dash.

Life was changing for all of them.

CHAPTER TWENTY-TWO
Five Years Later

Fannie was in her mid-fifties and had finished her graduate degree in English Literature. She accepted a position as a professor at the University of Missouri at Columbia. It had been her dream as well as Will's and Porter's. She had made it come true for all of them. During the week she stayed in a small apartment off campus and she came home most weekends. Every chance she got, she went to see Joseph and Mattie and her grandchildren. Wilke was now 12, Lilly was four and baby Thomas was just nine months. She had three grandchildren and adored them all.

The size of the Spenzi family had grown and so had the house they lived in. Joseph's business at the gas station prospered and he used the income to put a large addition on the house. As Mattie became a fulltime, stay-at-home mom, Joseph hired some help to fill in and take over the tasks she used to do at the station. This also gave him more time to get away and spend with the family. Life was good for the Spenzi family.

Wilke was in sixth grade at St. Bonaventure and had lived up to his Grandma Fannie's promises to Sister Mary Ellen. He had done remarkably well and his report cards demonstrated that. Fannie would stop by from time to time to chat with Sister Mary Ellen to see how he was doing. She would tell Fannie that Wilke was an inspiration to the other children and that one day in class he told them about somebody named Hobo Joe and Seth the coal miner. He had tried to impress upon them how important it was to read and write or they'd end up on the tracks or in a dead-end mine job. The only time Wilke got in trouble was once on show-and-tell day. He brought Chester to school. The cat caused quite a commotion and Wilke was asked to take him home.

Sometimes when Fannie was in town, Porter and Alfreda would drive with her to Marceline to have dinner with Mattie, Joseph and the kids. Porter and Alfreda were Lilly's godparents. They loved all the children, but always had a special affection for Wilke. Porter thought it was sad that just because of old drunk Homer Goss, Wilke had given up dancing. He thought he had a real talent for it, but decided not to bring it up. They had closed the dance studio and now just concentrated on enjoying their life together and tending to their gardens and hobbies. Once in awhile they would take the train to the Ozarks or drive to the nearest dance festival.

The times were changing. Seth the coal miner passed away from lung cancer and they had all gone to the funeral. Homer Goss remained the town drunk, but he knew enough to never come near Joseph's filling station. Sisters Leona and Viola were still teaching at St. Jude School in Kansas City. They had come down for the baptisms of Lilly and Thomas.

Wilke seemed to have adjusted well to having a sister and a brother. Lilly idolized her big brother and followed him everywhere like a shadow. He adored her. She was playful and he loved to tease her. He would tickle her and she'd giggle and plead, "Stop Wilke, stop!"

Even Chester took to two more kids around the house. Lily loved to lug Chester around in her doll carriage. Even when she would strap one of her doll's lace bonnets on his head, he didn't seem to mind. He loved the attention. Sometimes Wilke would get a little jealous because Chester seemed to spend more time with Lilly, but he still came to bed with Wilke every night.

Little did Wilke know that the clouds of change were forming on the horizon as the summer made way for fall and the new school year.

It was the first day at St. Bonaventure and all the students had taken their desks in the classroom. There were 12 students this year in Wilke's class. He knew most of them from previous years. They bowed their heads as Sister Mary Ellen said their morning prayer and then they recited the Pledge of Allegiance to the flag. They all took their seats. One by one, Sister Mary Ellen had each of them stand up by their desk and say their name and tell the other students what they wanted to be when they grew up.

Wilke always sat in the front row and therefore, he was first. In his strongest voice he said, "My name is Wilke Spenzi and I want to be a veterinarian." He acknowledged Sister Mary Ellen's smile of approval and sat down.

"My name is Bobby Crippen and I want to be a fireman." My name is Jenny Oakes and I want to be a nurse."

"My name's Sarah Ann Mills and I want to be a mother and have lots and lots of kids," which caused snickers to be heard around the classroom. Wilke was interested in what everyone said they wanted to be and on and on the introductions went until he was struck by the sound of a trembling voice from the back of the room, "Uh-h-h, my name is B-B-Betty Barnes and I want to be a ballerina."

Wilke's head snapped around and there she was…it was the first time he had seen Betty Barnes in five years! Their eyes connected immediately and as she took her seat at her desk, a smile for Wilke crept across her pretty face—a smile that he had never forgotten.

For the rest of that day Wilke was a mess. He found it hard to concentrate on his lessons that morning. He could hardly wait to talk to Betty.

When it was time for lunch, he made his way to the back of the classroom and asked Betty if he could walk with her to lunch. Nothing was said until they had found a place to sit in the lunchroom that was away from the other students.

"Betty…where have you been?" Wilke asked as he pulled his sandwich and apple out of his brown bag. "My Grandma and I tried to find you and we asked your parents and they just said you moved to Wichita. I found your ballet shoes in the dirt and took them home to save for you. I was worried. We even had the sheriff check on you."

"Wilke, my grandmother knew what was going on at our house. She knew I was in trouble with those parents of mine and she came to get me. She knew my parents drank too much. I'm sorry I didn't get to say good bye to you but it wasn't possible. Thank you for saving my ballet shoes. I don't think they will fit me anymore, but I appreciate it that you were thinking of me."

"Betty, I never stopped thinking of you," he said as he looked into her eyes. "Next to Chester, you were my best friend."

"Oh and how is Chester?" she asked as she opened her lunch bag and retrieved a sandwich wrapped in wax paper.

"He is fine, but he's still trying to adjust to my new sister and brother."

"Can I come see Chester sometime and meet your brother and sister?" she asked.

"Only if you eat lunch with me everyday," he said with a smile.

Betty laughed and said, "Wilke Spenzi, you are such a flirt! I would love to eat lunch with you everyday, even if I never got to see Chester or your brother and sister."

When school let out that day around 3 o'clock, Betty and Wilke gathered their books and walked out together.

Wilke asked Betty if he could walk with her. "Where do you live now?" he asked.

"I live in the same place you last saw me," she said.

As they walked Betty filled Wilke in on some of the changes that had happened in her life. "Wilke, about a month ago, several weeks had gone by and we hadn't heard from my parents," she related. "They usually called at least once a week to check on me. In their own way, they tried to be good parents."

"When we didn't hear from them, we got worried and we called and called and nobody ever answered the phone. My grandma called Sheriff Nelson and asked him to check on them.

"He went to the house and found my parents both passed out on the floor laying in their own vomit. I guess it was a real mess. He called an ambulance and they went to the hospital emergency room. The doctors and social worker there realized that they needed professional help, so they were committed to the state hospital in Brookfield. They are still there in some kind of alcohol recovery program. I haven't seen them yet.

"When my grandma and I heard what had happened, we took the train from Wichita to Marceline and got a ride from the station to my parent's house. Things were in shambles. Grandma and I spent a couple of days just cleaning up the mess and airing out the terrible smell in the house. We decided that we needed to stay in Wien for awhile, until we found out how my parents were.

"I had loved being in Wichita; the school I went to was great, and I was even taking a ballet class, but I knew that had to end for awhile. St. Mary's

School in Wien said they were glad to see me again, but I couldn't go to school there because the grades only went as high as fourth grade now. So, that's how I ended up at St. Bonaventure in Marceline."

Wilke was a little stunned by all of this information. He continued to walk but his mind was buzzing. Finally, he managed to ask, "How did you get from your house in Wien to St. Bonaventure for school today?"

Betty giggled and pointed her finger and said, "See that old, rusty blue and white Studebaker over there? Well, I drove that to school."

Wilke was astonished and stopped walking. "What?" he gulped. "Where'd you get a real car?"

"Oh it was my parent's car and when Grandma and I got here it was just sitting in the yard," Betty said. "Grandma showed me how to drive it so I'd have a way to get back and forth to school."

"You learned how to drive?" Wilke said incredulously.

"Of course Silly…It's really not that hard," she said. "There are just two pedals to push on—one to go and one to stop. And, of course, when you drive you have to steer and watch where you are going. I just go slow and make sure I stop when I should. I even know how to use the turn blinkers."

Wilke was flabbergasted. "Betty," he said. "You are only 12 years old. Aren't you going to get in trouble?"

"I will if they catch me," she said. "But that's not my biggest worry…"

"What's your biggest worry…?" he asked.

"Well I don't think I have enough gas in this old jalopy to get home tonight," she said with a grimace. "The gas gauge was on empty when I took off this morning. I don't think anyone is going to give a 12-year-old who is driving a car without a license any gasoline."

Wilke thought for a moment and said, "Well my dad owns the gas station in town. I'll probably have to tell a fib, but I think I can get you some gas. You wait here. I'll be back in about 10 minutes."

Before Betty could protest, Wilke dropped his school books at her feet and headed off in a slow, loping run across the street and down an alleyway. In just about three minutes, he made it to Joseph's filling station and as he walked in he could see his dad was working on a car that he had up on the lift rack. "Hi Dad! he chirped. "How's everything going around here?"

"Well, to be honest with ya'," Joseph replied over his shoulder. "This darn car is dripping all over me and I'm gettin' dirty and greasy. How was school today son?"

"The first day at school was great Dad, I think I'm going to do really good this year," Wilke said.

"Do you want a candy bar or Coke before you head home?" Joseph offered.

"No Dad, I'm trying to save my new teeth. I hear that's all the teeth I'm going to get," he said quickly. "I could use a can of gas though."

Before his dad could question him, he said, "There's a lady up the street near the school that ran out of gas and I told her I'd bring her a can. I'm sure she's good for the money. "

"Well that's mighty nice of you Wilke, just be sure to bring the can back."

"Will do Dad."

Wilke grabbed one of the red 5-gallon portable gas cans and quickly pumped it almost full. Then, without a further word to his father, he picked up the can and lugged it back up the street toward where he had left Betty.

As he rounded the corner and came out of the alleyway, he could see that Betty was still patiently waiting beside her car. "Here comes the gas man with a gas can," he sang out to her. She giggled at that and he remembered the sweet music of Betty's laughter when she was happy.

The large spout made it easy to pour the gas in the tank of the Studebaker. This should keep her going for nearly a week he thought.

"Wilke Spenzi, I'm so glad I found you again." she said as she gave him a hug. "Thank you for helping me out today. It's so nice to have my friend back." Wilke blushed and stuffed his hands into his pockets, but her words were simply more music to his ears.

"Well…I guess I better get going now," she said. "Don't worry I'll pay you back for the gas."

"Just consider it a welcome home present," he said as he pulled the car door open for her and she got into the driver's seat. He saw that she had a couple of hard pillows that she sat on to raise her up a bit and then he chuckled as she plopped an old floppy hat on her head and put on a pair of wire-rimmed, granny glasses.

"Now who would stop an old woman driver like me?" she said with a funny cackle in her voice.

Wilke said, "You be careful Betty" as she started the old car

"I will," she promised as she put the car in gear. "See you tomorrow—God willing and the creek don't rise. That's what my grandma always says." With that, she waved goodbye and took off down the road.

Wilke was astonished, but his heart was flying high. What a day it was he thought to himself—he'd found an old friend and become a gas thief.

CHAPTER TWENTY-THREE
Driving Through Life

Marceline was a nice, neat, tightly connected little community. People mowed their lawns in the summer, shoveled snow in winter, raked their leaves in the fall, painted their houses when they needed it. Marlon, the milkman delivered full glass bottles to the milk boxes on the front porches and Brown's Bread truck honked its way up and down the streets hawking the fresh loaves twice a week. In the summer, children played in their front yards with the great new invention, the Hula Hoop. They drank A&W root beer from big frosted mugs, caught fireflies in Ball jars and fell asleep to the sound of the crickets. Life was simple and good.

The folks in Marceline had either grown up there, moved from Wien or surrounding counties. Almost everyone went to church on Sunday and they all knew each other by their first names and pretty much knew most of their business. There was only one main street in town and that was fine, because all anybody seemed to need was on that street.

Marceline's only real claim to fame was that the cartoonist and entrepreneur Walt Disney had once lived there when he was a boy. He had been so impressed with the little town, that many years later he came back and had an elementary school, as well as a huge swimming pool, built for the community. Word was that he would be back for the dedication of the school and pool that bore his name. Everyone in town was excited.

Finally, it was announced that the dedication would be in the month of May. When that day arrived it was unseasonably warm and humid, but Main Street was lined by everybody waiting to see Walt Disney. Betty and Wilke were there holding hands and waiting for the makeshift parade and a glimpse of Walt. The whole world knew Walt Disney, and they were about to see him in person.

Wilke could see his parents about a block down the street. Lilly was sitting patiently on the curb at their feet and little Thomas was perched on Joseph's shoulders. He also spotted Porter and Alfreda as well. He hoped they didn't see him holding hands with Betty. It just wasn't the right time to bring Betty into their lives and try to explain her. Luckily Grandma Fannie wasn't there. Wilke knew she would probably recognize Betty.

And here came a ragtag marching band that the promoters had commandeered from a big high school in one of the larger cities nearby. Then came the Boy and Girl Scout troops from Salisbury followed by a bunch of local kids who had decorated doll carriages, bicycles and wagons. Bringing up the rear of the parade was none other than Walt Disney himself with his dark wavy hair and mustache. He was driving a Model T Ford and waving at the crowd and honking the ooga horn. Wilke thought that he looked like a very nice man and he wished he could tell him how much he liked Mickey Mouse and all of the other characters he had created.

The parade ended, the streets cleared and most of onlookers went to the dedication of the school and the swimming pool, just to get another glimpse of Walt. Betty and Wilke ducked off Main Street and made their way to where she had parked her old Studebaker. Along the way, they stopped at the Piggly Wiggly grocery and got a couple of sodas.

"So what did you think of Walt Disney?" Wilke asked as he took a swig of soda from the bottle.

"He was just what I pictured, nice and friendly," she said.

When they got to Betty's car, she took her place behind the wheel, silly disguise and all. Wilke, on the other hand, slouched down in the passenger's seat so no one would see him. "So, where are we going Betty?" he asked.

"We," she replied, "are going to give you a driving lesson Mr. Spenzi!"

Before he could say a word, she put the car in gear and headed for the back roads outside of town. Everybody would be busy in the downtown area with the dedication and she knew there wouldn't be any Sheriff Nelson or his deputy around. The sheriff was too busy looking officious for the crowds at the ceremony.

She drove about five miles on the gravel roads and then stopped and told Wilke to get in the driver's seat.

He was very apprehensive, but in front of Betty, he didn't want to appear weak. She showed him the brake and the gas pedal and he was glad he could reach them with his feet and still see over the dashboard without any of the pillows. She pulled the gear lever for him and the car started to move. Wilke was scared to death but he didn't let on at all. They chugged along slowly for a while and it seemed like he was getting the hang of it. It was exhilarating and almost made him dizzy with the power of being behind the wheel of a car for the first time. Imagine that, he thought, Wilke Spenzi driving a car!

After several miles, Betty said, "Wilke...do ya' want to try something really fun?"

"I'm already having fun Betty," he replied as he peered over the dash at the road ahead and turned the steering wheel ever so slightly.

"We are coming to the big hill at Stonewall's Tavern," she said. "I love to go over that hill fast because I found out that if you stomp on the gas pedal really hard, you can almost fly and the tires actually leave the road for a second and you get butterflies in your stomach until the tires touch down on the other side. I've done it before and it just scares me and excites me at the same time. Are you up for it?"

Wilke, not to be put off by a challenge, said, "Okay, but how much gas do I have to give it to fly over the hill?"

"Well, when you get to the bottom of the hill up here ahead of us, just stop and I'll show you," she said.

The sun was going down and the strong afternoon rays reflected off the tavern's tin roof. It was almost blinding.

Wilke came to a stop. "Okay," Betty instructed. "Let off on the brake pedal and push hard on the gas until I tell you when you are going fast enough." Wilke did exactly as she had told him to. They went faster and faster and she finally said "Okay, hold it there!" As they reached the crest, he thought he saw something in the road up ahead but with the sun being reflected from the tavern roof, he couldn't be sure what it was. In case it was another car, he steered Betty's car away from the middle of the road so he was hugging the shoulder. The car hurtled over the crest of the hill and the tires left the road for a split second and when they landed they heard a loud thud as if the car had bumped over something. Maybe it was a raccoon or a possum, Wilke thought.

Afraid that the strange bump had damaged the car, he pushed hard on the brakes and steered the car to a stop along the side of the road. When he shut off the engine, they both jumped out of the car.

Wilke walked quickly back toward the tavern and he could see something along the edge of the road on the shoulder. As he got closer, he could see that it was a man. He wore ragged baggy pants, an old dirty shirt and his shoes had been knocked off of him. "Oh my God Betty," he shouted. "Oh my God, we ran over somebody!"

Betty came running up to his side and they both stared at the person lying on the side of the road. There was blood running from the head. There was blood coming out of his mouth and nose. There was blood all over the chest, soaking the old shirt. It seemed like there was blood everywhere. The body was motionless and the man wasn't breathing. His head was near a concrete culvert where drain water would run under the road and his legs and lower body were on the shoulder along the edge of the gravel road.

Betty steadied herself by holding on to Wilke's arm and she said, "Wilke, I think we just killed this man."

"We just killed Homer Goss," he replied.

Betty was flustered and in shock and she asked, "Wilke, should I run to the tavern and get help? Should I have them call for an ambulance?"

"No Betty," Wilke replied as he wrapped his arms around her to steady her and give her some comfort. "If you go ask for help…you will never be a ballerina…and I'll never be a veterinarian."

"We have to face the facts," he said. "We are too young to be driving a car, that's bad enough and now we've killed somebody. We'll end up in jail and never see our families again."

"Oh my God Wilke," she said as she started to cry. "What should we do? We can't just leave a dead man along side the road."

"Betty, just so you know…this man was dead a long time ago," Wilke told her. "Nobody will miss him, believe me. I'm gonna' back the car up and you help me put this body in the trunk."

He ran to the car and started it and got it moving in reverse. They loaded Homer into the trunk and threw his shoes in as well. There was still some blood on the gravel and the culvert, but after a few cars passed by, in a short time that would be gone.

They jumped back in the car and Wilke slowly started down the road. Betty was in shock and hugged a pillow to her chest and whimpered. He knew where he was and he was heading for the big pond on the Schiltz's property. He had been fishing there many times and that's where his great-grandfather Edgar died. By the time they got there, it was almost dark. No one was around and the pond was quiet except for the sound of a few early crickets and some frogs and the usual mosquitoes. They hoisted Homer's body out of the trunk and both started to drag it toward the water.

Betty fell to her knees and sobbed into her hands uncontrollably, "I can't do this Wilke...I can't," she cried.

"Just go back and get in the car," Wilke said. "I'll do it myself."

She returned to the car and curled up on the front seat and cried even harder. Through her sobbing she heard the splash as Wilke rolled Homer's body off the dock into the murky water. It was over, the deed had been done, and their lives would never be the same again.

CHAPTER TWENTY-FOUR
One Bad Deed Begets Another

It was getting really dark when Wilke finally returned to the car. Betty was still curled up on the front seat. His hands were shaking. He got in the driver's seat and reached over and put his hand on Betty's head. It was not a time for conversation. He started the car and slowly drove away from the pond, with the headlights off, until he reached the main road. He knew his parents were probably worried sick about him.

Betty broke the silence saying, "Where are we going Wilke?"

"I'm going to drive us to Grandma Fannie's house," he said. "She's gone for the weekend with some professors to a conference in Seattle. I need to use her phone to call my parents and let them know I'm alright; well not really alright, but alive."

His mind was a jumble and all he could think to say was that they could get something to eat at Fannie's house.

He knew where Fannie hid the key to the house and he got it and let them in. The first thing he did was get on the phone to his parents. He'd been mulling over in his head what kind of story he was going to make up. He wasn't very good at this lying thing yet. He dialed the number and his mom answered.

Before he could get a word out of his mouth, his mother was yelling tearfully into the phone, "Wilke is that you, is that you? "Where are you? Your dad and I are frantic with worry."

"Mom, Mom, please settle down. I'm sorry I didn't call sooner, but I am fine. I was at the parade with a friend, and we decided we didn't want to go to the dedication. We just wanted to walk and talk," he said.

Mattie said, "So, why aren't you home? It's dark. Where are you?

"Well, we ended up at Grandma Fannie's," he said. My friend doesn't live too far from here, so he walked on home, and I was just too tired to walk the 10 miles back home, so I decided I'd just spend the night here."

"Wilke we're coming to get you right now," Mattie said.

"No Mom, it's dark and it's late and I know that Thomas and Lilly are probably already in bed. I'll be fine here for one night. You can pick me up tomorrow," he said.

"Let me check with your dad." She left the phone for what seemed like forever to Wilke.

When she came back on the line she said, "Okay, I talked to your dad and he says you can spend the night there, but we will be by early tomorrow morning to pick you up before church. And Wilke, just so you know, there will be consequences for what you have done."

Wilke thought to himself, Mom you have no idea what consequences there will be for what I have done.

"Thanks Mom...love you!" he said as he hung up the phone. He collapsed on a chair at the kitchen table and buried his face in his arms. Waves of fear and trepidation washed over him and he didn't know what on earth to say to Betty, but he knew she was sitting across from him and she was as anxious as he was. After what seemed like an eternity, he got up and went to Fannie's refrigerator. He pulled out a couple of sodas and opened them. Some slices of bologna piled on a piece of bread splashed with ketchup would have to serve as dinner. He sat back down at the table and he and Betty each pretended to nibble on a half of a sandwich while they twisted and turned the soda bottles in their palms.

They tried not to look directly at one another, but flashed their eyes around the room and studied their sandwich and their bottle of soda to keep from catching each others gaze. Finally, Betty got the urge to speak and she looked directly at Wilke and said, "Why didn't you let me go for help? I know we were too young to be driving and we don't have a license, but what happened was an accident. We didn't run over that man on purpose. I think the sheriff would have understood that we were just joy riding and something bad happened."

Wilke looked straight at her and said, "Betty…that wasn't just some guy I ran over. That was Homer Goss. Everybody in town knows he's a drunk, and everybody knows that I hate him for what he did to me six years ago. If they knew that I ran over Homer Goss, even though most of them wouldn't miss him, they sure wouldn't think it was no accident."

"What did he do to you that was so bad Wilke?" Betty asked.

"He was drunk at my dad's birthday party," Wilke said. "He called my dad and Porter Wilson and me some very bad names. I used to tap dance, and I was pretty good at it as you remember, but old Homer ruined that for me. I never danced again after he got through calling me names in front of so many people."

"But Wilke," Betty said. "Calling people names doesn't have to be so hurtful that you give up your dreams!"

"Oh Betty…it's all such a mess in my mind," he said. "Now we really have caused ourselves a problem. Look, it's late and I'm sure your grandma is really worried about you. You've gotta' get home as fast as you can…but we need to check the trunk of your car and make sure it's clean."

They went out in the back of Fannie's house and opened the trunk of the car. There were splotches of rusty, brown, dried blood in the trunk bed, but most of the stains were confined to an old dog blanket that Betty's father had kept in the trunk. They also found one of Homer's shoes. Wilke wadded the shoe up in the blanket and dropped the bundle beside Fannie's back porch. He figured he could bury the bundle somewhere on Grandma Fannie's property, until he could decide what else to do with them. He noticed that his own shirt was stained with blood from having heaved Homer's body into the trunk back out on that gravel road at the tavern. He'd have to soak the shirt in cold water to get the stains out. If they were still visible, he'd have to make up a story about that too. One lie just seemed to be leading quickly to another.

As Betty opened the driver's door and got behind the wheel he said, "Betty, I'm sorry about what happened tonight. God knows I didn't mean to get you involved in this. You had nothing to do with what happened. I was the one driving the car."

"Wilke," she said. "That's not true. I started it by giving you a driving lesson and then daring you to jump the big hill at Stonewall's. I'm as much to blame as you are. I just wish we could have told the truth, but now it's too late. We not only killed a man, we dumped him in a pond."

"Betty, I need you to drive home carefully," Wilke said. "Please don't drive the car to school anymore."

"But Wilke, how am I going to get to school?" she asked.

"Don't you understand," he said firmly. "You're not coming back to school Betty. You need to tell your grandma that you want to go back to Wichita right away. You are not happy here and you are not doing well in school. Tell her whatever works. You need to get as far away from here as possible, and quickly."

"But Wilke, what about our friendship? I care about you," she cried. "I just found you again!"

"Betty, I know...our friendship is important, but it can't be that important right now. Maybe someday we'll find each other again. Now go please. I have lots to do before my parents pick me up in the morning."

She reached out of the car window and gently took Wilke's face in her hands and pulled him close. She kissed him on the lips. It was a salty kiss as the tears rolled down her cheeks. She put the car in gear and slowly drove away.

Their joy ride had turned into a nightmare that would change both of their lives forever.

CHAPTER TWENTY-FIVE
As Lies Go By

Wilke Spenzi had suffered very few losses so far in his young life. He had lost Betty when he was 12, and now at 18, his good old faithful Chester had gone to sleep and never woke up. They buried him in the backyard with a very nice ceremony. Lilly and Thomas, now 10 and six carried lit candles and little bouquets of hand-picked wild flowers to put on the cat's grave. They all told a funny story they remembered about Chester. A small cross made out of a couple of sticks marked the spot where they buried him.

The last six years had gone poorly for Wilke. There wasn't a day that he didn't wake up with his heart beating fast and this dark cloud of fear hanging over him. He could never forget what happened on that warm May night in 1955.

Betty had left town with her grandmother as he had requested. They had driven the old Studebaker all the way to Wichita. It was good that the car was gone. Smart thinking on Betty's part Wilke thought. She had tried to contact him by phone and mail, but he never returned her letters or phone calls. He missed her, but had to make sure she was protected from what happened.

The blood stain never came totally out of his shirt, so he had to tell his parents that while he was eating a baloney and ketchup sandwich at Grandma Fannie's house, he spilled ketchup on his shirt and even though he tried to scrub it with water in the sink, it still showed a stain. They bought the story, but he was punished for staying out late and making his parents crazy with worry. He was denied numerous privileges and given many more chores to do around the house and the gas station.

After about four days at the bottom of the pond, Homer's bloated body floated to the surface. It was another five days before somebody found it. Jack Schiltz was fishing for catfish when he saw something floating along the weeds at the edge of the pond. The body was hardly recognizable after nine days in the water. Still, Jack could tell it was Homer Goss.

Sheriff Nelson came to the scene and called police from Brookfield and surrounding counties. It didn't seem like any of them could positively figure out what had happened to Homer, except that drunk, as usual, he probably walked to the pond and fell and hit his head on something and toppled into the water. The biggest mystery for them was what happened to Homer's shoe. When he was found floating in the pond, they were only able to recover one shoe.

Wilke thought it kind of sad in a way that no one really seemed to miss Homer and that nobody ever came to claim his body. He'd like to think he did the town a favor, but somehow it didn't feel like that.

There was one thing that still hung over Wilke's head. The night he and Betty were at Grandma Fannie's house, her Studebaker had been parked in the driveway. Jack and Larry Schiltz always checked on Fannie's place when they knew she was gone. They had driven by that night and saw a strange car in the driveway. A little concerned, they were going to check out the car but they could see through the kitchen window that Wilke Spenzi was there with a young lady. They figured that it was best not to make a big deal about it that evening, but they did tell Fannie about it later.

Fannie had asked Wilke about the Studebaker and he just made up another lie. Somebody had stopped by and saw the lights on in the house and they were lost and just needed directions. Wilke had become an expert at lying. He'd had plenty of practice. He was getting really good at it. Not a quality he was very proud of.

Through the last six years he had become more distant from his family and friends. His grades were so poor at Salisbury High School that he had little chance of getting into any good college. His parents and Fannie were worried about him and didn't know what to do to bring him around. He was belligerent to Mattie and Joseph and unkind to his sister and brother. Once again, Wilke was becoming a problem.

Fannie stepped in and tried to help. She was in her early sixties now and thinking of retiring in the next few years. One night, a couple of weeks before Christmas, she called Mattie and told her that she'd like to take Wilke away for a while. She thought that maybe a change of scenery would be good.

"I'd like to take Wilke to Kansas City and enjoy the Christmas lights and take him to see the Nutcracker and just spend some quality time with him," she said.

Joseph and Mattie agreed. Missing school for a few days wouldn't matter, since he was already doing so poorly. Maybe a trip away from home was just what he needed.

Fannie picked Wilke up on a cold Monday morning on December 18th. They took the train into Kansas City. Wilke had never been on a train and just kept looking out the window and watching the trees and farmland go by. Along the way he saw a lot of Hobo Joes. He wondered what it must feel like to jump on a train and not have any idea of where you were going. Maybe their life wasn't so bad after all, he thought. Just imagine not having to grow up to be somebody or answer to anybody or be responsible for anybody but yourself. He just wanted to bury the past, but he didn't know how. Maybe the Hobo Joes knew the secret.

The train rolled into Kansas City about 5 o'clock. They took a taxi from the station to the Royal Hotel in the downtown area. It was a nice place, all decorated with Christmas lights and garland and there was a beautiful Christmas tree in the lobby. Fannie checked them in and a uniformed man took their bags to their rooms. Wilke had never slept in a hotel before. He was glad he had his own room. Maybe this trip wouldn't be so bad after all. Just maybe he'd get a good night sleep for a change.

After Fannie got settled in her room she made a phone call to Jack Schiltz.

"Hello Jack, this is Fannie," she said. "I need a little favor from you. I left a few bills to mail on the dining room table and forgot to put them in the mailbox before I left today. Could you please stop by the house tomorrow and get them and put them in the mailbox. I don't want to have my electricity shut off while I'm gone," she said with a chuckle.

"No problem Fannie," Jack said. "You know, I'm glad you called. We were plowing some ground on the property today. It's that parcel just west of your backyard. We thought we'd try some watermelon and muskmelon this year. The plow turned up a dirty, old blanket and a shoe that looks like they had blood or something on them. What would you like for us to do with the stuff?"

Fannie's face drained of color but she remained calm. She had known the Schiltz boys most of her life. She took a deep breath and said, "Jack, I want you to burn the items…and never talk of it again. Do you understand?"

"Yes ma'am, I understand," Jack said. "Not to worry Miss Fannie. We are burning a bunch of stumps that we pulled last week and we'll just throw those things on the fire."

"Thanks Jack, you're a good man and a good friend." Fannie said as she hung up.

It had passed through her mind more than once that maybe Wilke had something to do with what happened to Homer Goss. She had just let the thought pass on by, because no matter what, Homer Goss wasn't worth what would happen to her grandson if the truth was known. She had never believed Wilke's story of the lost girl in a Studebaker stopping by the house for directions. Nobody got lost in Wien.

That night Fannie and Wilke dined at a nice restaurant at the hotel. They were both tired from the trip and needed to go to bed early. The next day Fannie would take Wilke shopping and that evening they were going to see the Nutcracker Suite.

Wilke said, "Grandma, I so appreciate you bringing me here. You always come to my rescue. I would enjoy some shopping with you tomorrow and seeing the city, but I really don't want to go to this Nutcracker thing. I don't like opera music."

"Wilke this is not opera music," she said. "It's a ballet and it's beautiful. The Nutcracker Suite is famous, and tomorrow is a special performance. There is a young woman playing the lead female ballerina role. She's supposed to be amazing and only 18 years old. Her name is Barnes…Elizabeth Barnes."

Wilke looked at his Grandma and his face was pale. "Grandma, I don't feel so well, may I be excused and go to bed?"

Fannie said, "Of course Wilke, I'll check in on you later to make sure you are okay. Sleep in tomorrow and I'll plan on seeing you around 9 o'clock for breakfast downstairs."

Wilke went to his room and didn't get the restful sleep he was hoping for.

He tossed and turned all night and dreamed of Betty Barnes and their last salty kiss and sad goodbye.

The next day in the city was snowy and cold. They did some shopping, stopped for hot chocolate and then just went back to the hotel to sit in front of the big fireplace. Wilke thought Kansas City was too big for him, and he'd really seen all he'd wanted to see except, Elizabeth Barnes.

The performance of the Nutcracker Suite started at 7 sharp. Fannie had bought the expensive seats so they could see the performance up close, and she had even brought her small binoculars in case it wasn't close enough. Grandma Fannie thought of everything. She had even bought Wilke a new suit that day while they were out shopping. It was a dark suit and it came with a sharp looking tie and new black leather shoes. Wilke had never had that kind of dress clothes.

"You look very handsome Wilke," she said as they got into the cab for the theatre.

"Thanks Grandma, I think tonight will be a special night; my first ballet."

"Don't make fun Wilke. I think you'll enjoy it a lot more than you think."

They took their seats about 15 minutes before show time. Wilke looked over the program and saw Elizabeth Barnes name. He just stared at it and then the music started and the dancing began.

It really was beautiful, like Grandma Fannie had said. Wilke had never seen anything like it and then he saw Betty…his Betty. She danced like an angel, so graceful, like her feet were floating on air. He was mesmerized by her and so was the rest of the audience. He thought how proud he was of her that she had gone on to live her dream and make it happen. Her life had not been easy and she had overcome it all to be here at this moment.

After the performance, there were three standing ovations and she was presented with several huge bunches of red roses. She continued to give bows and wave and throw kisses to the audience.

"Grandma, can we go backstage to see if we can meet Elizabeth?" he asked.

"Wilke I'm not sure I have those kinds of connections. It's very difficult to get back stage to see the performers."

"Grandma, I'll meet you outside, just give me a few minutes. I'll find a way to get backstage," he said.

Wilke walked up the side steps to the stage as the audience was filing out.

He ran into some stagehands and asked how to get back to the dressing rooms.

One rough looking fellow said, "You ain't gittin' to the dressing rooms son, unless maybe yer' the Pope or somethin'."

"Well, I'm not the Pope," Wilke said confidently, "but I am Elizabeth Barnes' brother and since she didn't know I would be here tonight, I wanted to surprise her. Can you just point me to her room?"

"You jest hang on sonny boy, let me go check with the stage manager," the gruff fellow said.

A few minutes passed and a very officious looking man came walking toward Wilke.

"Mr. Barnes, I'm so sorry, we didn't know that Elizabeth had a brother," he said.

"Well, yes she does, and I'm here to see her and take her out to a dinner. We haven't seen each on in a long time—way too long. I think she'll be pleasantly surprised."

The stage manager escorted Wilke to the door of Betty's dressing room. Inside, there were a dozen or so people crowded all around her. There were special fans from the audience with backstage passes, photographers and news people from the *Kansas City Star.*

She was grasping hands and smiling and looking more beautiful than he could ever have imagined. She was signing some autographs for a few people and looked up for just a split-second and spied Wilke in the crowd. Even though it had been six years, he could see that she still recognized him.

In an instant, she edged through the crowd and headed directly toward him. She stopped and met his gaze saying, "Are you here for an autograph?"

"Betty, it's me…Wilke Spenzi," he said.

She looked him straight in the eyes and said very quietly, "My name is Elizabeth…not Betty…and I don't know any Wilke Spenzi. Do you want an autograph?"

He was confused, but it was what she went on to say that really dumbfounded him. She leaned forward and whispered something in his ear that he'd never forget.

"Get the hell out of here and don't ever come back," she said with conviction. "I don't know you and I don't want to know you. Get a life and stay out of mine."

CHAPTER TWENTY-SIX
Train Leaving—All Aboard

When Wilke made his way from backstage to the front of the theater, he saw that Fannie was patiently waiting for him. She had perched herself on a bench near the cab stand and as he approached, she could see that he was pale and visibly shaken.

He collapsed on the bench beside her as she said, "Wilke what happened, did you make it to see Elizabeth back stage?

"No Grandma, it was too crowded and I couldn't get through," he lied.

"I know why you wanted to go backstage," she said. "You wanted to see Betty."

This insight from his Grandma caught Wilke by surprise. He was stunned and felt as if another knife had been driven into his chest: one from Betty and now one from Fannie.

"How did you know Grandma?" he asked.

"Wilke, I'm not just some old lady. I am actually a pretty smart old lady.

"I recognized Betty right away. She's grown into a beautiful young woman, but there are some features you never forget. The Betty I remember always had a small mole above her right eyebrow. I saw the mole tonight with my binoculars.

"Was she the girl parked at my house with the Studebaker, and was she the reason you tried to hide a bloody blanket and shoe in the field?"

He was speechless as Fannie stepped up and hailed a taxi. They both piled into the back seat and nothing was said on the short ride back to their hotel.

They crossed the lobby and waited at the elevator. Wilke finally spoke, "Yes Grandma that was Betty and, just so you know…it was an accident."

"I know Wilke," Fannie said. "It was an accident, and we need to put it behind us. Can you do that?"

The elevator door opened and they got on. The doors closed and they were alone. "I don't know Grandma. I still hear the thud of his body hitting the car. I see his bloody face and the sound the water made as his body rolled in."

Fannie said, "Wilke it's time we bury Homer Goss for good. He was a poor excuse for a human being and I'm sorry you were involved in all of this, but it's time to put it behind us and move on with our lives."

Wilke watched the lights blink on and blink off as the elevator moved upward. The chime rang at their floor and the door opened. "Goodnight Grandma, I love you. Thanks for everything." He hugged her, turned and headed for his room.

After he peeled off his jacket and kicked off his shoes, he just sat on the edge of the bed. His breath came in gasps. The shirt collar and tie were stifling him and he tore off the tie and pulled the shirt collar open. He looked at the ceiling and tried to take in a couple of deep breaths. He felt like he was buried alive in a tomb filled with guilt. It was strange to be alive, but yet feel dead.

The longer he sat on the bed, the more his thoughts went back to his family and all that they had brought to his life. He felt at that moment like he had brought nothing to theirs but trouble.

The night wore on and Wilke paced the room. He stood at the window and watched the lights of the traffic in the streets below. About 2 o'clock, he laid out his small travel bag on the bed and dropped in a few essential items of clothing. He checked his wallet and found $42. It was the most he'd ever had in his wallet at one time. In the desk in the corner of his room he found a clean sheet of hotel stationary paper and he penned a note to Fannie and his family.

At about 3:00 a.m., he left the room and walked down the hall toward the elevator. As he passed Fannie's door, he reached out and touched his fingers to the door and silently said goodbye to her.

The elevator dropped him down to the lobby and it was empty at that hour, except for a fellow behind the front desk. Wilke just waved at him and walked out the front door. On the street, he took a deep breath of the early morning air and tuned into the sounds of the railroad tracks off to his left. With the small travel bag in his hands, he turned and headed down the street.

It was a long walk, but he finally got to where he could see the railroad station. He angled over a few streets and arrived at the tracks just below the bright lights of the station. In the pitch dark, he found a sheltered area under a large tree and sat down clutching his sole possession, his travel bag, on his lap. He didn't know what to expect, he just knew that he needed to make some major changes in his life.

It wasn't long before a Hobo Joe came along. He sat down beside Wilke and said, "Hey boy, what you name?"

"My name is Sam," Wilke said.

"Well my name is Lazrus," the Hobo Joe said.

"That's a nice name, Lazrus, kind of like the guy that was raised from the dead," Wilke said.

"Oh yes sir, I been raised from the dead many times."

"Where you going Sam?" Hobo Joe asked.

"I'm going some place, any place, no place."

"Well that zactly where I'm going Sam."

"You look like you kinda' new at this thing," Lazrus said.

"What makes you say that?" Wilke asked.

"Well, you carrying way too much baggage," he said with a grin.

Wilke said, "I just have what I need in here, and don't get any ideas about stealing my bag."

"Now, that ain't no way to treat a fellow Hobo," Lazrus said.

Before any more conversation, they both could hear a train coming down the tracks. They got up and moved toward the tracks but still stayed inside the cover of the trees along the right-of-way.

Lazrus piped up to Wilke, "Now Sam, just in case you need some advice, which I'm sure you don't...but just in case. Wait until you see an open boxcar as the train is starting to pull out of the station. We'll run along side that car and throw our bag in and then jump in after it. We'll be safe until we get to the next station and then we have to be careful that the railroad cops, we call them "bulls," don't go down the line car by car and find us. Don't be surprised if you find other Hobo Joes already in the boxcar. They'll make room for us...we're a family you know."

"It's nice to have family," Wilke said, as they walked toward the train track and waited to time their run to catch the right boxcar.

CHAPTER TWENTY-SEVEN
The Note

Fannie, unaware of Wilke's activity in the night, slept in the next morning until about 7:30. She got dressed and went down for breakfast and thought she would just let Wilke sleep until he was ready to get up. He needed the rest. It had been a long night for both of them. After breakfast she went back up to her room and lounged in the easy chair beside the window. She started to read a book she had brought along but she was soon interrupted by a knock at the door to her room. She thought perhaps it was Wilke. When she opened the door, she saw that it was one of the hotel's housekeepers.

"Mrs. Spenzi, I worried. I go to clean your boy's room and he no there," she said. "His bed is made and there is a note with your name on it lying on the pillow. His clothes and bag are gone too. I had to come tell you, Mrs. Spenzi."

Fannie was upset but was intently trying to remain calm. She managed to ask, "Can you please let me into his room?"

The two women went quickly down the hall to Wilke's room. The maid opened the door and Fannie went in. Just a quick look around proved to her that Wilke was not there and his clothes and travel bag were not in sight but the new suit she had bought him was neatly hanging in the closet. On the pillow of a bed that hadn't been slept in was a folded sheet of paper addressed to her.

She asked the maid if she could be alone and the maid turned and left the room, closing the door behind her. Fannie sat on the edge of the bed where Wilke had sat the night before. She slowly opened the note. Her hands were shaking. On a sheet of the embossed hotel stationery, in Wilke's schoolboy handwriting, the note said:

> *Grandma, thank you for this trip and for everything. You have taught me so much and given me so much. I love you and I know you will understand. Like you said, You are one smart "Old lady."*

In the middle of the page was a circle and inside the circle he had written the names of his family with a little arrow pointing to each one's name. The first one was Grandpa Will, then Fannie and his parents, Joseph and Mattie, Lilly, Thomas, Leona, Viola, Porter and Alfreda. One part of the circle was broken and the arrow pointed outside of the circle to his name, Wilke Spenzi. Below the circle he had written.

> *Keep the circle open for me. I love you all and your love will keep me strong. Please don't try to find me. I need to find myself first.*
> *Love,*
> *Your Wilke*

Fannie remained seated on the bed as she read the note over and over. When her tears finally stopped, she neatly folded the note and put it in her pocket. She went to the closet and picked up the suit and shoes and then slowly walked back to her room. The housekeeper was in the hallway, but she knew enough not to interfere.

Fannie called Mattie and Joseph to let them know that she was headed home in a few hours and needed them to pick her up at the station. She asked them to get someone to watch the kids since it was important for her to spend some time with them over dinner. When Mattie sensed by the tone of her voice that something was wrong, she wanted to know if everything was okay and all that Fannie replied was, "There are some things we need to talk about."

She packed her bags and checked out of the hotel, catching a cab back to the train station and then waiting for the next train to Marceline.

As the train rocked and clicked and clacked through the Missouri countryside, she stared out the window at the changing landscape. Small towns along the way whizzed past her window and often she glimpsed people along the track. She thought many of them were Hobo Joes and that reminded her that Wilke was probably out there with them...somewhere. As the shadows lengthened and the sky darkened, tears of sadness streamed down her cheeks.

The train pulled in about 5:30 at the Marceline station and Mattie and Joseph were there waiting. When they saw Fannie get off the train without Wilke, they were alarmed.

"Mom, where's Wilke?" Joseph asked.

"I'll tell you over dinner son. Would Drennen's be okay with you and Mattie? It's quiet there and usually not too crowded, and I would love to have their fried catfish with hushpuppies."

They drove to Drennen's and were seated at a nice table in the back of the restaurant. It was early, so there were only a few other diners. Mattie and Joseph hardly looked at the menu and quickly ordered. They were both anxious to hear what Fannie had to say about Wilke. Fannie ordered her favorite meal and tried to stay calm.

While they waited for the food, Fannie began to speak, and she told them the whole story of Wilke, what had happened in Kansas City, his meeting with Betty Barnes and then the final and most difficult part of the story. She told them about Wilke's involvement in the death of Homer Goss, about how it had been an accident, but covered up and the Studebaker in her driveway the night of Homer's death and the bloody blanket and shoe that Jack Schiltz had dug up in the field. Mattie and Joseph didn't say a word...they were truly in shock.

The food came and they all just sat there in silence. Fannie was able to eat a few bites, but Mattie and Joseph didn't even touch theirs.

Finally, Joseph spoke up, "Mom, we need to find this Barnes girl. She may know where he is."

"Joseph, you aren't listening clearly and you're not thinking straight," Fannie said. "Betty Barnes wants nothing to do with Wilke. I think that's part of what finally broke the straw for him. I think it's what drove him to the tracks."

"The tracks?" Joseph asked incredulously. "Did you say on the tracks?

You mean the railroad tracks? Do you mean he's a Hobo Joe?"

Joseph angrily stood up and threw his napkin on the table. "Well, my son can't get involved with the likes of them that's good-for-nothing' hooligans!" he said. "I'm going looking for him and call Sheriff Nelson to get his people to start looking."

Fannie grabbed his wrist and shook his arm saying, "Joseph, listen…you have to understand what's going on from Wilke's point of view. Here," as she stuffed the folded sheet of paper in Joseph's hand. "Read this note that he left for all of us.

Joseph sat back down at the table and opened the note. He read it and slid it across the table in front of Mattie. Joseph put his head in his hands as Mattie read the note. Fannie waited until the right moment and said, "Our Wilke is almost a grown up. He's 18 years old. He's experienced a lot and he's got to figure this out for himself. He's not missing, he's just searching."

"Mom, I don't care if he is almost an adult," Joseph said. "He's out there alone and anything could happen to him. He won't finish high school. He won't graduate. What will become of him?"

"Son, I feel your pain," said Fannie. "It's my pain and Mattie's pain. Go ahead…call Sheriff Nelson. Round up a posse and go looking for him. He won't be found…until he's found himself and then he'll come home to us."

"But Mom, I'm worried about him. I'm worried about what could happen to him," Joseph said as he wiped tears from his eyes.

"Son, I have worried about Wilke from the day he was born. I knew then that he was different and special, but right now it's up to him…he needs to get himself through this challenge in his life."

Fannie paid the bill and Joseph and Mattie drove her to their house so she could pick up her car and go back to Wien. She hugged them both goodbye and said she'd talk to them in the morning. As she drove the 10 miles home, she looked on the dash at Wilke's miracle Jesus statue and said a prayer.

"Jesus, please keep our Wilke safe tonight and all the nights to come," she prayed. "Show him the way home when he is ready."

CHAPTER TWENTY-EIGHT
Life Without Wilke

Mattie and Joseph realized that they had to accept what Fannie had said about Wilke. They talked to Sheriff Nelson and he said he'd look into it, but he admitted that he didn't have the manpower to check the hobo jungles along the miles and miles of train track in the area.

When it came to Lily and Thomas, they were told that their big brother Wilke had gone on a trip. He'd always wanted to travel so this was something that he wanted to do and that he'd be back sometime soon.

Lilly wanted to know if Wilke would be back in time to see her perform in the Christmas play and Joseph told her that Wilke probably wouldn't be back by then but he'd be thinking about her and wishing her well.

Porter and Alfreda were aware that Wilke was gone. They didn't know the whole story about Homer Goss and Betty Barnes, but Fannie had told them about the trip to Kansas City and the note Wilke had left. On Christmas Eve, Porter and Alfreda came by the Spenzi house with a big basket covered with a blanket. Mattie let them in and thought they had a basket full of goodies for the children, but then she heard a strange sound coming from under the blanket.

Lilly and Thomas had heard them come in and came running to hug Alfreda and Porter. Joseph was right behind them.

Lilly asked, "What's in the basket Aunt Alfreda?"

"Well, Lilly it's a surprise from Santa that he wanted us to drop off," Alfreda said with a wink to the other adults. "Go ahead and see what it is."

She put the basket down on the kitchen floor and Lilly walked over and carefully lifted the blanket. There she saw an orange-striped kitten that looked like a baby Chester. Both children squealed with delight and immediately fought over who could pick it up first.

Mattie looked at Porter and Alfreda and said, "You two are so good and so bad."

"That's what we thought you'd say," Porter said with a grin. "So, we brought a nice bottle of wine to dull the shock."

They all laughed and enjoyed the wine while the kids loved up the new kitten and tried to decide on a name.

Lilly said she wanted to name it Wilke. Thomas wanted to name it Chester two. They finally decided on KC for kitty cat. So, KC joined the Spenzi family. He made Christmas a little more bearable for all of them. They missed Wilke. The ache of his absence would not go away.

The days came and went with no word from Wilke. Fannie had gone back to Mizzou, but came to visit as often as she could. Joseph kept busy at the station and Mattie's time was spent with Lilly and Thomas and KC. Never a day went by that they didn't think of Wilke and wonder about him and pray for him. Every time they heard the Santa Fe train whistle, they thought of him. Was he safe? Was he alive? Would Wilke ever come back to them?

CHAPTER TWENTY-NINE
Life Along the Tracks

In a very short period of time, Wilke and Lazrus had become fast friends. Lazrus showed Wilke how to survive as a Hobo Joe.

From that first boxcar just outside of Kansas City that they had jumped on together, Lazrus showed Wilke the way of the tracks. Lazrus knew from the beginning that Sam, as he called himself, had no idea of how to jump on a train or survive in the hobo jungle. He knew that Sam was running away from something…but weren't they all.

Many nights, as they would rock rhythmically to the clickety-clack in the darkness of the boxcar or as they would gather around a smoky campfire along the tracks, the hobos would drink and talk and tell their tall tales.

Wilke couldn't believe that one Hobo Joe said he had killed his wife, another said he had been in prison for rape, escaped and was on the run, and one told the story that he found out he had bad cancer and he just wanted to get away from all the seriousness of his own deathwatch and live out his days having a little fun. They all had a story…even Wilke. He just used his imagination and made up a story to tell. He said he had been attacked by a drunk in town and just had to get away. He supposed, he told them, the guy was probably queer. The hobos didn't really care if it was true or not, they all just wanted to tell their story and have somebody feel sorry for them.

Some hobos travelled alone while others stuck together in small groups.

Some preferred to ride the rails for weeks on end and then stop and rest for a spell. When a specific train ride came to an end, usually at a larger station, the danger of getting caught intensified because some railroad cars were rolled off on a side track and others were hooked on. The hobos who had been stowed away had to get clear of the cars before they were seen, chased and sometimes caught by the railroad cops and switch yard engineers. It was like the proverbial game of cat and mouse…and the hobos were the mice.

As a train would slow as it approached a town or a switching yard, the hobos would throw their packs out the door of the boxcar and jump after them, sometimes hitting the rough turf and gravel along the track and rolling down the embankment. Broken fingers, wrists, arms, ankles, and sometimes heads were commonplace and at any gathering of hobos, slings and bandages were typical wearing apparel.

Every so often, the hobos had to make it to a larger town. The larger town meant more people and more commercial businesses and therefore more opportunity for them to come up with a free meal, a change of clothes or just a chance for a much-needed bath or shower. Though some of the Hobo Joes survived by stealing money, clothes and food, others tried to earn some cash or a meal by panhandling or by demonstrating a skill to an audience and then passing-the-hat. In most instances, they just did whatever worked.

One of the regulars who travelled with Wilke and Lazrus was Marco. He had been an auto mechanic in his younger days and found it easy to pick up some cash by offering his tune-up or tire changing skills at various repair shops. In many of the towns along the track in the Midwest, Marco was well-known and in demand by several regular customers who valued his talents. They would put out the word when they needed Marco to come by and work on their car. He'd stay for a few days, make a few bucks, buy some fresh clothes and a couple of good meals and a bottle or two of good hooch and catch the next train out of town. No matter what…Marco kept running. He was always trying to get away from something or someone.

Wilke's friend and mentor Lazrus used to be a janitor and he knew where he could get cleaning jobs where he'd work using equipment and cleaning supplies provided by the customer. He took great pride in his skills…but he too, was always on the run.

At one stop, Lazrus returned to the hobo jungle along the tracks outside of town after he had just finished a big cleaning job at an apartment building and had been paid handsomely. He strutted up to Wilke and the other hobos and did a pirouette to show off the new clothes that he had bought. "Whoo-Whee!" he shouted. "Look'it me! I'm the best-lookin' hobo on these here tracks!" After much ribbing and good-natured hooting and hollering, he plunked down beside Wilke and pulled two fresh sandwiches out of his shoulder bag. "One for me and one for you, my friend," he said. Wilke's eyes got as big as saucers as he took one of the sandwiches and held it close to his nose. The smell of a fresh sandwich was almost too much for him. He was so hungry. "Thank you, thank you, thank you," he told Lazrus as he took the first delicious bite. "I wish I had skills to make money like you do," he said through the next mouthful of food.

"Well, Mr. Sam," Lazrus asked as he chewed on his own sandwich. "What can you do? You must know how to do somethin'"

Wilke kept eating, but he thought long and hard before he blurted out "Well Lazrus, I used to be able to do a mean tap dance," he said. "But I can't do it without any tap shoes."

"Now that gives me a great idea," said Lazrus with a smile. "I know jus' the place to get the shoes and I knows jus' the place to have you do your dancin'. A fine-lookin' young fella' like you could make some big bucks tapping away for people with coins in their pockets. People pay to see performers...especially poor, starving ones. You finish up that sandwich and you and I are going to go and do somethin' about this."

They walked back to town with Lazrus leading the way. He knew right where the Goodwill Thrift Shop was located and when he walked in, the workers knew him by name. "Hey Lazrus, what you doin'? We haven't seen you for a while. How are you? To which he replied, "Oh I'm jes' doin' fine and me and my friend Mr. Sam need some shoes for him...but they needs to be special shoes...they needs to be dancin' shoes with taps on'em. Whatchathinkaboutthat?"

One especially matronly worker looked down at Wilke's feet and with a big smile on her face exclaimed, "You ain't gonna' believe this, but I think I have an old pair of tap shoes that might fit his big dancin' feet." She disappeared down one of the cluttered aisles and emerged from the mess with an old...very used...pair of tap shoes. There was hardly any tap left on them, but the price was right at $2.00.

Wilke sat down on the floor and pulled off his old shoes and tried on one of the tap shoes. It fit!…sort of. He was sure they would work. At that, Lazrus picked up a battered gray fedora hat that was on a shelf and beamed as he pulled three $1 bills out of his pocket and gave them to the lady. "These shoes are on me and I'll give you a dollar for the hat," he announced.

Lazrus led the way wearing the slouchy fedora hat at a jaunty angle as they left the Goodwill store. "Follow me Mr. Tap Man Sam, follow me roun'," he said with a sing-song. "You gonna' tap man, all over the town!" Wilke laughed and he and Lazrus hightailed it down the street toward an outdoor shopping area where Lazrus hoped the crowds would be willing to stop and appreciate a rousing street performance by Mr. Tap Man Sam.

They immediately found an area where the sidewalks curving toward the various groups of shops converged and lo and behold, what did they find but a wide iron grate that covered a utility box. This would be and ideal stage for Mr. Tap Man Sam. Wilke sat down on a bench and put on the tap shoes while Lazrus started to attract a crowd with his sing-song routine while tossing his hat up in the air and catching it on his head. "Hey you people…come aroun'," he chanted. "You gonna' get to see the best tap dancer in town. He's Tap Man Sam…he's where it's at. You like what he does, jes' fill up da' hat!"

Wilke moved to the iron grate and clicked his taps a few times to get the feel of the shoes and he was thrilled that the grate had space below it and the sound resonated and intensified like dancing on a sounding board…or like the hollow top of the pop case in his dad's filling station. The memories came flooding back to him. He could hear the old guys at the station egging the little boy on, cheering for him to tap faster and louder. He could feel and hear the staccato sounds as he and Porter danced to Alfreda's tinkling piano's ragtime melody. Ratta tat ratta tap ratta ta ratta ta tat, he went.

The crowd gathered. They began to clap and stomp their feet along with the rhythm of Mr. Tap Man Sam's ratta tat tat. He tapped and tapped until the sweat flowed down his neck and then he tapped some more. The more he tapped, the more the crowds clapped and when he closed the routine with a double clamproll that Porter had taught him, the audience roared their approval. Lazrus worked the crowd offering the gray fedora for donations and when the dance routine was over and the crowd had dispersed, many still snapping their fingers and clicking their heels like Mr. Tap Man Sam, the coins and bills had almost filled the hat.

Lazrus and Wilke collapsed on a bench to count their spoils. "Man oh man," said Lazrus with an affectionate slap on Wilke's back. "You some kind of dancin' mashine, Mr. Sam! You some kind of money mashine too! Look'it this!"

Wilke beamed as he studied a fistful of dollar bills as Lazrus busied himself counting the pile of change. "Whoo-Whee! Almost thirty bucks…we gonna' have a nice dinner tonight," he said.

Lazrus was Wilke's agent of sorts. At many of their stops they would pile off the boxcar and make their way to a busy downtown area where Lazrus would draw a crowd and pass the old fedora while Wilke tapped away. Ratta tatta tap tap he went. The audience chanted and clapped and cheered, especially when he rounded out the routine with what became his double clamproll finale. They usually brought in between 10 and 20 dollars every time Mr. Tap Man Sam performed. Sometimes they would stay several days in a good area and do several performances a day. It really was a good living for a couple of Hobo Joes. Every so often, they actually made enough money to check in to a seedy motel and spend a luxurious night where each of them had a soft double bed with clean sheets and they both took several hot soapy baths and spent the evening watching anything and everything on the television.

But luxury was at a premium. They usually had just enough to get by. When Wilke didn't feel like dancing or when the weather didn't allow them to perform outdoors on the streets, Lazrus would busy himself with odd cleaning jobs and whatever he earned would be shared. When money or food or items of clothing were left over, they always shared with the other Hobo Joes. After all, they were a family and family always looked after one another.

Wilke missed his other family. He thought of them often. He hoped someday he would see them again.

CHAPTER THIRTY
The Circle

Wilke had been gone for over two years. Mattie and Joseph had not heard a word from him—not a postcard, a letter or a phone call. They had tried to move on with their lives, but he was never far away from their thoughts.

Grandma Fannie had gone on to complete her doctorate degree and was on her way to be a full professor at the University of Missouri. Sisters Viola and Leona were still teaching at St. Jude's School in Kansas City, but only on a part-time basis. They were in their seventies now and life was moving a bit slower for them.

It was the spring of 1960 when Alfreda and Porter were doing their usual gardening, which they loved to do. Porter went out to pick some strawberries from the patch and Alfreda brought out a pitcher of iced tea. She called to Porter to let him know she had brought some cold tea for him. There was no answer.

"Porter, are you ignoring me?" she asked. "Come get your tea, you need a break."

Still there was no answer so she went to check on him.

As she approached the strawberry patch, she saw Porter laying face down on the ground. She ran to him and dropped to her knees grabbing his shoulders to turn him over. His face was pale and his lips were blue.

She ran into the house and called the emergency number for the ambulance. They were there in eight minutes, but it was too late for Porter. The doctors at the Brookfield Memorial Hospital said he had died of a massive heart attack. At 67 years old, Porter Wilson was dead and Alfreda was a widow.

The news of his death spread quickly; after all he had been a well-known and respected member of the community and the former mayor of Salisbury. His obituary was in all of the county papers.

Alfreda was too devastated with grief to make any of the arrangements, so Fannie, Joseph and Mattie stepped in to help. They contacted St. Mary of the Angels Church for the service and sent the body to the Otto Brothers Funeral Home in Marceline. Melvin and Jacob Otto helped them pick out a nice casket for Porter and handled the rest of the arrangements.

They asked Alfreda if there was a special suit Porter would like to be buried in.

She went to Porter's closet and picked out his nice navy blue suit and the cute little pink tie he liked to wear with it and a freshly starched white shirt. She also gave them his favorite dancing shoes. She knew he would like to be buried in those special shoes. The service was scheduled for Saturday, the 29th of April.

St. Mary of the Angels Church held about 200 people, but on April 29th it was overflowing with twice that many people and there were still some milling around outside. They had all come to show their love and respect for Porter Wilson.

Immediate family and acquaintances, Alfreda, Mattie, Joseph and the children, sat in the front pew. Joseph was to deliver the eulogy. He thought it only appropriate since Porter had delivered the eulogy for his father Will and his Grandpa Edgar. Joseph wondered what to say about a man who had given so much to him and so many others. How could anyone say enough about a man like Porter, he thought?

Father Luther was still the priest at St. Mary's. He was in his eighties and feeble, but his sermons were always strong and uplifting. On that day he talked about Porter Wilson and all of his good deeds and how much he had brought to everyone's life. He blessed the coffin with the sprinkling of holy water.

It was Joseph's turn to speak. He walked to the podium and gazed at the huge congregation and thought about how many people's lives Porter had touched. As he looked over the crowd, he saw a strange young man standing in the doorway at the back of the church. At first he didn't recognize who it was. The long dark hair framed an unshaven and weather-beaten face.

Without a word, the young man made his way slowly down the aisle toward the front of the church. There was a murmur from the crowd as this scene played out. As he got closer, Joseph knew who would be delivering a perfect eulogy for Porter. He stepped back and the young man took the podium. A hush fell over the congregation.

"My name is Wilke Spenzi," he said. "Porter Wilson was one of my best friends. He taught me to dance and gave me the strength and courage to believe in myself. I think he was everybody's best friend. I wish I could have been here to see him one more time and thank him for all he did for me. In memory of Porter, I want to do a little dance routine he taught me many years ago."

Ratta tat tatta tat tat went Wilke's feet in the tattered old tap shoes from the Goodwill store. Ratta tat went Wilke as the tears streamed down his cheeks and ratta tat tat he went as he remembered the flashy finale that Porter had taught him how to do. Ratta tat tatta tat tat! went the double clamproll.

The audience couldn't contain itself. They jumped to their feet and clapped and cheered and many were in tears as Joseph grabbed Wilke and they hugged and cried in each others grasp. Fannie, Mattie, Thomas and Lily bolted from their seats in the front pew and lunged up to the podium to wrap hugs and plant kisses on Wilke.

As the greeting subsided and Fannie found herself face to face with her grandson, she looked deeply into his eyes and said, "Wilke, tell me…are you here to stay?"

"Yes, grandma," he said. "I'm here to stay, if you still have room for me in the circle."

Fannie kissed him and replied, "Wilke you never left the circle. You just walked outside of it for a while."

CHAPTER THIRTY-ONE
Life after Porter

When the memorial service for Porter had ended, everyone got in their cars for the drive to the Wien cemetery. Porter would be laid to rest in the same ground that his dear friends, Edgar Clark, Hannah Clark and Jack Keenan had been buried. The sky was dark and a light rain was falling. Hundreds of people stood around the gravesite and Father Luther intoned his final blessings. Alfreda, dressed in black with a veil that covered her face and hung down on her shoulders, approached the casket and then she leaned forward and hugged the shiny wood as if she was giving a final hug to her beloved Porter. She kissed the casket and laid a single white rose on top of it. The white rose was Porter's favorite flower. Fannie followed and laid a brown and wrinkled photo of herself, Porter, Joseph and Molly that had been taken years ago when Molly was just a pup. Joseph and Mattie offered a Christmas picture taken four years ago with Porter, Alfreda, Wilke, Lilly, Thomas and Chester. Sisters Leona and Viola had come for the service from Kansas City. Viola was now in a wheelchair. Leona wheeled her up and Viola put a rosary blessed by the Father's of St. Jude School on the casket. Wilke was the last to step forward. He had taken off his tattered, old tap shoes and now he put them on top of the coffin.

He said, "Goodbye old friend. I know you'll be the best tap dancer in heaven." He turned and walked away, feeling the cool wet grass under his bare feet and he couldn't hold back the tears any longer. He sobbed, not just for Porter, but for his own pain, loss and loneliness these past two years.

The wake following the burial was at Grandma Fannie's house. The Wien community had all chipped in and brought so much food to her house. It was a good thing because almost 200 or more people stopped by. The house was full, the yard was full. There were people everywhere. Wilke was overwhelmed and he could tell that Alfreda was as well.

He went over to her and hugged her. His eyes were still wet from tears and so were hers.

"I love you Alfreda. You are so special to our family." he said. "I know how much we will both miss Porter. He made such a difference in all of our lives."

She was crying as she said, "Wilke, Porter saved my life when I was just a girl and then he saved my life again when he married me. I don't know how I'm going to live without him."

"Alfreda, you know I've been on the tracks the past few years and I've learned a lot from the Hobo Joes," Wilke said. "One thing I know is that they all are really just trying to find somebody to love and somebody that will love them...They are all so lonely and lost. I wish Porter could have touched all of their lives, like he did mine. Porter is what brought me back home."

"Thanks Wilke. Porter loved you so much and was so proud you," she said.

Fannie insisted that Alfreda stay with her until she felt ready to go back to her own home and she agreed. She didn't have the strength to disagree.

When all the guests had left, Mattie and Joseph said their goodbyes and drove home with Wilke, Lilly and Thomas. It was a quiet and solemn ride. Mattie and Joseph felt joy at getting their son back and sorrow at the loss of their dear friend.

Wilke was afraid of how he would feel on actually being back in his own home. When he walked in, he saw that a few things had changed. A new addition had made the house much bigger and then he saw the new cat. He looked a little like Chester but Wilke knew there would never be another Chester. Lilly ran and picked up the cat and brought it to Wilke. "Look Wilke," she said. "This is KC and he looks like Chester."

"Yes Lilly, he does look exactly like Chester," Wilke fibbed. "Where'd the name KC come from?"

"Well," Lily replied very seriously. "KC is for kitty cat. I really wanted to name him Wilke, but Mom said that wasn't a good idea."

Mattie interrupted saying, "Lilly and Thomas...it's time for bed. It's been a long day for all of us and we need some rest—especially Wilke. Please go put your pajamas on, brush your teeth and we'll all catch up with Wilke in the morning."

As the younger kids scattered into the back of the house, Wilke reached out and wrapped his arms around his mom. As he held her close, Joseph came over and wrapped his arms around both of them. They were together again.

"I am beat," Wilke said. "Do you mind if I get a good night's sleep and we'll talk tomorrow and start to catch up? By the way, what room do you want me to sleep in?"

"You'll sleep in your own bed in your old room, of course," Joseph said. "It's always been your room and it always will be."

Mattie and Joseph hugged him tightly one more time and they all headed for bed. Wilke was surprised to see that nothing had changed in his room. The same pictures were on the wall, his comic books were neatly stacked by his bed and the same bedspread was there, along with the little nightstand with a small lamp on it. He slipped under the covers and for the first time in several years, he slept a deep and dreamless sleep.

CHAPTER THIRTY-TWO
Life After Death

Lilly and Thomas were up early the next day. It was a school day for them but neither wanted to go. They begged to stay home and listen to Wilke's stories and just be around him. They had missed him. Mattie and Joseph understood, but also knew that Wilke would need some time to himself and they wanted life to continue to be as normal as possible for Lilly and Thomas. So, off to school they went with a promise from Mattie that they would have a nice family reunion dinner that night for Wilke and there would be cherry cobbler with candles.

Joseph went off to the station about 8 o'clock that morning. Mattie said she would wait for Wilke to get up and she'd be over to help. It was past 10 when Wilke finally wandered into the kitchen. The house was quiet and no one seemed to be around. He saw some coffee that looked like it still might be drinkable and a note on the table from Mattie that said breakfast is in the oven and she'd be back by lunchtime.

Wilke sat at the kitchen table and drank the lukewarm coffee and ate the hash browns, eggs and bacon that Mattie had left for him. He found some bread in the fridge and popped a few slices in the toaster. He didn't realize just how hungry he was.

It felt good to be home, but also strange. He had traveled to so many places with the Hobo Joes and they had become his friends. They were in one world and he was a part of their world and now he had crossed back to his former life. It was a good decision for him because he knew in the end that he loved his real family and missed them and needed to be back with them, but he didn't know where coming back would take him.

He didn't realize how long he had sat at the kitchen table, slowly eating his food and daydreaming about his life backwards and forwards. It was almost lunchtime and Mattie came in the back door. It snapped him back to reality when he saw his mom. He knew she was happy by the beautiful smile on her face.

"Mom, it's good to be home with all of you," he said. "Thanks for the good breakfast. You can forget about lunch. Just sit down and talk to me. How are you and Dad?"

"Wilke, it's hard for me to even talk right now," she said. "I just want to sit and look at you and realize that you are truly home with us. You don't have to tell us about your travels or where you have been. I know that will all come in time. Let's just enjoy being back together."

"I appreciate that Mom," he said. "I'm really not up to long conversations or explanations right now. Like you said, that will come in time."

"I know you are going to rustle up some lunch and take it to Dad," he told her. "While you do that, I'm going to go take a nice long hot shower and get on some clean clothes and then I'll come over and see you and Dad at the station."

"That's fine Wilke. We'll see you at the station when you're ready," Mattie said. "We love you so."

"I love you Mom, and thanks for keeping my room just the same," he said. "It made me feel so comfortable last night."

"Wilke, like Grandma Fannie said, you never left our circle, you just walked outside of it for awhile."

Wilke hugged her and went off to take a shower. He wished coming back could be this easy, but he knew he had to deal with life after the death of Homer Goss.

When he went over to his dad's station, his mom was busy behind the counter and there were people lined up to pay for gas or get cigarettes or candy bars. It seemed to be busier than he ever remembered. When there seemed to be a lull in the business, he told Mattie to take a break and he'd run the counter for awhile. He loved the smile of relief that he saw in her face…it was so good to be back home.

That evening Mattie made a pot roast with potatoes and green beans for dinner with the famous cherry cobbler for dessert. They would put candles on it to celebrate Wilke's homecoming. They all sat around the old learning table. Lilly and Thomas had all kinds of questions about the Hobo Joes.

Wilke told them that they were very nice people and had become his friends. He said that many of them were lonely and had no family and reminded Lilly and Thomas how lucky they were to have such a good family. "Not everybody has *that*," he said.

They finished dinner and Wilke blew out the candles on the cobbler and everybody had a piece. When dessert was done, Mattie sent Lilly and Thomas off to bed after they gave Wilke a big hug. KC was still hanging around the table hoping for one more scrap. He finally gave up and followed Lilly to bed.

Mattie started cleaning up the dishes and Wilke was at last alone with his father. Joseph reached over and took hold of his son's hand. He gave it a hard, and meaningful, squeeze. "Thanks for coming home to us," he said.

"I missed you all Dad, but it was just something I had to do," Wilke said. "I didn't want to cause you and the family pain, but I had to deal with my own pain."

"I understand son," Joseph said.

"Dad, I hope you will understand what I'm going to say," Wilke said. "I want to finish high school and I want to go to college and I want to be a veterinarian but I can't do any of that until I put this Homer Goss thing behind me." He took a very deep breath and continued, "I killed a man, Dad…it may have been an accident, but I did it and I need to face that before I can go on with my life. I've run away from it for too long.

Joseph looked intently into his son's eyes and he wanted to say that Homer Goss was dead and gone, water under the bridge, history, and everybody had already forgotten about him, but Joseph knew that this was something Wilke was going to have to deal with to finally purge the guilt from himself.

"What do you want to do son?" Joseph asked. "Whatever it is, I will support you."

"I want to go to the police Dad and tell them exactly what happened," he said.

"Now think about it…you know that you were not in this situation alone," Joseph said. "The Barnes girl was with you. I don't know how much she was involved, but you can't tell the truth without implicating her. Are you prepared to do that?"

"I have to Dad," said Wilke. "I don't want to get Betty in trouble, but she was with me and there is no denying that. She didn't hit Homer, but she was there when it happened."

Joseph said, "Wilke remember that we're going to have to talk to your Grandma Fannie about this. I'm afraid she may be implicated as well. She's known the truth for quite some time, and even had the Schiltz boys cover up some of the evidence."

"That's going to be the hardest part for me Dad," Wilke admitted. "I don't want Grandma to be involved. She's been so wonderful to me. I guess all we can do is talk to her and see what she thinks."

"Son, remember…we'll get through this together," Joseph said. "Let's all sleep on it tonight and the situation will be much clearer tomorrow. We'll talk about it again and if you still feel the same way, we'll decide where to go from there."

"I love you Dad, and I'm so glad to be home," Wilke said. "Thanks for understanding. Once this is over and done, I promise I'll make you proud of me."

"I've always been proud of you Wilke. I just wish I could have understood you better and maybe none of this would have happened," Joseph said as he stood up and gave his son a hug.

They both headed for bed with their minds full of worry and confusion and hearts full of trepidation about the truth and how it could be such a double-edged sword. It can hurt some, and heal others.

PART IV

A NEW BEGINNING TO THE END

CHAPTER THIRTY-THREE
The Truth May or May Not Set You Free

The next morning, Wilke got up with the rest of the family and had breakfast. He told Lilly and Thomas a few Hobo Joe stories and promised more later on. He hugged them goodbye as they left for school and then he helped Mattie clean off the table and do the dishes. Joseph sat at the table finishing off the coffee in the pot and reading the morning paper.

When Wilke went to take a shower, Joseph got on the phone to Fannie and asked her if she could come for lunch. He explained that they needed to have a family meeting.

She could sense that something big was brewing and said, "Okay son, I will be there at noon."

Wilke took a long, hot shower. He was stressed and just couldn't keep his mind off what he and Joseph had talked about the previous night. He knew it was the right thing to do for him...but was it the right thing for everyone else?

When he walked back into the kitchen, the die was cast. Joseph let him know that he had called Fannie and she would be coming for lunch and they would all talk.

Mattie wasn't sure exactly what was going on since she had not been privy to the conversation between Wilke and his father but she did have some brief conversations with Joseph and she knew that whatever it was specifically, it was very important.

Wilke put on his sneakers and said he needed to take a walk and he told his mom that he'd be back in time for lunch. He explained that he needed some time to think and clear his head before they all met with Fannie.

He headed out the door and walked toward town. He passed Drennan's diner and Lohman's drugstore, where he got a soda and just sat on the bench outside the front door quietly for awhile. When he left there he cut up a side street that he knew would take him to the railroad overpass where he stood on the bridge and gazed up and down the silver tracks that stretched off into the distant countryside. There were no Hobo Joes around that day. He walked back to Main Street and when he got to St. Bonaventure, he decided to stop in to see if Sister Mary Ellen was still teaching there. As he came through the familiar front entrance, one of his favorite nuns was coming down the hallway. When she saw Wilke she rushed up to him and gave him a big hug. Her class was at recess so that gave them a few minutes to chat. He thought about opening up to her about his situation, but decided he really should discuss it with his family first. Their conversation was interrupted by the bell announcing the end of recess and the Sister patted Wilke on the shoulder and went to her classroom.

He went back out into the sunshine and continued his walk up the street. He knew it was still early and it was over two hours until lunch so he decided he felt like running. He headed for Wien. It was still easy for him to do 10 miles in an hour, if he kept up a steady pace. Jumping the trains and eating lean meals had kept him in good shape. He ran on the gravel roads like he was running for his life.

He made it to Grandma Fannie's house about 11 o'clock and knocked on the door but she apparently wasn't home. Knowing where she kept the spare key, he let himself in. He heard the shower running in her bathroom and didn't want to frighten here, so he found a piece of paper and wrote her a note telling her he'd be back shortly, and could he please ride back to Marceline with her. He left the note where he knew she would see it, and went out and locked the door quietly behind him.

He ran down the gravel road and up the hill toward Stonewall's Tavern and the memories came flooding back. As he came over the crest of the hill he recalled the sound of the thud under the front of Betty's' car, he saw the blood and he saw the crumpled body of Homer Goss lying dead on the shoulder of the road. He walked down the side road to the Schiltz pond and just stood in silence. He remembered how it felt to roll Homer's heavy body into the water, and the splash that it made. He had taken a life, perhaps a useless life, but a life nonetheless.

He made it back to Fannie's just before noon. She had gotten his note and was waiting for him. She, luckily, didn't ask any questions. They got in the car and drove to Marceline passing minor pleasantries along the way. Fannie had known Wilke long enough to know when he was up for serious talking and when he wasn't. Actually, she felt like being quiet herself. She was worried about what this lunch meeting was about.

Wilke did make a few comments about the miracle Jesus statue on Fannie's dashboard and she engaged him by saying, "Yes, he's still there for us. Are we going to need a miracle Wilke?"

That remark stifled any further conversation and they rode along in total silence for the remainder of the trip. Fannie sensed the seriousness of the impending meeting with him and Joseph and Mattie.

Mattie had Joseph and Wilke's favorite lunch waiting—like father like son, grilled cheese, hot tomato soup and left over cherry cobbler. She had also set out a bowl of cut up melon and some strawberries.

They all hugged and sat down around the kitchen table. The tension was palpable…no one spoke…everyone pushed the food around their plates with their fork or spoon. Throats were cleared, drinks were sipped and Joseph even got up and went into the other room to blow his nose into his handkerchief.

He came back to the table and took it upon himself to not only bait the hook, but to cast it out…"Mom…Mattie…," he cleared his throat again…, "Wilke has something very important that he needs to talk to us about. He and I went into it a little last night, but we decided that we all need to talk about it."

After further silence and tension, Wilke managed to swallow a small bite of the sandwich and he cleared his throat and started to speak. "Grandma, Mom, you know I've been running from the truth for a long time. I just couldn't face it. You all know that I killed Homer Goss. It was an accident, but then I covered it up. It was a big mistake on my part and I've had to live with it for years."

His train of thought was now in overdrive and he continued, "I told Dad that I want to finish high school and go to college and get to be a veterinarian, but I can't do any of that until I get in the clear of what I have done." He took this opportunity to take another bite of his sandwich and finished the thought by saying, "I need to do the right thing."

The room was silent. Wilke looked up and glanced around the table at his mother and his dad and at Fannie. He was looking for approval, understanding or perhaps, support. But his jaw dropped as he met Fannie's gaze…he had never seen her face so red, like it was on fire and her eyes just stared ahead and her jaw was set tight.

She leaned forward in her chair almost coming to her feet and turned to level her eyes directly at Wilke's face. As she began to speak, her diction was clipped by the tension in her jaw…"So now Wilke you want to do the right thing? Don't you think that you should have thought of that years ago? A man is dead and buried. Nobody cared about him when he was alive and they certainly don't care about him now."

She continued, her voice rising in intensity and volume, "I told you when we were in Kansas City that I had figured all of this out and I told you that you needed to put it behind you and move on. So…your reaction was that you decided to run the tracks for a couple of years and worry all of us sick and now you come home and want to do the *right thing*?" By now, her nose was almost touching Wilke's nose.

Joseph came to Wilke's defense saying, "C'mon Mom, you don't need to be so harsh on the boy."

"You think I'm being harsh Joseph?" said Fannie as she sat back in her chair gesturing wildly with both her hands. "Let me tell you what harsh is. Harsh is covering up for a grandson that you love and having him come back and stab you in the heart for it. If Wilke goes to the police now, he not only implicates me, but you and Mattie and the Schiltz brothers and Betty Barnes. We'll all be charged as accomplices."

"Grandma, I thought you'd want me to do the right thing," Wilke interrupted. "You go to church every Sunday and believe in being a righteous person. What I did was wrong and I should pay for it."

"What you say is right Wilke," she replied. What you did was wrong, but if you pay for it, so do a lot of other people. I'm a respected professor at a prestigious university and your parents have two young children to raise.

The Schiltz brothers now have families of their own and Betty Barnes is on her way to be a famous ballerina. So, when you do the right thing for you, think about all the people you are doing the wrong thing for."

With that she banged both palms flat on the table, making the dishes jump, as she quickly got up from the table and walked toward the front door. She looked back at Wilke and said, "Just so you know Wilke, that miracle statue on my dashboard has been glued there for years. It's no miracle. There is no such thing as a miracle."

CHAPTER THIRTY-FOUR
The Devil Works in Mysterious Ways

In a second, Fannie was out the door and the screen slammed shut. Wilke, Joseph and Mattie sat in silence at the kitchen table. Mattie had tears in her eyes and she started to sob uncontrollably. She had never seen Fannie act like that and it scared her to think that she finally got her son back and now he may be taken from her again. Joseph got up and went around the table, leaning down to try and console Mattie. Wilke got up from the table, went to his room and closed the door and didn't come out the rest of the day. When Joseph checked on him later, he found him fast asleep with his clothes on, just lying on top of the covers. He let him sleep. They all needed time to think.

The next morning Wilke woke early and made the coffee and brought in the newspaper. When the others in the family got to the kitchen, he made sure that they sat down to a plate of bacon and scrambled eggs and fresh toast. There wasn't much talk. There was tension in the air and everyone could feel it. Mattie's eyes were swollen from crying and Lilly and Thomas could sense that something was wrong, so they kept quiet. Joseph thanked Wilke for the breakfast and headed out the door to go to work. The children straightened their rooms and got dressed and headed off to school. Mattie and Wilke were left alone.

"Mom, I'm so sorry for all the trouble I've caused," Wilke said. "I never meant to hurt the family or you or Grandma Fannie. I just didn't know what to do with all of my guilt."

"I understand," Mattie said as she reached across the table and put her hands on top of his. "Wilke, I know that you want to do the right thing, but I'm just as confused as you are at this moment as to what the right thing is. You could not only ruin your own life, but the lives of many others. We've got to face the fact that there really isn't an easy answer here."

He helped her with the breakfast dishes and then said he was going to go talk to someone outside of the family that might be able to help with this dilemma.

"Who do you have in mind?" Mattie asked.

"I'm going to confession Mom," he said. "At this point, I think I need to get some inspiration and some help from someone higher up."

"You're probably right Wilke, but I don't think it would be a good idea for you to go to St. Mary of the Angels," she said. "Father Luther always does the confession and he'd recognize you. Go to St. Jude's, the new church in Marceline. I don't think the priest there would know you.

Wilke took a shower, made his bed and got dressed. He gave his mom a kiss and headed out the door. The church was about a mile away and it felt good for him to get some exercise and breathe big gulps of fresh air. He recalled that all of his significant religious events such as his baptism and first communion had been at St. Mary of the Angels Church, so going to this other church would keep his identity a secret for sure.

He walked through the big, heavy glass doors of St. Jude's Catholic Church into the cold and sterile lobby. He could see a plump lady dusting off the pews and there were several people waiting in line for confession. He took his place at the end of the line and saw that the name posted next to the confessional door read "Father Ludwig." Beneath it was a sign that flipped over and it read, "Confession in Session."

He figured with a name like Ludwig, the priest must be German. Whatever nationality, he was just glad they didn't know each other.

A small bent-over man came out of the confessional and the next person in line went in. It was an old woman with a scarf on her head. The old woman must not have had too many sins to confess because she was in and out in just a few minutes. The older man ahead of Wilke took a little bit longer. Wilke fidgeted and wondered if any of their sins could have been as bad as his. Did any of them confess to killing someone? Before he knew it, it was his turn.

He went into the small confessional and knelt down. As he had done several times before, he recited, "Bless me Father for I have sinned. It has been many years since my last confession."

It was silent for a few moments and then Father Ludwig, in a slight German accent, quietly asked, "Why have you waited so long to come to confession?"

"I have been away Father," Wilke replied. "Actually...I ran away."

Father Ludwig said, "What were you running from my son?"

Okay, thought Wilke...here we go...His hands were sweating and his voice was shaky when he gave his answer. "I hit a man with a car and I killed him. It was an accident, but I covered it up and got rid of his body. It really was an accident Father."

There was a long silence, but Wilke could hear his own heart beating wildly and his breathing was strained. When the priest finally spoke, he said, "An accident is one thing, but covering it up was your sin. You have sinned greatly my son and there is no greater penance I can give you than to tell you that God wants you to tell the truth and take your punishment."

Wilke gulped at that and said, "Father, it's not that simple. I am willing to do that, but there are other innocent people involved. They weren't responsible for what I did, but they helped cover it up. I don't want them to get hurt for what I did."

"They are already hurt for what you did," replied the priest. "And now you have put your sin upon them and they are no longer innocent. You must save all of their souls and tell the truth. Do you understand son...do you understand?"

"Yes Father," Wilke said hurriedly. Before the priest could offer another comment Wilke bolted from the confessional and down the aisle and out of the church into the street.

He walked for a while trying to compose his thoughts. The priest was right—he needed to tell about his sin and in doing so remove all the innocent ones from their sin. Although it seemed like he was walking aimlessly, he knew exactly where he was going. Sheriff Nelson's office was located on the first floor of the building beneath Dr. Red's dental office. There was a sign on the door that said *Office of the Sheriff*.

Wilke walked in and found himself staring at a very plump woman with large breasts at the front desk. It was Gloria Wilson, the sheriff's niece. The story had gone around town several years ago that Gloria had gotten into some trouble back in Georgia and had come to live with her uncle for awhile. Awhile had ended up being three years. Bud Nelson, as he was known without his sheriff's badge, was not happy about it. He hadn't thought her visit would drag on this long.

Sheriff Nelson never married. Rumor was that Bud preferred men to women, but nobody ever dared bring that up. After all, he was the sheriff. Rumor also had it that Gloria was having an affair with the sheriff's deputy, Benny White. At this point in time Wilke didn't care about any of that. He just wanted to see Sheriff Nelson and tell the truth.

Wilke remembered Gloria from about a year before his hobo adventures on the tracks. She had come to their house to drop off some legal papers from the sheriff regarding some property he and Joseph were buying together. He didn't like her then and he didn't like her now. She was known as the town gossip and he didn't trust her.

He remembered that after the incident at his dad's birthday party with Homer Goss, when he had run away to hide at Fannie's house, Sheriff Nelson had been called in to help look for Wilke. He heard later that Gloria had overheard some of the information that came and went through the dispatch lines and she made up stories about how Wilke was probably queer because he was a dancer and was probably molested by the old, one-eyed Porter Wilson and how Joseph Spenzi had beaten poor, drunk Homer Goss to a pulp. It was terrible stuff that she spread, and even though nobody seemed to believe her, it still hurt Wilke's family and he never forgot it.

Gloria looked up and saw Wilke. "My gosh," she said. "Do my eyes deceive me or is this Wilke Spenzi? You've certainly grown up since I last saw you—y'er a little on the skinny side, but nice looking like your Pops."

"Hello Gloria," Wilke said.

"I hear you caused your family a lot of worry, you running away and all. What got into you boy?" she quizzed.

Wilke responded curtly, "May I please speak to Sheriff Nelson?"

"Why, boy, he's just not available on a moment's notice ya' know," she replied. "If you wanna' see an important man like Sheriff Nelson, you gotta' make an appointment. "Why don't you just tell Auntie Gloria what's going on with you," she continued. "Maybe I can help. I'm a good listener ya' know."

"Well…," Wilke shot back through clenched teeth. "First of all Gloria, you are not my aunt and second of all I know you are a nosey parker, a gossip and a big mouth. Now once again, is Sheriff Nelson here or not?"

"Well you certainly have grown up to be one nasty and mean young man," she said.

The volume of their voices was intensifying, but before Wilke could respond, Sheriff Nelson breezed in the front door. "Wilke Spenzi," he said as he gripped Wilke on the shoulder with one hand and grabbed his bicep with the other in a kind of a friendly wrestling motion. "Good to see you again. I heard you were home. Come on into my so called office. Gloria…get us a couple of sodas."

She just glared at both of them.

The sheriff ignored her attitude and led Wilke into his office where he plopped down at the chair behind his desk and motioned for Wilke to take the other chair. As Wilke looked around he could see stacks of papers and files all over the place. On the walls were several pictures of chimpanzees and one of a gorilla and another of the sheriff and Walt Disney posed in his Model T parade car. Wilke didn't want to ask and didn't want to know. He just wanted to confess.

"So what brought you to my dumpy old office?" Sheriff Nelson asked as he took off his hat and scaled it on to a stack of file folders on a side table. Hearing no immediate answer, he leaned back in his chair and balanced his clasped hands on his ample belly as he propped his boots on an open desk drawer.

"Well sheriff…I came here to confess to a crime." Wilke blurted out. "I ran over Homer Goss with a friend's car. It was an accident, but I got scared and threw his body into the Schiltz pond." As the words tumbled out of his mouth, he didn't feel like he was even talking. He felt like he was vomiting the words.

The sheriff didn't move and didn't say a word. He just sat there in his chair without changing the expression on his face. There wasn't a look of surprise or any emotion at all.

Wilke stared wide-eyed at the sheriff and the sheriff stared back at him. Wilke was even afraid to blink. The sheriff finally broke the silence saying, "I was wondering how long it would take for you to come to me with this."

Wilke was shocked. "How did you know Sheriff? Why didn't you come after me?"

"Son, your family and I go back a long ways," he explained as he dropped his feet to the floor and leaned forward over his desk. "I've known your Grandma Fannie for years. Your dad and mom are good, upstanding members of the community. I knew they hadn't raised a cold-blooded killer. I wanted to wait it out and have you come forward when you were ready. I knew that would be better for you. Plus, just so you know, that damn Homer Goss has been a pain in the ass to me for years and years. It's been like I'm always responding to calls reporting him for some stupid thing or another. We'd arrest him and throw him in the holding cell and he sobered up and then cried like a baby and swear'd he'll never touch another drop of hooch and then he did it all over again. The way I figure it…nobody really misses him…especially me. I know it sounds bad, especially coming from a man sworn to the badge, but you may have done us all a favor."

Wilke just couldn't believe what he was hearing. "But Sheriff, how did you know it was me?" he said.

"That was the easy part Wilke," he said with a grin. "Even though everyone has been covering up for you, you left a pretty obvious clue at the scene of the crime. You were in such a hurry to get Homer's body in the pond that you weren't aware that you dropped something."

"I what?" said Wilke. "I dropped something? What did I drop?"

"Well, it was small and you probably never missed it and to be honest, I almost missed it," admitted the sheriff. "You're just lucky it was me that found it!" With that said, he pulled an envelope out of his desk drawer and dug a scrap of paper out of it as he continued, "You and the Barnes girl apparently stopped at the grocery store and bought a couple of sodas before you hit the road." He slid the scrap of paper across the desk toward Wilke. "I talked to Miranda, the checker who waited on you, and she told me that the cash register had run out of receipt tape, so she wrote on a scrap of paper and gave it to you Wilke Spenzi—PAID—75 cents—2 sodas. I found the receipt under a shrub near the edge of the Schiltz pond where you pushed the body in. I've saved it all of these years."

Wilke looked at the incriminating scrap of paper. They both just looked at one another. The game was up, the showdown was over and the cover up was uncovered.

CHAPTER THIRTY-FIVE
The Circle of Deceit

"So Sheriff...where do we go from here?" Wilke said as he slid the scrap of paper back across the desk. "What a mess I've created. It looks like even you have been involved in the cover up. I've not only got my family in it, and then the Schiltz brothers, Betty Barnes, Grandma Fannie and now you. I'm more confused than ever about the right thing to do."

Sheriff Nelson leaned back in his old leather chair and propped his boots back up on the open desk drawer. "Wilke, let's look at the facts as we know them. I'm due to retire this year with a nice pension. If this should get out, I will lose all that. Your grandmother has a great job that she loves; teaching at Mizzou...and that will be ruined for her. Your parents have a great business and a fine reputation in this town. The Schiltz brothers have children of their own now and their farm business is going very well for them. This Barnes girl sounds like she's got a pretty good dancing career ahead of her. So, think about it. You tell me...what's the right thing to do?

You gonna' trade all these lives for one dead drunk?" the sheriff asked.

Wilke put both hands on the sides of his head as if trying to control the rising pressure. "But Sheriff, you're an officer of the law," he cried out. "I committed a crime. Are you telling me I should just forget about it and walk away?"

"I'm not telling you nothin' young man," Bud said with a snort as he fished a half-smoked cigar out of the huge ashtray on the corner of his desk. "I'm leaving the decision up to you. I was just trying to fill you in on what the consequences will be, not just for you, but for a lot of other folks too."

He bit into the cigar butt, scratched a kitchen match into a flame and lighted the cigar creating clouds of acrid white pillows of smoke that headed for the ceiling. He eased even farther back in his chair to the degree that Wilke was afraid he and the cigar would just topple over backwards.

After what seemed like an hour, the sheriff blew a huge cloud of cigar smoke at the ceiling as he said, "Do you want me to arrest you now Wilke?"

Wilke almost fell off his chair as the sheriff, in one quick motion, dropped his feet to the floor and rocked his chair forward as he leaned across the desk with the cigar clenched in the side of his mouth. "I can read you your Miranda rights, slap the cuffs on you and away to the jail in Brookfield we'll go," he threatened. "After bookin', you'll wait in a cell until your parents come to bail you out. Then you'll have to get an expensive attorney because you'll be indicted and your trial date will be set and eventually a jury will get selected. Then the trial will go on and on and you can watch your Grandma Fannie, Mattie, Joseph—hell, maybe even Lilly and Thomas, and me and the Schiltz brothers and that cute little ballerina girl all be paraded in front of the jury."

This was too much for Wilke to handle. He had a splitting headache and the cigar smoke had seized up in his nose and his chest. As he bolted from the chair and headed out the door of the office he almost bowled over Gloria Wilson who was standing just outside the door with two soda cans in her hands.

Wilke glared at her and said, "How long you been hiding there Gloria? Long enough to get some more gossip to spread around? You can drink my soda. You're lookin' a little parched." With that he turned and made his way out the door.

As he walked back toward home his mind was in overdrive. He realized that Grandma Fannie was right, as usual. He had made a mistake several years ago and now he expected everybody else to pay for it so that he could feel better about himself. It was selfish of him to expect them all to make such a big sacrifice for him. They had already sacrificed enough. If they could get beyond the guilt, then he would have to also. He loved his family too much to put them through any more pain.

He could see his dad's gas station up ahead at the corner where the blinking red stop light was located. When he got there he stopped in to let them know that he felt he had come up with a decision on what to do. Mattie was seated on a tall stool behind the counter as usual. She was busy sorting sales slips and Joseph was changing a tire on an old rusty car that he had lifted up with the power jack. Wilke walked into the mechanic's bay area and asked his dad if he needed any help with the tire.

"No thanks, son," he said. "I've gotten pretty good at changing a tire after 20 some years, but I appreciate the offer. What'cha been up to today?"

"Well Dad, I've made a decision," Wilke said in a very determined tone of voice. "I'm gonna' finish high school and get a job to support myself through college and then I'll get to be a veterinarian. I also want to leave Homer Goss dead and buried for all of our sakes."

Joseph stopped what he was doing and said, "That's great news, son! I wanted this to be your choice, and if this is what you want...then I'll support you in it. Thank you for making a difficult and unselfish decision for all of us."

"Dad, let Mom know I'm headed home now and I'll make dinner tonight," Wilke said. "I think she needs a night off."

"You're a good son Wilke Spenzi and I'm not going to tell your mom a thing—you surprise her," Joseph said. "We'll be home about five."

When Wilke got home, he called Grandma Fannie. She answered the phone and when she heard that it was him, she was quiet.

"Grandma, you were right," he said. "I've caused enough pain for this family and I'm not going to cause any more. The past is the past and it'll just stay that way. I'm making a dinner to surprise Mom. Would you like to come?"

"Yes Wilke, I'd like to come," she said.

"Thanks Grandma, I love you," Wilke said. "Oh, and could you bring a salad?"

"Yes Wilke, I'll bring a salad and I'll bring dessert. I love you too," she said.

Wilke wasn't much of a cook. He and his hobo friends had roasted hotdogs over an open campfire or just made a meal out of what they scavenged from here or there. He was amazed at the quantity and quality of food that they could turn up from an alley behind a grocery store or a busy restaurant.

At home in Mattie's kitchen, he scoured the cupboards and the refrigerator for possibilities that would go with a salad and dessert that Fannie was bringing. There were a couple of boxes of macaroni and cheese and some hotdog buns in one of the cupboards. He decided that he could do that…it would at least be a good start. The hotdogs to fit the buns had to be around somewhere. Water and a little butter in a saucepan would handle the mac 'n cheese course and when he found a package of wieners in the refrigerator, he knew that he had a complete meal. He could boil a few wieners. Grandma would bring the salad and dessert. That should be enough. He set the table for six.

When Lilly and Thomas got off the bus from school, they were surprised to find Wilke in the kitchen and they knew something special must be going on. He told them Grandma Fannie was coming and he was surprising Mom with dinner.

"What's for dessert?" Lilly wanted to know.

"I don't know," Wilke said as he noticed Fannie's car pull in the driveway. "Here comes your Grandma, ask her."

Fannie came in carrying a couple of big bowls, one stacked on top of the other. She put the salad bowl on the table and slid a big bowl of tapioca pudding into the refrigerator. As she turned to greet the children, Lily and Thomas beat her to it with their hugs and kisses. "Grandma, Grandma," squealed Lily. "I just love, love, love your pudding! How did you know that's what I wanted for dessert? This must be a special night."

Fannie said, "Yes, Lilly, it is a special night. Your big brother is truly back to us and he's going to stay."

Mattie and Joseph came home around 5:15 and everything was ready for them. Wilke had even found a candle to light in the middle of the table. They had turned the lights off in the kitchen and when Mattie and Joseph walked in, they all yelled "SURPRISE!"

"I don't believe this," said Mattie with a big grin and hugs for all the children. "What a wonderful surprise. Thank you all for this. Did I forget my birthday?"

"Not at all," Fannie said as she put her arms around Mattie. "Your son Wilke just wanted to make this a special night for all of us. It was his idea. He's decided to leave the past buried and work on his future."

Mattie hugged Fannie and the tears streamed down her cheeks as she turned and threw her arms around Wilke. She leaned back and held her son by his broad shoulders and looked him directly in the eye saying, "Thank you son. I know this wasn't an easy decision for you. You've made a very big difference in all of our lives tonight. I love you."

They all ate and enjoyed the dinner. Fannie left for home. Lilly and Thomas went to their rooms to finish up their homework and then to a bath before bed. As the table cleared, Wilke steered his dad and mom into the front room and told them to just go relax. He made it clear that he'd made the dinner and now he planned to clean up his mess and wash the dishes.

With those chores done, Wilke sat down at the kitchen table to rest and he decided to see if Sheriff Nelson happened to be still in his office. Even though it was almost 8 o'clock, Bud Nelson answered.

"Hello Sheriff, it's me Wilke Spenzi," he said.

"Well Wilke," he said. "Good to hear from you. What's up son?"

"Thanks for our talk today," Wilke said. "I just wanted you to know that if you're okay with the way things are, then so am I. Let's all get on with our lives. Maybe someday after you retire we can go fishing together, just so it's not at the Schiltz pond," he added with a chuckle.

"That's a good decision Wilke," said the sheriff. "You go forward now and don't look back."

"Will do Sheriff…Good night," he said. Oh, and if I were you, I'd quit smoking those nasty cigars!"

"Good night Wilke Spenzi," the sheriff replied, adding "You mind your own business Boy." They both chuckled and hung up.

The next morning Wilke got up feeling lighter and better than he had in a long time. His headache was gone and he just couldn't help smiling at himself in the bathroom mirror as he brushed his teeth. After he finished a cup of coffee, he got on the phone to Fannie and asked her what she thought was the best way for him to finish his last year of high school.

She said she would check with the registrar at Salisbury High and find out how many classes he had to complete and see about the best way to do that.

Wilke could finally see a future for himself. He'd finish high school and then probably get an AA degree at the community college in Brookfield. With some decent grades he'd be accepted in the bachelor's program and that would lead to vet school. He knew it was a long road, but at least he had a chance for a new beginning and he had a goal to achieve. He felt such an unfamiliar emotion…excitement.

CHAPTER THIRTY-SIX
About Gloria Wilson

Bob and Judy Wilson were both successful professionals who lived in Roswell, Georgia, a very affluent suburb just north of Atlanta. Judy owned and operated a well-known antique store in the area, called "The Old Treasure House," and Bob was in his twentieth year as CPA for a large construction company. It was late in life when they had Gloria. They really had not had time for children and they still didn't. To make up for what little time they had to spend with her, they spoiled her rotten. Gloria had the best toys, the best clothes, and she could eat anything she wanted, anytime she wanted.

By the age of 12, Gloria had bulged to 160 pounds. All of her beautiful clothes looked terrible on her. The kids at her private school made fun of her and would chant, "Gloria, Gloria, can there be any moreaya." Gloria was overweight, unpopular, unloved and unhappy.

By the age of 13, when she was in the 7th grade, she took up smoking. Her father Bob had always been a smoker and kept cartons of cigarettes in his fancy study. He never noticed when a pack or two of cigarettes was missing, so Gloria had a reliable source of supply. She smoked in the girl's bathroom at school and some of the other girls wanted to learn how to do it. Several of them tried a few puffs and thought it was pretty neat. Gloria always had cigarettes, so she became the supplier for her classmates. That seemed to make them like her. She felt important.

At this same time in her life, she was so unhappy and was always looking for new ways to make herself feel better in addition to being the students' source of cigarettes and constantly stuffing herself with candy and doughnuts. She discovered that if she made up fantastic and juicy stories about fellow students, others flocked to hear the latest news from Gloria regarding what was going on. As time went on, she not only created more and more stories, but the subject matter became more and more outlandish. She'd spin a yarn like the best tabloid reporter. She'd tell them that she saw Carol Weidum, who was going steady with Billy Hughes, making out with Tom Winford at the football game. Lacy Smith, according to Gloria, stuffed her training bra with athletic socks to make herself look stacked. These pieces of gossip spread like wildfire around the school. Gloria became very popular since her fellow students realized how important it was to remain on her good side and not make her mad.

When it came to her relationship with the boys at school, she had several things going in her favor. Most of the boys heard the stories she spread and they knew that they didn't want to be the butt of Gloria's wrath, so they did all they could to placate her with their attention. In addition to that, one of her more admiring suitors invited her into the boy's bathroom one day during recess and as she hid with him in one of the toilet stalls, he felt her up and kissed her. Other boys heard about what Gloria would do and she soon became a regular attraction in the boy's bathroom at every recess. She'd hide in a stall and the boys would come in one at a time to ogle and squeeze her naked breasts and she even let some of them reach up under her skirt to touch her panties.

Gloria was in her "glory" until she got expelled.

Of course, Bob and Judy were horrified at the reports of her smoking, spreading false stories and letting the boys touch her in all the wrong places. She was ruining their reputation in Roswell and they just wouldn't have it. So, at the ripe old age of 15, off to an all-girls boarding school she went. Her parents espoused the age-old adage—out of sight—out of mind. But, it seems that Gloria, though out of mind, was incorrigible.

Over the next 10 years, her behavior certainly changed…it got worse instead of better. Her smoking cigarettes escalated to pot and then to drugs. Her touchy-feely sexual play branded her as "easy" and before very long, she was doing oral sex and having sexual intercourse with many willing partners before her sixteenth birthday. And, regarding her obsession for telling tall tales and spinning tabloid-style rumors, Gloria's-gift-of-gossip became pathological. She found that she couldn't tell the truth about much of anything because she'd crisscross a lie that she'd recently fabricated. Her whole life had spun out of control.

She was in and out of several boarding schools, in and out of abortion clinics and in and out of jail. She never lasted long enough in a single school to get her high school diploma. She just seemed to bounce around from one place and one eyebrow-raising dilemma to another. The straw that finally broke her parent's strained support was her arrest in New York City at Macy's department store. She had shoplifted a fake diamond bracelet and had been nabbed red-handed by the security staff as she made her way out the door. The police took her into custody and during her questioning she rolled her eyes and hyperventilated and cried and pretended to faint. When that didn't elicit any sympathy, she fabricated terrible stories of how she had been set up and how it wasn't her fault and how she didn't know it was in her pocket…and, when all of those antics didn't sway anyone to her side; she admitted that she didn't want the bracelet for herself, she just she wanted to give it to a new friend for her birthday. The bracelet was returned to Macy's and Gloria was booked into a holding cell awaiting a decision from the department store as to whether they wanted to press theft charges over a rhinestone-encrusted, gold-plated bracelet.

Bob and Judy bailed her out once again and sent her a plane ticket to fly home. They had also sent her a MARTA ticket that would get her from Hartsfield International Airport to the Dunwoody transit train station. She took a taxi from the station to the house in Roswell and her dad came out when she arrived and paid the taxi driver. She was expecting a half-baked homecoming due to the circumstances, but what she discovered was certainly less than half-baked.

There was a small, older car in the driveway that she didn't recognize as belonging to her parents. She walked with her father over to the car and she saw it was stuffed with her clothing, some blankets, towels and a couple of pillows and a few small pieces of furniture from her old bedroom. As he handed her a thick envelope, Bob said, "Gloria…here's $5,000. Take the money and get in the car and just get out of here. Your mother and I have had enough of your behavior. We're through with you. You're on your own. Go! And don't come back!"

He turned and strode across the driveway to the porch and went into the house, shutting the door, both figuratively and literally, with a slam.

Gloria was stunned. She finally got in the car and sat massaging the steering wheel with trembling hands, trying to sort out what was happening to her. After what seemed like an hour, she started the car and pulled out of the driveway and on to the street. The names of streets and roads blurred. She found herself on the I-285 and knew that it was a major interstate, but she wasn't sure if she was going east or west, but then again…that wouldn't have mattered since she had no idea of where she was going or what she was going to do. She just drove and drove and drove.

After several hours, she was thirsty and needed to pee, so she got off the highway and pulled into a service station. She used the rest room and went into the minimart and got a soda. Near the front door she spotted a pay phone and an idea crossed her mind. She fished around in her purse and came up with a tattered address book. By balancing the receiver between her ear and her shoulder, she managed to hold on to her purse, the address book, the soda and still dial "O." "Buzz, buzz, buzz…operator" "Hello," she said. "I'd like to place a collect call to Missouri; the number is 417 929 0868." A man answered and conversed with the operator. He hesitated, but finally said he would accept the charges.

"Hello Uncle Buddy," she chirped. "It's me…it's your niece Gloria!"

"Gloria," he stammered. "Uh well…gee…It's certainly been a month of Sundays since I've heard from you girl or your mom or old Bob."

"I know Uncle Buddy, things haven't been good. I didn't know who else to talk to. You're the only real family I have besides Mom and Dad," she said convincingly.

"What's up Gloria…," he said with a serious tone in his voice. "Is Judy alright? Tell me, is something wrong?

"No it's not your sister," she lied as she added sniffs and snorts of breaking down in tears. "It's my dad."

"Why, what's wrong with your dad Gloria? Buddy asked.

"Uncle Buddy, my dad has been molesting me for years," she cried. "I didn't know who to tell and my mom knew about it and…I just can't be with them anymore. I know she's your sister, but my God…they're both sick people!"

"G-g-g-good heavens G-g-gloria," Buddy stammered. "I had no idea. This makes no sense at all, but where are you now?"

"I'm at a gas station on some highway outside of Atlanta," she sniffled as she pleaded, "Can I come stay with you for awhile? I have to get away and I really have no place to go."

"Well of course Gloria," he replied. "You can come stay with me until we get this straightened out," he said. "Do you have a way to get here?"

"Yes, Uncle Buddy, I have a car," she said. "I'll get a map and I'll give you another call when I get closer."

"When you get the map Gloria," he advised. "Just find the Interstate marked I-24 and take it northwest from where you are in Georgia. The Interstates are the safest routes...especially for a single young lady like you. It'll be about a three to four hour drive and then look for the I-55 west into Missouri. Call me again after you get on the 55."

"Oh-h-h...thank you-u-u...Uncle Buddy," she oozed. "I knew I could count on you. See ya' soon."

When this strange and shocking call ended, Bud went to his wet bar and poured himself a stiff drink. He sat down at his kitchen table for fifteen minutes or so, contemplating what had just occurred and getting his wits about him. He picked up his phone and called his sister.

The conversation was a total disaster. Judy couldn't believe that Bud could think such a horrible thing about Bob and proceeded to tell him some of the terrible things Gloria had done.

The call ended abruptly with Judy saying, "Fine Bud, you see what you can do with God's biggest mistake on earth," and with that challenge...she hung up.

And so it was, that's how Gloria came to live with Sheriff Nelson. He had no skills at raising a child...especially not a conniver like Gloria had become. He confronted her several times on her reports about her dad's behavior and she weaseled out of much of what she had said by telling even more strange tales about how she had always been misunderstood and mistreated. She regaled him with explanations of how it wasn't her fault that she got into trouble when she was away at school. After all, she said, it was because she got to hanging around with the wrong crowd and they are the ones who made her do things that she got in trouble for.

Since he didn't know what to believe and he didn't know what to do with her, he reluctantly decided that he could possibly keep her out of trouble by having her answer the phone at the sheriff's office and do other odd jobs that he needed done.

He hoped and prayed that the uncomfortable situation would get straightened out and that Gloria would get bored with life in small-town Missouri and move on…but she didn't budge. Several times he tried to call his sister or his brother-in-law Bob, but when they answered their phone and found out it was him, they immediately hung up. Sheriff Bud Nelson was stuck with Gloria.

Gloria really hadn't changed a bit. She was now 24 years old and still very overweight and, most importantly, she was still the game player she had learned to be. Any friends or acquaintances she made in town were the result of her tabloid-mentality that led to reckless storytelling, and it seemed that many of the small town Missouri folks loved juicy gossip, whether it turned out to have a speck of truth or not. Working for the sheriff gave her plenty of fuel for her fire. She knew just about everything that was going on with everybody in town. When she ran into people in town that she knew and who wanted to know the "latest," she was more than happy to tell them stories like the guy who got picked up driving drunk last night and you won't believe who he had in the car with him. They'd all hang on her every word. She'd go on to tell them it was Ted Winslow's wife Mary and how disheveled Mary looked. She left the rest of the lurid details to their imagination. Gloria was a walking, talking self-made tabloid reporter.

In order to get the info that she needed to concoct her wild and wicked tales, Gloria had become a professional eavesdropper. She not only had developed hearing like a barn owl, she had mastered the technique of listening in on Sheriff Nelson's phone calls from her desk in the outer office without him being any the wiser that she was on the line. When it came to his candid conversation with the Spenzi boy, that was an easy one. She waited to bring the sodas to the sheriff's office and then loitered out of sight behind the open door, soaking in every detail of Wilke's confession and the various cover ups that the sheriff had condoned. What a story she had now…this information would really make her special…everyone in town would be impressed and want to be Gloria Wilson's friend.

CHAPTER THIRTY-SEVEN
"Freedom" of the Press

The Marceline Register was the only local newspaper in town and it had five people on staff. The editorial offices were located on the floor above the Midland Printing Company on Main Street across from the First Missouri Savings and Loan. Midland was an outfit that not only ran the weekly newspaper on its presses, but they printed many of the school yearbooks from a tri-state area. They were the main employer in Marceline.

The paper came out once a week on Thursday because, well, in a small town like Marceline, there just wasn't much to report on a daily basis. *The Register*, as it is referred to in town, covers the usual statistics of who was born and who died and who got married and who got divorced. Interspersed with this kind of local trivia, readers can find newswire blah-blah-like reports on politics from the state capital in Jefferson City or boilerplate features on recipes, finance and health. Occasionally, major breaking news like car wrecks in town, a local farmer's 1,200 pound squash that takes the blue ribbon at the Missouri State Fair or the Boy Scout troop's annual Mother's Day pancake breakfast photos are featured on the front page. Usually, on page two the paper reserves a column for the police blotter, detailing crimes and misdeeds large and small in the area. It's here that Sheriff Nelson's office was always consulted. The rest of the paper featured week-old cartoons, a crossword puzzle, the weather report and the local church schedules.

It was truly a local paper. If people really wanted to read about world news, they got the *Kansas City Star*, which was the "newsy" paper.

On Wednesday afternoon, Gloria knew that *The Marceline Register* would be finalizing the news for their Thursday edition of the paper. The sheriff had left the office early and when he went out the door it was without a goodbye to Gloria or even a simple thank you. She usually stayed at the office until around five, but she locked up early because, this day, she was truly on a mission.

She got over to the newspaper's office about 4 o'clock and as she came through the door she was met by the editor, Elmo Crippen. He'd been in charge of the paper for the last seven years. A heavy, balding, jovial man, Elmo was liked by everyone in town.

"So Gloria," he said with a grin. "How's our star reporter? Any hot news to report today?"

"Well…actually Elmo," said Gloria officiously, her voice trailing to almost a whisper. "Yer hardly going to believe it…but…I've got some very disturbing news for you today. I feel it is my duty to report it."

"Oh my Gloria, did the sheriff pick up another drunk that has been sleeping with somebody else's wife?" Elmo joked. "I'm afraid that's probably old news my dear."

"Nope…this is serious stuff," she said as she motioned the editor toward the sanctity of his own office and as they sat in a couple of chairs at a small table in the corner, she continued. "As you know Elmo, I have access to a lot of information, working for the sheriff and all, and usually I would be sworn to secrecy, but what I overheard today, just can't be kept secret."

He looked at her wide-eyed and wondered what was coming next. She really looked like she had a serious story. "What will you pay me for a really big story?" she asked. "I mean a really big story that will turn this town inside out!"

"Gloria, Gloria…," he said."You have been around here long enough to know that we don't pay money for stories. We just look and listen and report the news. Now, I have work to do and a deadline to meet. If you have a credible story, let's have it."

She figured that she'd try to get some money, but when that didn't work; she decided that being identified as the reporter of the story was worth it. She told him what she had heard being said in the sheriff's office, with a few embellishments of course. She implicated Wilke, the whole Spenzi family and Fannie, and the sheriff himself. The only people she wasn't clear on was how the ballerina girl or the Schiltz brothers were involved.

When she was done Elmo was dumbfounded, but he managed to say, "Gloria these are very serious accusations that could hurt a lot of people. Are you absolutely sure about this?"

"Oh yes Elmo, I'm absolutely sure," she said. "I heard it all loud and clear. Sheriff Nelson's even got the evidence in his desk drawer."

"Why are you doing this Gloria?" Elmo wanted to know. "You're not going to get any money for it and you'll probably lose your job."

"Well…everybody knows that crime don't pay," she said. "I just want all of Marceline to know that Gloria Wilson did some good here. When you print my name on the story, everyone will know me and they'll know that it's true."

"Oh yes Gloria," he assured her. "Your name will be the source of the story. We'll make sure you get the credit."

"Oh goody," she said with an air of satisfaction as she rubbed her palms together in front of her face.

After she left, Elmo immediately put in a call for Bud Nelson. He called the office and he rang Bud's home number. There was no answer at either phone. He tried to verify the story and he wanted to let the sheriff know that he would be implicated but he was never able to reach him.

And so… *The Marceline Register* went to press on Wednesday night with the biggest front page news they'd had in the last 20 years.

CHAPTER THIRTY-EIGHT
The Morning News

Bobby Torres was a seasoned newspaper carrier and had been delivering papers around his Marceline neighborhood for the last three years. Every morning at 5:30, he went to *The Register's* loading dock at the back of the Midland Printing building and folded and banded the papers, layering them into the bins on his bicycle. On most days, he never paid much attention to what was printed in the paper, but that morning something caught his eye; he read a little bit and then saw the name Spenzi on the front page. He knew Wilke Spenzi from grade school and he had liked him. Bobby thought to himself that this was not going to be good news he was delivering. He wished he could burn all of the papers, but he knew he had a job to do.

Mattie was generally the first to rise in the Spenzi household. She started the coffee and went out near the front porch to get the paper on Thursday mornings. They got the *Kansas City Star* on Sundays, but looked forward to the local news in *The Register* on Thursday. On this day, she got the paper and laid it on the kitchen table as Joseph wandered into the kitchen. As she got a cup from the cupboard and poured him a cup of coffee there was a knock at the back screen door. It was Sheriff Nelson.

Mattie opened the door and said, "Hey Bud, come on in. What brings you here so early? I have fresh coffee, sit down and join us."

After the sheriff came in and eased himself into a chair at the table across from Joseph he admitted, "I wanted to be here when you see *The Register* this morning."

"Why Bud, what's happening?" Joseph said as he sipped his coffee and flipped open the paper that was on the table. "Oh my God!" he said as he sat staring at the front page that stared back at him. The headline read…SPENZI BOY KILLED HOMER GOSS and in a font below it that was almost as large: FAMILY COVERED IT UP, ALONG WITH THE SHERIFF'S HELP

Joseph flipped the paper over on the table and looked away from it. He wasn't able to read any farther.

Mattie who was standing at the table almost dropped the coffee pot from which she was pouring the sheriff's coffee and she picked up the paper and read the headline aloud. With the stinging words ringing in their ears, they all were frozen in total silence.

Wilke, in his pajamas, ambled into the kitchen following the smell of fresh coffee. He had heard Sheriff Nelson's distinct voice and wondered what he was doing here so early on a Thursday morning. "Hey Sheriff Nelson," he said as he grabbed a cup from the cupboard and picked up the coffee pot that Mattie had set down. "What brings you around here today?"

Still no words were spoken from those at the table as he settled in a chair and glanced at the paper that Mattie had dropped. The headline screamed at him and his face turned ashen white. As he grasped the meaning of the words in large black letters, he could hear his heart booming in his ears and his eyes refused to focus.

He blurted out the first thing that rushed into his mind, "Sheriff…oh my God, I thought this was settled?" he exclaimed. "We came to a decision yesterday. I talked to you last night and I thought this whole thing was supposed to be done and buried."

"So did I Wilke," Sheriff Nelson said hurriedly. "You have my word that I had nothing to do with this, but I know who did. It was my slut of a niece, Gloria. The article gives her full credit for the information. She must have listened in on our conversation yesterday and decided to make a name for herself."

He got up from the table, paused and said to everyone around the table, "I don't want you all to worry; I will take care of this."

Wilke looked up at him saying, "Sheriff, the damage is done. I don't know what you can do to fix it. Gloria has ruined all of our lives."

"I'll take care of it," the sheriff said over his shoulder as he walked out the door.

The loud voices and the slam of the kitchen screen door woke Lily and Thomas. They headed for the kitchen where they found everyone just staring off into space. Joseph quickly rolled the newspaper up and put it down beside his chair.

"Hello my morning bunnies," he said. "Guess what? I have a surprise for you…no school today. We're taking a family day. Watch some TV and your mom and I will make some breakfast for you."

"Yay," chimed the children in unison. "Yippee-skippy…no school today!" They tumbled onto the couch in front of the TV in the living room. What a treat they thought and wasn't it strange that adults were so hard to understand sometimes.

Back in the kitchen, Joseph got Fannie on the phone and told her to come over immediately. He knew that she did not get the local paper regularly, so he knew she had no idea what trouble was brewing. Wilke had picked up the paper and was intently reading the details in the article, and all the while he was twisting and pulling on a thick strand of hair behind his ear.

Sheriff Nelson left the Spenzi's kitchen, but he did not go directly back to his office. He stopped off at Benny White's place, his deputy for the last five years. Benny was a big guy and somebody you'd like to have as backup because his 250 pounds intimated most people. He wasn't the smartest guy on the block, but his bulk made up for it.

Benny's wife Lois came to the door. She was, in contrast to Benny, skinny as a rail—she probably weighed 90 pounds…soaking wet. She was not a very attractive woman with scraggly, dirty blonde hair and crooked teeth stained yellow from years of smoking. Benny and she had twin girls named Lisa and Liza. They were about four years old and looked a lot like their mother…unfortunately.

"Well, Sheriff, good morning to you," she said through a cloud of cigarette smoke. "We just finished breakfast. Would you like some leftovers?"

"Nope…thanks anyway Lois," he said. "I need to talk to Benny for a few minutes outside privately—police business you know."

"Hey Benny…get yer ass out here," she screeched toward the interior of the double-wide trailer they called home. "Yer boss is here and wants to talk to you."

Benny ambled out of the back room wearing a bulging white T-shirt and the wrinkled trousers of his deputy's uniform. He was chewing on a greasy piece of link sausage. "Hey Bud, what's up?" he asked.

"C'mon outside with me, Benny," the sheriff said. "I need to talk with you."

They both walked across the brown patch of dirt and dead grass that Benny called a front yard, but not a word was said by either of them. Benny was getting worried about what was up. He couldn't figure out why his boss had come to his house for the first time since he had been sworn in as deputy. In the past, no matter what the situation, they always communicated by the handheld 2-way radio that they both carried on and off duty. Something big must be up he thought.

"Benny, I know you been doing my niece," Bud began as they reached the corner of the so-called yard. "I just let it go because I figured it was none of my business as long as it didn't interfere with what we were doing on the force. But some things have come up and I need to know, and it's very important that you tell me the truth, did you ever give Gloria either gifts or money as part of your, er…uh…romantic activities?"

Benny stopped in his tracks. He was speechless. He had no idea that Bud Nelson knew about he and Gloria. They had always made it a point to be very careful. They met late at night when Benny wasn't near his own home and when he had the excuse that he was out on patrol. The fact was that there wasn't much to patrol in and around Marceline so Benny would generally cruise around the reservoir outside of town and Gloria would meet him out there. Since they were too big to both squeeze into the back seat of the patrol car, Gloria always had a couple of blankets in the trunk of her car and she'd bring a bottle of vodka or a few beers and they'd drink and talk and go at it on the blanket along the bank of the reservoir for hours.

"Benny, I asked you a question," the sheriff snapped. "Answer it."

"Well Bud, gee…ya' kinda' caught me by surprise…," Benny began. "Gloria was always short on money, so,,, yes, I gave her money to help her out and I guess I gave her a few trinkets like for her birthday and for Valentine's Day. Don't tell anybody but it was stuff that I filched out of Lois's jewelry box."

"Okay Benny…thanks for leveling with me," the sheriff said. "You've given me all I need to know." He reached out and put one hand on Benny's broad shoulder as he said, "If I were you, I'd go back inside and say goodbye to your family, because you and Gloria are going to be spending some real quality time together in jail."

With that the sheriff opened the door and slid into his patrol car that was nearby and headed for his office.

As he walked in, earlier than usual, he encountered Gloria cleaning out her desk.

"There's no need to do that," he announced. "You're wasting your time. I just talked to your boyfriend Benny White and I'm arresting you for prostitution. You're nothing but a slut, Gloria, and I'm ashamed to say that you are my niece. I should have listened to your mother years ago. But don't worry, I will be calling her and finding out all of the other charges that we might be able to bring against you."

"Uncle Buddy, you've got me all wrong," she pleaded as she reached out to her uncle. "I was just trying to do the right thing."

He grabbed her outstretched arm as he leaned his face close to hers and growled, "Gloria, you wouldn't know the *right thing* if it hit you smack in your ugly, fat face." And with that he snapped handcuffs on one of her wrists and spun her around to complete the cuffing behind her back. "Sit your fat ass down in that chair and shut up!"

"You know what I heard was the truth," she argued as she plopped into a chair.

"Gloria…I said shut up!" he snarled. "Shut your goddam mouth!"

The sheriff went into his office and sat down on the edge of his desk. He picked up his phone and dialed.

"Bob…Bob…wait…don't…please don't hang up on me!" he said. "Bob, listen to me. I'm in my office and I've arrested Gloria. She's sitting in the next room and she's in handcuffs. Yes I know you and Judy warned me Bob…I'm sorry. I should've listened. Please may I speak with Judy?"

Judy got on the phone and Bud apologized to her for not listening to her warnings over three years ago. He told her what had happened with Benny and with the newspaper and he wanted to know what else Gloria had done that made them kick her out. Judy was more than happy to tell him.

He left his office and walked Gloria out to his police car. But before he took her to the Brookfield jail to be booked, he made one important stop.

He drove a short way down the street where he parked and marched Gloria, in her handcuffs, up the stairs to the offices of the *Marceline Register*. Miriam Miller was at the front desk. She was one of the reporters at the paper.

"Miriam, I need to see Elmo," the sheriff announced.

"Sure thing Sheriff, I'll go get him," she said as she jumped up from the desk and headed down the hallway.

In a few moments, Elmo Crippen hustled into the reception area and his eyes bugged out when he saw the sheriff and Gloria beside him in handcuffs.

The sheriff spoke first. "Elmo, how long have I known you…10 years? Or has it been longer? If I recall correctly, I helped you get the editor's job on this rag of a paper. I just have one question. Why the hell after all these years of friendship would you not have come to me before you printed such a ridiculous story in today's paper?"

"Elmo," he continued. "I can't believe you took the word of this tramp of a woman who is now going to jail for prostitution, before you talked to me. This woman is a liar, a cheater and a thief, and you were willing to destroy innocent people's reputations based on her lizard tongue."

Elmo was visibly shaken by Bud's accusations but he managed to stammer, "Bud, her information seemed to be accurate. I thought she was telling the truth or I never would have printed the story."

"Elmo, I thought she was telling the truth when she told me three years ago that her father was molesting her," Bud said. "Now I know that wasn't the truth and neither was anything else she told me. I talked to her mother this morning and before they kicked her out three years ago, Gloria had been expelled from three boarding schools, had two abortions, was arrested four times for shoplifting, and was involved in a hit and run accident and got a DUI. Gloria Wilson doesn't have any concept of the truth or the difference between good and evil."

"So, Bud what do you want me to do?" Elmo asked.

"I want you to print a retraction of the story. Apologize to the Spenzi family, and let everybody in this town know that Gloria makes up stories just to get friends and attention," Bud said. "I want you tell them that she slept with Deputy Benny White for money and that she has been arrested for prostitution and that her story had no credibility. She is a sick and needy person, who will be going to the state mental hospital for evaluation. Is that clear enough Elmo?"

"Yes, Sheriff, I understand," Elmo said.

"Oh, and Elmo," the sheriff added. "Before I cart this poor excuse for a human being off to jail, I'd like your photographer to take a real nice picture of her. I think Gloria deserves the attention she really wanted. I want to see her picture on the front page of the retraction story. Make sure they see her nice, greasy, matted black hair and her sweet pudgy face and those eyes that are the windows to a very sad soul."

After the photographer came to the reception area and snapped a photo of Gloria, Sheriff Nelson dragged her down the stairs and stuffed her into the rear seat of his patrol car. On the way to the Brookfield jail, he called Benny White on the police radio.

Benny was still at home mopping the dust off his patrol car with an old towel when he heard the radio crackle and then he heard Sheriff Nelson's voice, "Pick up Benny…If you are there, pick up! Over!"

"Sheriff…, Benny here. Over," he said.

"Benny, get down to my office," said the sheriff. "Bring your badge and gun. You'll be turning them in. Over."

When he got no response, he continued, "You were a good deputy Benny, but you went too far with this. There's a good chance that you will do some jail time for solicitation. Over…Benny, are you there? Over."

"But Sheriff," Benny pleaded. "I didn't solicit sex from her. She was always willing. She wanted it. Over."

"Benny, listen to me," the sheriff said. "You gave it to her and you gave her cash. That's solicitation. If I were you, I'd have a heart to heart talk with Lois and try to explain things the best you can, because once I get Gloria booked I'll meet you at my office. Out."

The radio crackled and went dead. Benny just stood there in his dusty yard next to his patrol car. His felt like his whole life had just gone dead, as well.

He couldn't imagine facing Lois's wrath when he had to tell her about his escapades with Gloria. Sure, he was a big guy, but when it came to dealing with Lois, he felt like a whipped mouse. She made a daily task out of bad mouthing, ridiculing and nagging him. Their relationship went from bad to very bad and he had fallen out of love with her even before the twins were born. They were really the only reason he stuck around, but even they had turned into whiners and fighters like their miserable mother.

He didn't consider Gloria to be good looking but he sure relished the attention she gave him. She always said nice things and gave him compliments and, of course, the sex was great. The only reason he gave her money was to insure that she'd keep carrying on with him. He just needed somebody to hold onto, somebody that wouldn't say bad things to him. And now, Gloria was gone and he'd lost his job and his wife was going to make his life even more miserable. If Lois thought he was a loser before, she'd be totally convinced after this.

He fondled the grip of the revolver on his belt and contemplated killing himself with it, but he knew he didn't have the guts to pull the trigger.

His thoughts were jerked back to reality as Lois screeched at him from the porch, "Benny, if yer done talkin' to the sheriff on that there radio, git your lardass back in here and help with the dishes and the girls. I can't do everything."

"The sheriff needs me," he yelled back at her. "He wants me to meet him at the office. I've gotta' get goin' and I don't know when I'll be back. Give the girls a hug for me and tell them I'll see them later."

Before she could reply, he slid his bulky frame into the front seat of his patrol car and headed toward Brookfield. He planned to meet the sheriff at the jail where he'd turn himself in and give up his badge and gun. He figured that it would be better than facing up to Lois and continuing to live this miserable life."

Benny's intentions were good, but his timing was bad...very bad. In order to get from where he lived to Brookfield, he had to go through the north edge of town and then head north about 20 miles or so through the corn and wheat fields that stretched for miles in all directions. As he turned onto Eastern, his mind was racing as he imagined what was going to happen in his life and how he would accept losing much of what he had. He knew that Lois wasn't going to be a loss, but he'd sure miss Lisa and Liza. When it came to Gloria, he knew that he'd miss the passionate nights at the reservoir. His wandering mind played back how Gloria would talk softly to him as they had sex and as their rhythm increased, her soft talk changed to hot talk and then it reached a fever pitch...and...the last thing he heard was the horrendous, grinding, metal-smash-metal impact of Benson's bread truck...and Benny was dead.

Benson's veteran driver, Les Weaver, had completed the daily run from the factory bakery to several large grocery stores and small markets in Wien, Marceline, Crescent City, Claiborne and Salisbury and he was headed back to pick up the afternoon delivery. It was going to be lunchtime by the time he got to the bakery and he hoped he'd have time to grab a bite to eat at the diner across the street. He raced up Main Street and was glad to see that he'd catch the green light at the corner of Eastern. From experience, he knew that a red light stop at Eastern would set him back at least 5 minutes by the time he stopped and then got the big truck going full speed again. He accelerated to make sure he got to the light while it was still green and flashed into the intersection. He had no idea that Benny's police car would be ignoring the red light. The big truck impacted the smaller vehicle right in the driver's door. The collision made a terrible noise.

Les, in the much larger vehicle, had hit his head on the visor above the steering wheel and his right knee was bloodied when it caromed off the dash, but he wasn't seriously hurt. The front of the truck was a mess. Les got down out of the truck and limped over to the police car. Deputy White was still in the driver's seat with his arms draped over the steering wheel. A steady stream of bright red blood was pulsating out of the deputy's neck and ear where the side of his head and neck had slammed against the broken window on impact. There was broken glass and blood everywhere. Les tried to yank open the driver's door, but it was twisted and crumpled and wouldn't budge. He broke several remaining chunks of window glass out with his elbow and this allowed him to reach into the car to ease Benny's head back and see if he was still breathing. Bloody foam bubbled out of Benny's mouth, but he didn't appear to be breathing.

As people who had heard or seen the crash gathered around the vehicles, it seemed like everyone was screaming at everyone else. "Call an ambulance!" "Get Dr. Null."

Les made his way around the patrol car to the passenger's door since he could see the deputy's 2-way radio on the seat. He reached in through the broken window and picked up the radio. "Calling Sheriff Nelson," he said into the radio. "Calling Sheriff Nelson. Come in Sheriff."

The radio crackled and Sheriff Nelson's voice could be heard as he said, "Benny, I hear you. Over."

Les pushed the transmit pad and said, "Sheriff, it's not Benny. It's me…Les Weaver the Benson Bakery driver. Your deputy has been in a bad accident at Main and Eastern and…and…I think he's dead! Over."

"Did you call an ambulance?" the sheriff said. "Over."

"Yes sir, I think an ambulance is on the way. There's a bunch of people here," Les reported. "Where are you? Over."

"I'm just getting ready to leave the jail in Brookfield and I'll be there in about 20 minutes. Out," the sheriff said through some radio static.

Les dropped the radio back on the seat in the crumpled patrol car. He could hear a siren in the distance and figured that it must be the ambulance. He slumped to the pavement and thought to himself. How could this have happened? He had always prided himself on a clean driving record for the bakery for the 7 years he'd been driving the bread truck. No accidents and not even any tickets, he recalled. He knew the light was green, so he figured the deputy must have run a red light.

The sheriff had just finished processing Gloria into the jail for booking when he got the radio call from Les. He ran to his patrol car and screeched the tires on the pavement as he left the parking lot. His mind was aflutter with thoughts of Gloria behind bars and now this, his star witness, deputy and friend may be dead. It had been a hell of a morning…and now the afternoon wasn't looking much better.

When Sheriff Nelson pulled up to Main and Eastern, the ambulance had come and gone with Benny's body. Les was still sitting on the pavement and someone had thrown a blanket over his shoulders and got him a paper cup of water. Doc Null had heard the commotion and ran over from his office with one of his nurses. He checked Benny and verified to the ambulance staff that nothing could be done for the deputy. They pulled Benny's large body out of the mangled patrol car and strapped it on a gurney. The stretcher was loaded into the ambulance and they headed for the hospital in Brookfield. Doc Null's nurse checked Les for his injuries and bandaged the cut on his knee. He refused any further care since he wanted to wait for Sheriff Nelson.

"Les Weaver…," said the sheriff as got out of his car and knelt down on the pavement beside him. "My God…are you alright? What happened?"

"Benny's dead Sheriff…, he cried. "Benny died! It was an accident. I didn't mean to hit his car. I was going through the green light and he ran the red light…it happened so fast.

"Take it easy Les, I know you are shaken up over this," the sheriff said as he helped the injured man to his feet. I want you to get home and get some rest and we'll talk about this tomorrow when we are both fresh. I radioed Ron's Tow Service as I was getting here and they will tow the patrol car and your truck to Peavey's Collision yard. Do you have a way to get home?"

"Yes sir," Les said. "Dr. Null's nurse is right over there and she offered to give me a lift home. She'll also check my cut knee and see if it needs a new bandage tonight. I think I'll be fine."

"Okay Les, you do that," he said. "We'll talk tomorrow. I'm sure this was just an unfortunate accident."

As Les headed off in the direction of Dr. Null's office, Sheriff Nelson was pleased to see that the tow truck was pulling up on the scene. "Drag both of them to Peavey's, will ya' Ron?" he yelled at the driver. "And when you are done, I'd appreciate it if you would shovel up this broken glass and wash the area down."

"Will do Sheriff," said the tow truck driver. "Hey...is Benny alright?"

"Nope Ron," the sheriff replied. "Benny didn't make it. He's dead."

Bud Nelson dreaded his next duty—telling Lois. He sensed that there wasn't much love lost between her and Benny, but still she had just become a widow with two small kids. He knew her main concern would be Benny's last check and what about his life insurance and he knew she'd ask him if he thought it would do her any good to sue Benson's Bakery. Knowing Lois, there probably wouldn't be much grief on her part.

He was right. She did shed a few tears, but only when she was at the hospital where she was asked to identify Benny's body. He guessed that Lois decided it only seemed appropriate.

CHAPTER THIRTY-NINE
Wait and Worry

The Spenzi family holed up in the house all day. The curtains were closed and the doors were locked. When the phone rang the first few times, Joseph answered it thinking it was Sheriff Nelson. Each time it was somebody asking about the story in the paper and was it true and they told how shocked they were. After that, Joseph didn't answer the phone even though it rang every five minutes or so. Lilly and Thomas were really confused. They couldn't quite figure out what was going on, but they were happy to be home from school and watching TV.

Then the doorbell rang and when Joseph parted the living room drapes, he saw at least 10 people standing in the front yard. They all had cameras or recording equipment and were obviously reporters who were working with their assigned video crews. A news van from Channel 5 Nightline News in Kansas City was parked across the road. Joseph was at a loss as to what to do.

Mattie, Fannie and Wilke had argued throughout the day about what their options were. Wilke just kept saying he thought he should just tell the truth, and then Grandma Fannie would go into her tirade again how this wasn't just about him. A lot more people were involved and sure to get hurt by all of this.

Where was Sheriff Nelson? He was the one who had headed out the door assuring everyone that he was going to "take care of it." Hours had passed and no contact from the sheriff. Little did they know all that he was dealing with.

At about 8 o'clock that evening, Joseph peeked through the curtain and was surprised to discover that all the reporters were gone. He figured they had either given up on getting additional tidbits for the story or they were assigned to a bigger story that was brewing. Whatever the reason, he was relieved but he still kept the doors locked and the drapes drawn.

As it got later, Mattie put Lilly and Thomas to bed. She came back into the front room and collapsed with a loud sigh on the couch. She had made dinner for everyone and was emotionally exhausted from the day's wondering and waiting. There was a loud knock on the backdoor that disturbed everyone. Joseph jumped up…more nosey reporters? "It's okay Joseph, let me in," the sheriff said.

Joseph opened the backdoor and pushed open the screen, letting Bud come staggering in. He had never seen the sheriff so haggard looking. His eyes were bloodshot, his hair was disheveled and he seemed to be visibly shaken. "Bud, come on in," he said. "My God…we've been waiting to hear from you all day."

The sheriff made his way to the nearest kitchen chair and collapsed, resting his upper body on the table. "Mattie…," he said. "Can you get me some water and a couple of aspirin? This headache is killing me."

Mattie got the aspirins and drew a glass of water at the kitchen sink. They all congregated in the kitchen around the table. Sheriff Nelson was, obviously, the center of attention.

"I'm sorry it took me so long to get back to all of you," he said as he popped the aspirins in his mouth and washed them down with a swig of water. "It's been one hell of a day. Let me try to tell you what happened in the short version and we'll talk more about it tomorrow. I'm way too tired and I know all of you are as well."

With the rapt attention of the Spenzi family audience, he related the events of the day. Gloria Wilson had been arrested for prostitution and had been booked and locked up at the Brookfield jail. He told them about his conversation with Elmo Crippen at the *Marceline Register* and promised them that there would be a retraction and an apology from the paper. "Unfortunately," he concluded, "the retraction story will share the front page with the fact that Benny White was killed in a car accident this afternoon."

The Spenzi's just sat dumbfounded. None of them really quite knew how to respond.

When he realized that everyone was completely overloaded, including himself, the sheriff said, "I'm headed for home now and I'll be back tomorrow. Don't answer the door to anybody but me. If I need to contact you by phone, I'll give one ring, hang up, and you'll know it's me when I call back. Let's all stick together and we'll get through this."

He got up from the table and without a further word to anyone, he went out the door, got in his patrol car and left. The Spenzi's went to bed. Grandma Fannie spent the night and slept with Lilly. They were all afraid of what tomorrow might bring...

Sheriff Nelson was dead tired. Every cell and fiber in his body had been challenged by the stresses of the day and he felt like he had been rubbed raw. As he drove back to town he wanted to continue on to his own home and sit down with a stiff drink and forget what he had endured for the previous 12 hours or so. But, he knew he had one more stop to make. It was nearly 10 o'clock when he pulled his patrol car into the parking lot and climbed the stairs to the offices of the *Marceline Register*. He could see the lights were still on and he knew Elmo Crippen would still be there. The front reception area was empty but he could see lights down the hall.

He yelled, "Hey Elmo, you in here somewhere?"

Elmo appeared in a doorway and replied, "Hey there Bud. Of course I'm here and I think I will be for the rest of the night, thanks to you and all of the news you've given us to print. This is the only Saturday edition we've ever run."

"Elmo," the sheriff offered, "I appreciate you printing this retraction and picking up on all the other news, but you know Benny White is dead, and I was just thinking maybe in respect to his wife and kids, we shouldn't mention about him being involved in solicitation of prostitution."

"Bud, I'd like to do that for you but the paper is already on the press downstairs," Elmo said. "I did the retraction edition exactly as you wanted and that's what will be in the paper tomorrow morning."

"Elmo thanks for what you did," Bud said as he gave him a bear hug. "I know I asked a lot of you. I'm going home and we'll just leave things the way they are and let the cards land the way they fall."

"Oh Bud, you are certainly welcome," Elmo replied. "I can't thank you for the biggest piece of news this paper has ever reported. I'm just sorry it was bad news. Now, you git out of here," he added as he grabbed Bud's broad shoulders and spun him around and playfully pushed him toward the door. "Go home Sheriff! "Pour yourself a stiff one and get some sleep. You look exhausted."

Bud Nelson headed back down the stairs and out to his patrol car in the parking lot. He was exhausted, but his mind was still buzzing with thoughts of all that had happened in one day. As he pulled out on the street he wondered how long he could keep Gloria locked up, now that the prostitution charge didn't hold much water. The solicitor was dead. Oh man, what a mess, he concluded. Maybe after some sleep, he'd figure it all out.

Many of Marceline's town folk awoke Saturday morning and noticed a newspaper on their porch or driveway. What was going on? You can imagine their interest was piqued when they discovered that the strange Saturday paper that was delivered was a special edition of the *Marceline Register.*

Prominently placed on the front page was a 4"X5" headshot of Gloria Wilson, in all her homely glory. She wasn't happy about the circumstances of getting this photo taken, so the expression that was caught was one of her glowering in disdain at the camera. It was such an unglamorous shot to say the least. The accompanying story under the photo described how and why Gloria could never be considered to be mentally stable. There were details of her sexual escapades with Deputy Benny White and information about how he paid her for her favors like anyone would pay a common whore. It went into detail regarding how Gloria had made up the information about Wilke Spenzi and the Spenzi family and Sheriff Bud Nelson and made it clear that they were not involved in the death of the town drunk Homer Goss. All the information she had given *The Register* was totally false and she and *The Register* apologized to the Spenzi family.

In a whole separate paragraph, details about Gloria's past and her run in with her family and the reasons why they had disowned her before she moved to Marceline were described graphically. It was clear that Gloria Wilson did what she did to get attention.

On the lower section of the front page was a stock photo of Deputy Benny White, taken years ago when he graduated from the police academy. In those days, Benny was a svelte 180 pounds and the headshot photo of him in his uniform made him look like Adonis. The story attached to the photo was his obituary. It told about Deputy White's death in the traffic accident at Main and Eastern. It described how he accidentally collided at the intersection with the Benson Bakery truck driven by Les Weaver. Mr. Weaver was not injured seriously and the accident was deemed the fault of the deputy who had not stopped at the red light. The article ruined the potential for a lawsuit from Lois.

This was the most news this little community and this little paper had ever experienced. The whole town was abuzz.

Speaking of buzz, when Lois White read her copy of the special edition she was seated at her dinette table in her tiny kitchen, slurping down her third cup of coffee and puffing on her fifth cigarette. She'd accidentally spilled the box of the kids' morning cereal on the floor and they were busy picking up the little Cheerio donut-shaped pieces and stuffing their mouths. Lois was half-interested in the information about Gloria, but when she got to the part about Gloria getting paid for sex with Benny White...her mind went into overdrive...Benny WHO she thought! Benny White? My fat husband Benny White? She went ballistic! The coffee cup flew across the kitchen and crashed into the front of the refrigerator, splattering coffee all over the billboard of crayon drawings plastered there by the twins. She grabbed the phone and dialed Sheriff Nelson. After several rings she slammed the phone down because there was still no answer. She picked up one twin under each arm and bolted out the door. When she got to the car she pulled open the back door and shoved the kids on the seat. "Sit down and shut up," she yelled at them and once in the driver's seat, she roared the car out the dusty driveway and down the street. She was headed for Sheriff Nelson's house where she planned on telling him a thing or two.

It was about 7:30 that morning and the sheriff was just waking up. He got a couple of aspirins from the medicine cabinet in his bathroom and headed for the kitchen where he looked forward to peace and quiet and a strong cup of hot coffee. He just knew it would be another grueling day. As he was getting the coffee grounds arranged in the coffee pot, he was interrupted by the sound of frantic knocking on his front door. Oh no, he thought...not another reporter. He tried to stay hidden in the kitchen and ignore the rapping, but soon the rapping became pounding...bang-bang-bang it went...bang-bang-bang! He finally gave in and went to answer the door and when he opened it, there was Lois White and her two scraggly kids on his front porch. He actually wished now it had been a reporter.

"Good morning Lois. I'm making myself some coffee," he said as calmly as he could. Would you like some?"

While waving the *Marceline Register* in his face, she screeched. "What's this shit about my Benny being involved in prostitution with your crazy secretary?

"Lois," he responded. "I haven't seen any paper this morning. Do you want to come in and have some coffee or do you just want to keep yelling at me and waving the paper in my face? Either way…I definitely need a cup of coffee." He turned and headed back to his kitchen.

She yanked the screen door open and shooed her two Lois-lookalikes inside. "Sit down," she screamed at them. "Sit right there and stay there." As they obeyed with big-eyed frowns and shaky lower lips, she stormed into Bud's kitchen and plopped down at his kitchen table, the wadded up newspaper still clutched in her fist.

He looked over his shoulder at her as he supervised the first few perks of the chrome coffeemaker that sat on the counter and said, "Lois, I know you've had some bad news with the loss of Benny and all, but Benny had been sleeping with Gloria for some time. He wasn't happy with you, and you had to know that."

Lois appeared like she was shocked at what the sheriff had to say. "What on earth do you mean? She screeched. "Benny? Not happy with me? How could Benny not be happy with a woman like me?"

He bit the side of his lip as he answered that question…"Lois…I'll let you figure that one out for yourself."

"So where is this Gloria Wilson now?" she asked.

"She's in jail," he replied. "In Brookfield. Right where she belongs."

There was a minute or so of silence, except for the wheezing and coughing of the final perks of the coffeemaker and Lois spoke up first. "So, yer telling me that my Benny screwed around and paid a woman our hard-earned money to give him sex. Money that could have helped support me and my kids. And…And then the fat bastard gets himself killed and I can't sue anybody because he caused the accident?"

Bud listened to her wailing as he poured two cups of coffee and said, "That's what happened Lois. If it's any help to you, I have Benny's last paycheck at the office and I'll drop it in the mail tomorrow. I know he had some kind of life insurance. You should check into that."

He had no sooner placed her cup of coffee in front of her and sat down with his cup when she pointed a cigarette-stained finger at him and exploded, "Bud Nelson, you're a sonofabitch!"

Taken aback by this attack he fired back at her saying, "No Lois, you're the bitch and always have been. Being honest with you, I really don't know how Benny put up with you all of these years."

She was furious and immediately picked up the cup of coffee that he had placed in front of her and threw the coffee at him. Luckily, he had a terrycloth robe on and the material absorbed most of the hot liquid before it burned his skin.

As he stood up, she bolted from her chair grabbing the twins by the arms and dragged them screaming out the front door. She tossed them into the back of her car and headed for the Brookfield jail. Hell hath no fury like a woman scorned.

The Brookfield jail was designed to house 10 total prisoners, five cells with two to a cell. There was the main jail block and a couple of short-term holding cells. Gloria was in a holding cell pending her indictment and her possible assignment to the psych ward at Brookfield General Hospital that was located about six miles from the jail. She was all alone in her cell and she was very lonely...she needed someone to talk to.

Little did she know who would be her first visitor on that Saturday morning. The rule was that only family members could visit prisoners in the holding cells. Lois had told the desk clerk that she was family to Gloria Wilson because, as she told it, "Gloria was screwing my husband and so I guess that makes us family." The desk clerk thought that was a novel answer, so she paged the intercom in Gloria's cell and said, "Wilson...you have a visitor."

Gloria got up from the bunk and walked to the bars at the front of her cell. A buzzer sounded and she heard a loud clank as an outer barred door slid open. She was confronted by a short, scraggly, dirty-blonde haired woman and two similar-looking kids. The woman and the kids, one holding each of her hands, walked to the cell and stopped and just stared through the bars at Gloria.

Lois had the crumpled Marceline newspaper tucked in her armpit. She dropped the children's hands and spread the newspaper and held the front page against the bars in front of Gloria's face. "Is this your ugly face, bitch? she yelled.

"Oh my God," Gloria said. "That's me!" This was the first she had seen the paper and she was amazed that her photo was right there on the front page. She looked at it and wished she had smiled more naturally and thought she probably should have washed her hair that day, but, the picture wasn't that bad.

Lois pulled the paper down out of Gloria's narcissistic gaze and spewed, "Is it true that it was you that was screwing my husband Benny?"

Gloria jammed her face against the bars and spit her answer back at Lois, "Oh...so you're the scrawny piece of crap with the two whiny kids he was so unhappy with."

Lois blew up. She slapped the paper against the metal bars trying to hit Gloria in the face. Gloria stepped back away from the onslaught but she reached through the bars and grabbed the paper pulling it out of Lois hands and into the cell. She opened the full front page again and admired her photo, and it was then she saw the photo of Benny and the headline that read that he had died in an accident.

She was devastated. Her sweet Benny was gone. They had such great sex and for the first time Gloria had felt special and understood and almost loved. She had appreciated the money and trinkets Benny had given her, but she mostly appreciated that he was imperfect like her. They were imperfect people—damaged, yet so perfect together.

Meanwhile, Lois was screaming at Gloria and banging her fists on the bars. Lisa and Liza were scared by all this activity and yelling and they began to scream as only a couple of upset four-year-olds can scream. The one guard on duty at that section of the jail heard the commotion and came running. It was pandemonium. "Give me the newspaper," screamed Lois as she reached through the bars and tried to get a hold of Gloria. "Give it back to me!"

But Gloria wasn't about to give the paper back. She paid no attention to Lois as she retreated to her bunk and laid down clutching the picture of her beloved Benny, who she realized was now dead, to her breast. "Benny, my Benny," she moaned.

The guard grabbed Lois and Lois grabbed her kids. "It's time for you to leave," he said. "I want you out of here...now!"

As Lois and the children were escorted out of the area of the holding cell, Lois screamed one more obscenity at Gloria, "You'll pay for this you butt-ugly bitch."

Gloria closed her eyes as she lay on her bunk. She clutched the newspaper even tighter as Lois's screams faded into the distance. Oh how true those screams really were…as the tears rolled down her cheeks she knew that she would pay for this. She'd been paying for something like this all of her life. Mostly she'd been paying the price for parents that didn't want her and never had a clue how to love her.

CHAPTER FORTY
1968

Richard Milhous Nixon, alias "Tricky Dick," won the November election and would become the 37th President of the United States. The Vietnam War was in full swing and Americans would be shocked to hear of the My Lai Massacre and the Tet Offensive. Rowan and Martin's *Laugh In* debuted on TV. Senator Robert Kennedy and Martin Luther King, Jr. were assassinated in the prime of their life. It was a year of change, hope, tension, deception, laughter and needless death.

Wilke Spenzi turned 25 that year. He had finished his AA degree at Brookfield Community College and, thanks to Grandma Fannie, was accepted into the University of Missouri. He was in the last year of his bachelor's degree in biology and veterinary science.

Five years had passed since the Gloria Wilson fiasco. The retraction from the *Marceline Register* had completely exonerated the Spenzi family and the reputation of Sheriff Bud Nelson. The matter was never brought up again. Gloria spent six months locked up at the Brookfield General psych ward as a prisoner inpatient and she endured a battery of tests and hours and hours of counseling. When she was finally released from custody, Sheriff Nelson signed the release papers for her and drove her back to his place. Much to her surprise, there in the driveway was her car, stuffed with everything she owned and gassed up ready to go. Bud had anticipated her release and removed any excuse she may have had for staying in Marceline any longer. For Gloria, regardless of her current mental health, it felt like déjà vu as he handed her a little cash as severance pay and told her to drive out of town and never come back. He warned her that if he ever saw her face again, he'd trump up whatever charges were necessary to put her back behind bars, and if that happened, it would be for a very long time. Gloria was done with Marceline and Uncle Buddy. She drove out of town and never looked back. Everything she owned was in the car, including a tattered memento on the seat next to her. It was a wrinkled and faded copy of the *Marceline Register* special edition from 1963. She needed something to hang onto.

Regarding Benny White, the sheriff was forced to allocate some city funds for a pauper's burial in the Marceline cemetery. He offered a short prayer over Benny's pine box at the burial service that was attended by about 10 townsfolk who knew Benny, including Les Weaver. Benny White's jilted and scorned wife Lois never claimed his body for burial and didn't attend the makeshift service, but she did track down and cash in his life insurance policy. That gave her enough money to relocate her miserable self and two kids to her mother's place in Arkansas. Next to Gloria, Bud Nelson had never been so happy to see someone leave town.

Bud himself retired with the pension he had earned. He wasn't much of a fisherman, but he thought he could learn, so he and his friend Elmo Crippen moved to the Ozarks together. They would learn to fish and just enjoy the rest of their lives away from the pressures of newspaper deadlines and crime.

Lilly and Thomas entered Salisbury High the year after Joseph and Mattie expanded their filling station and auto repair shop business to a second location at the north end of town. They hired Ray McGanna to run the new station and both businesses were doing good.

Grandma Fannie had retired from the University of Missouri, but still dabbled with guest lectures and tutoring for some graduate students. She also was working on writing a book about overcoming obstacles to teach. Alfreda had taken a fall and broke a hip on the leg that caused her limp. She really couldn't fully care for herself so she was forced to sell her and Porter's home and move in permanently with Fannie. It was a nice arrangement as they always enjoyed one another and now could grow older together.

The twin Sisters, Leona and Viola, had both passed away gently, just six months apart. They were incredible women who had such a positive influence on so many people. They were missed by many who knew and loved them.

In April, it was unseasonably warm and humid in Missouri. Marceline was gearing up for another Walt Disney's visit. The streets and building façades were washed down with fire hoses, the band gazebo in the park got a fresh coat of paint and Walt's namesake elementary school and community pool that he had donated over 10 years ago were spruced up as they readied for his arrival. This year Walt was being heralded for his lifetime accomplishments with the planned release of a commemorative postage stamp with a face value of six cents, the current going rate for first class mail in 1968. Also, while he was in Marceline, one of his film companies would be involved shooting a biographical documentary in and around his boyhood home.

College student Wilke Spenzi was home from Mizzou on spring break. Grandma Fannie had made plans for all of them to go to the celebration and get to see the Walt Disney downtown parade once again. This year, Salisbury High had its own marching band and it would be joined by bands from several high schools from the larger cities nearby. Of course, the Boy and Girl Scout troops with their Cubs and Brownies would have a few hundred ragtag, flag-waving marchers and there would be clowns with balloons and magic tricks and kids on decorated bicycles and dressed-up pets in arms and on leashes. There was to be an open house with food and drink stands and live entertainment at Walt's old farmhouse homestead.

It was Saturday afternoon on April 10th, when Grandma Fannie and Alfreda arrived at the Spenzi home. "Are you all set for the big parade?" Fannie asked Lilly and Thomas who met them at the door.

"Yes! Yes!...Grandma!" they cheered in unison as they jumped and ran circles around the two women. "Let's go see the parade!"

"Where's my grandson Wilke? Fannie asked.

"Oh Fannie," Mattie said. "Wilke is in his room and I don't think he's up to going to the parade. He said he's afraid it will bring up old, bad memories for him."

"Nonsense," Fannie chided as she headed for Wilke's room. "It's high time that boy forgets about his past and gets busy making new memories."

She stopped at the door to his room and knocked. "Wilke Spenzi...you get out here right now," she said.

The door opened and Wilke stood looking at his grandmother sheepishly. "Aww Grandma...just leave me be," he pleaded.

Fannie would hear none of it. "Listen to me now," she said. "It's been over 10 years and there's been a lot of water gone over that dam. Things have changed and, I must say, they've changed for the better. You've moved on with your life and so has everyone else. Now c'mon...let's go to the parade and have some fun."

"Okay Grandma," he offered. "I'll think about it and if I decide to come, I'll meet you guys there later."

So, the Spenzi family and Alfreda, minus Wilke, headed out to join the throng of people on both sides of Main Street waiting to see the parade and especially the celebrity bringing up the rear, Walt Disney in his Model T Ford.

The house was quiet and Wilke lay on his bed, flipping through old comic books. He recalled what his grandma had said and agreed that his life had really changed for the better and he had a bunch of things to be thankful for. So he thought, why not...it was time to put old and cloudy memories to rest. After all, who doesn't love a parade? The sound of a marching band quickens the beat of anyone's heart. The flame of patriotism burns in the breast as the American flag flaps on its pole carried by soldiers in the color guard. He was getting excited just thinking about it.

He pulled on his shoes and headed for the parade route. As he paced down the street, his mind wandered to old memories. He shook his head and they disappeared. He knew he had to erase those old scenes. Walt Disney he thought. It'll be good to see Walt Disney again. Pictures flashed through his mind and memories clouded his thoughts. Turn them off...turn them off...he pleaded. Don't recall the soft feel of Betty Barnes's hand or the taste of the sodas they shared or the sound of tires grating along a gravel road or the thrill of the joy ride and the sound of Homer's body as the car bumped over it and then...and then...the salty tear-stained kiss goodbye. He stopped and placed both hands against a huge elm tree that stood along the street. "Go away...," he said to the thoughts. "Go away!" Then he heard one of the marching bands as it turned the corner, way down the street. The bleating of the horns and umm paas of the sousaphones blended with the crashing cymbals and the boomp boomp bass drums and ratta tat tat of the snares and it captivated his thoughts and filled his brain and the old memories were gone.

Wilke jogged down the parade route, waving to people he knew, then he saw the Spenzi family along the curb and he took his place wrapping a grateful arm around his Grandma Fannie. When he looked at her she could see in his eyes that he had conquered some demons, and she knew he had done it very recently. She was amazed how much he looked like his dad…so tall and straight with jet black hair and blue eyes. Wilke was movie-star handsome and everybody knew it but him. He always stood out in a crowd.

It was impossible to hold a foot still as the bands played their tunes and paraded down the street. Horns honked, balloons popped, fire truck sirens wailed and kids screamed in delight at the marchers and the silly clowns and the parading kids and animals. Then there was Walt with his wavy dark shock of hair and trademark mustache, in a Model T Ford putt-putting slowly down the street. He looked just like everyone remembered him over ten years before. He was wearing a straw hat with a wide brim and a candy-striped jacket with white duck pants. He waved to the crowds on both sides of the street and oogaed the big brass horn to the delight of everyone

As the car got closer, they could see that Walt was driving the car but he shared the Model-T with a bevy of three beautiful young ladies. The girl seated next to him in the front seat looked like one of the Mouseketeers from the popular Disney TV show. In the backseat, a blonde in a gorgeous ball gown with elbow-length white gloves and a sparkling tiara waved to the crowd. As she turned her attention to the side of the parade route where Wilke and his family were standing, he almost fell over. It was Betty Barnes! At the instant their eyes met, she looked shocked and stopped waving but quickly turned her attention to the other side of the street as the Model T continued down Main Street.

Wilke could hardly catch his breath and began to hyperventilate. He bent over at the waist and tried to refocus his thoughts. He felt a soothing hand on his back and knew that his Grandma Fannie recognized Betty also and he knew she understood his reaction. "Wilke," she whispered in his ear. "Why don't you just go on home and we'll meet you there later."

He straightened up and put his arms around Fannie and whispered back to her, "No Grandma, I need to see her one more time and finish all of this."

With the passing of Walt's car, the parade had officially ended and waves of people flowed into the street. Many of them went to their cars to drive a few miles outside of town to Walt's boyhood home where the party was just getting started.

The Spenzi's planned on enjoying the food and drinks and entertainment at the party so when they got home they made a stop so they could all go to the bathroom and then, except for Alfreda, they all piled into Grandma Fannie's old Mercury. Fannie, Lilly and Joseph sat in the front seat and Wilke, Thomas and Mattie sat in the back. Alfreda would have loved to be included, but her hip was hurting and she decided that it was best that she just rest.

When they arrived at the party, the place was packed. There were hundreds of people just wandering around the property with paper plates full of food and cups full of cold fruit punch. The party was well-organized and the lines waiting for food and drink were short. Walt himself was seated at a table on the old front porch of his beloved childhood home. He was signing autographs and having his picture taken with anyone and everyone. Professional photographers from various media outlets knew a photo op when they saw one and the flashes and snapping never seemed to stop. There were also movie cameras and big lighting equipment to film for the upcoming documentary on Walt Disney. Walt sure loved Marceline and the people of Marceline loved Walt.

Wilke wandered around aimlessly. He got himself a plate of food and a cold drink. He could see that a film crew was getting set up and pretended that he wasn't looking for anyone special, like maybe Betty Barnes, but his eyes kept searching the crowd. Of course it wasn't long before he spotted her. She was at a small table signing autographs mostly for an admiring audience of teenage girls. He could see that she still had her tiara on and the long white gloves with the tight bodice of the sequined gown accentuated her toned and fit figure.

He slowly made his way toward her table. Since Wilke always stood out in a crowd, it wasn't long before she glanced up and noticed him. Their eyes met for a heartbeat. She signed a few more autographs and then excused herself and walked toward a quiet corner of the yard. He followed her and when she rounded the corner of a large food tent, she turned and as he approached she said, "Wilke Spenzi...I asked you the last time we saw each other if you wanted an autograph? You never answered me. Would you like one now?"

"No Betty or Elizabeth or whoever you are now," he said confidently as he leaned his face close to hers. "I don't need an autograph, your face lives in my mind every day. And the last time we saw each other, well…you didn't seem too pleased to see me."

"I'm truly sorry Wilke," she said as she reached out and put her hand on his arm. "With all that had happened, you were the last person I expected to see in Kansas City. It caught me by surprise and I thought you were there to ruin my career. After five years, I hadn't heard a word from you. I tried calling you and sent letters, but you never replied. My parents were committed to a sanitarium, my grandmother had died and I was all alone. All I had was my dancing."

Wilke put his hand on top of hers as he replied, "I didn't return your calls or letters because I wanted to protect you. I figured if nobody knew that we were connected, you'd be safe."

"Did you know when I kissed you that night in front of your grandmother's house that I loved you?" she asked.

"Betty, both of us were young and I'm not sure we knew what love was then, but yes, I felt with you the most special connection I had ever had with anyone," he said. "If that's what love feels like, then yes, I loved you too.

"I have to perform a short ballet tonight about 7," she said. "When I'm done with that, let's go for a drive and maybe sort things out? I have a rental car. We can take that. Will you wait for me?"

"I'll watch you dance and I'll wait," he said.

Betty returned to her autograph table and Wilke wandered around until he spotted his family. It was getting dark and Lilly and Thomas wanted to go home and Grandma Fannie was getting tired. Wilke told them to go on, that he wanted to see the entertainment and he'd be home later. "How will you get home Wilke? asked Fannie.

"Oh, don't worry about me Grandma," he said. "I met a friend here and she'll give me a ride home."

Fannie gave him a hug with a warning, "Just be careful."

As he watched them walk back to Fannie's car, he thought to himself what a wonderful family I've got.

Betty's performance was beautiful and elegant—like her. It was short, but the audience clapped and clapped.

He waited while Betty went to a dressing room and changed out of her ballerina outfit into a cute little skirt and top and she had a sweater draped around her neck. She met him at an area that was roped off for the vehicles belonging to the cast and crew of the entertainment production. Her rental was a small black sedan. They both got in and Betty insisted that she would do the driving. "See if there's a cooler in the backseat," she told Wilke. "I asked the caterer to put some cold drinks in the backseat for us."

He leaned his lanky frame over the seat and sure enough, there was a cooler that held a six-pack of beer on ice.

"So ballerinas drink beer? "he asked.

"Only if there isn't an expensive bottle of champagne available," she answered with a grin.

"So, I guess we'll just have to settle for poor man's champagne tonight," he said as he popped the caps off a couple of bottles of beer. "By the way...where are we going and should I call you Elizabeth or Betty?"

"Wilke, I'll always be Betty to you," she replied as she pulled the car out of the lot and headed onto the gravel road "And if you must know where we are going, how about a drive down "memory lane?"

It was quiet in the car as they were both locked up in their own thoughts and sipping on their beer. She drove slowly toward Wien on the same gravel roads they were on 13 years before. She broke the silence by asking, "Wilke...do you have a girlfriend?"

"Well," he stammered, not quite sure how honest she wanted him to be or how honest he wanted to be. "I have a girl at college that I'm fond of, but I wouldn't call her a girlfriend," he said. "We enjoy one another and have sex now and then, but we're both just dedicated to our studies. What about you Betty?"

"I'm very much in love with a wonderful dancer," she said. "His name is Valdov Kaminsky. Have you heard of him?"

"No Betty, I can't say that I have heard of him. I don't travel in the ballet circle," he replied. "You certainly have come a long way from the Betty Barnes I used to know."

"Yes Wilke, that's true, she agreed. "And I want to keep as far away from that old Betty Barnes as I can. Valdov and I are going to be married in a few months. I am carrying his child. I'm going to be rich and famous, Wilke. And what about you?"

"Betty, you're a hard act to follow. I'm just going to be a veterinarian and take care of sick animals. I doubt I'll be rich and famous," he said.

They drove several more miles in silence. She pulled into a driveway and

Wilke recognized it as her old home. The yard was overgrown with weeds and the house looked more like an old shed that was falling down. She didn't bother to get out. She just wanted to see it one more time.

"See why I want to forget about Betty Barnes?" she said as she pulled out of the driveway and headed down the road.

"We need to let go of the past and you need to let go of me," she said. "You've been like a time-bomb ticking over my head for so long. A few years back, the sheriff in Marceline got in touch with me. He wanted to know about my involvement with the death of Homer Goss. He even tried to get me to talk by telling me that you wanted to come clean. I just played dumb, like I didn't know what he was talking about. I guess he believed me and he just went away. Then I heard there was a big write up in the Marceline paper and the name Betty Barnes was mentioned. Wilke, I don't need this in my life. I'm about to marry a very famous dancer and have his child. I don't need any scandals to ruin it."

"Betty, I told you all I ever wanted to do was protect you," Wilke said.

As he looked out the window at the passing landscape, he realized that she was headed back toward Marceline. She broke the tension as they passed by his Grandma Fannie's house by saying, "We should stop there and break in again. You can make me a bologna and catsup sandwich?"

He smiled at her and commented, "No, Betty I think you are on to better days of caviar and champagne, which is just what you deserve."

"And Wilke, what do you deserve?" she asked.

"I'm really not sure what I deserve," he said. "But I do know what I want. I want to be a good veterinarian. I want to hang onto the love of my family. And someday…I want to have a family of my own."

They pulled up in front of Wilke's parent's home. She shut off the engine and they just sat quietly, listening to the evening crickets.

Wilke looked across the front seat of the car at her and said, "Betty, I'll never forget the first day I saw you at Porter Wilson's dance studio. I was so nervous, and after I danced, you clapped for me. I never knew how good it felt to be clapped at."

She returned his gaze and reached over and took his hand between her two hands, "Wilke Spenzi, I'll always be clapping for you," she said.

"I'll always be clapping for you too Betty," he said. "I'll clap when I hear you have married this famous ballet fellow and I'll clap when I hear you have had his baby. I'll just clap knowing that you are happy."

As he leaned across the seat and gave her a kiss on the cheek, she gently squeezed his hand.

He sat back and looked at her again, "Betty…now that you're rich and famous," he deadpanned. "Don't you forget that you owe my dad two bucks for the five gallons of gas I stole for your old Studebaker."

"I'm good for it Wilke," she said. "The check's in the mail."

"Goodnight Betty Barnes," he said.

"Goodnight Wilke Spenzi."

EPILOGUE

Marty Biggs was born and raised in Marceline. He married his high school sweetheart and seven months later had a daughter they named Peggy. The young couple struggled and tried to make the marriage work, but they split up after six years. Marty was devastated and swore he'd never marry again. For 25 years he had been a mail carrier in town and handled routes in Marceline and Wien. He loved his job but hadn't been feeling up to par lately. Lethargy and bouts with shortness of breath, especially when he was forced to carry heavy trays of mail, had turned into a nagging pain that radiated across his chest and into his left shoulder area. He was seriously considering retiring and just taking it easy. His doctor made that decision for him. The doctor did some tests and referred him to a specialist in Kansas City. After several tests, he was told that he had advanced lung cancer that had already spread to several other organs. It was inoperable and incurable and therefore, he received his death sentence at age 46.

As he lay alone in a hospital bed, stewing over the bad news, he realized that he probably had very little time left on this earth and, because of something that had happened in his past, not much of a shot at getting into heaven. He asked his nurse if she would contact Father Ludwig at the Catholic church in Marceline to hear his last confession and perform the sacrament of extreme unction. There was something Marty needed to get off his chest before he passed on…whether or not it would save his soul from eternal damnation.

The following day, Father Ludwig drove to Kansas City and went to Marty's bedside.

"Tell me Son," the Father said as he laid his rosary on Marty's heaving chest. "I can feel that your heart and soul are heavy with the burden of something in your past."

"Father…I killed a man. His name was Homer Goss," Marty blurted out.

The priest was shocked by Marty's blunt confession, but he managed to say, "Tell me about how that happened."

Marty recalled that he had stopped at Stonewall's Tavern in the late afternoon, as he had developed the habit of doing almost every day after his route was done. He downed the usual two shots of Irish whisky and washed them down with a big frosty mug of draft beer. Homer Goss, one of the tavern's regular customers was at the bar, already drunk as usual. When the bartender asked Marty how his beautiful daughter Peggy was doing at college, Homer butted in with a slurry-voiced remark that he would bet that if Peggy was so good looking, she was probably making the rounds of the fraternity houses and getting laid every night.

Marty blew up and with one swing of his fist, he knocked Homer off the barstool and on to his back on the floor. Homer staggered to his feet and swung a feeble punch back at Marty. Ben, the bartender told them to take it outside. "That piece of crap isn't worth a good fight," Marty said as he dropped a twenty dollar bill on the bar. "Keep the change Ben. I'm going home." He pushed open the back door that connected the bar area with the small parking lot around the back of the tavern along the gravel road to town.

As he was walking toward his car, Homer stumbled up behind him and punched him in the middle of the back. By this time, the alcohol in Marty had started to kick in and in a rage, he turned and delivered a powerful punch to the side of Homer's face. The drunk staggered a few more steps and tumbled down the embankment where his head struck a concrete culvert at the side of the gravel road. Blood was pouring from the side of his head as he lay in a heap, totally unconscious. His head was on the culvert, but his legs were protruding on to the shoulder of the road.

It had all taken place so fast and so violently that it took Marty a few moments to realize what had happened. He climbed down the embankment and could see that Homer wasn't breathing and his head was in a pool of blood.

Before he could do anything, he heard the sound of a car approaching on the gravel road at the bottom of the big hill. If he was connected to this unfortunate accident, he knew he'd lose his job with the post office and his government pension. Surely someone coming down the road would spot the body and call for help. He quickly scrambled back up the embankment to his car and took off out of the parking lot and down the road toward his home in Marceline.

Little did he know that Wilke Spenzi was driving the next car that came over the hill. Father Ludwig was the only one that would ever know the truth about the death of Homer Goss...and he was obligated by his vows to remain silent.